The Beauty Within

H.L Day

Other books by H.L Day

EagerBoyz series

Eager To Try (EagerBoyz 0.5)

Eager For You (EagerBoyz 1)

Eager For More (EagerBoyz 2)

Too Far series

A Dance too Far (Too Far #1)

A Step too Far (Too Far #2)

Temporary Series

A Temporary Situation (Temporary; Tristan and Dom #1)

A Christmas Situation (Temporary; Tristan and Dom #1.5)

Temporary Insanity (Temporary; Paul and Indy #1)

Fight for Survival series

Refuge (Fight for Survival #1)

Rebellion (Fight for Survival #2)

Standalones

Time for a Change

Kept in the Dark

Taking Love's Lead

Edge of Living

Christmas Riches

Exposed

The Longest Night

Short story

The Second Act

Other books by H.L Night

Shai

Copyright

Cover Art by Jo Clement at Covers by Jo

Edited by Alyson Roy - Royal Editing Services

Proofreading by Kate Flo Wood

The Beauty Within © 2021 H.L Day

All Rights Reserved:

This literary work may not be reproduced or transmitted in any form or by any means including electronic or photographic reproduction, in whole or in part, without express written permission.

The Beauty Within is a work of fiction. Names, characters, places, and incidents either are the product of the author's imagination or are used fictitiously, and any resemblance to actual persons, living or dead, business establishments, events, or locales is entirely coincidental.

Warning

Intended for an 18+ audience. This book contains material that may be offensive to some and is intended for a mature, adult audience. It contains graphic language, explicit sexual content, and adult situations.

Thanks

Huge thanks to my beta readers Barbara, Sherry, and Jill.

KEEP IN TOUCH WITH H.L

Join Day's Den

Get H.L's newsletter

Subscribe to H.L's Patreon

Like H.L's Facebook page

Follow H.L on Bookbub

Follow H.L on Goodreads

Follow H.L on Amazon

Follow H.L on Twitter

Follow H.L on Instagram

Visit H.L's website or Amazon page to see her other books and audios

Blurb

"You will be trapped in stone forevermore, your beauty hidden by a façade so ugly that people will not like to look upon it. You will feel, but you will not be able to speak. You will hear, but you will not be able to communicate. You will endure across the ages, a silent witness to the decades that go by."

François Damont's only crime was loving the son of a witch in a time when it wasn't permitted. For that sin, he's been cursed to spend eternity locked inside the body of a gargoyle. A chance to break the curse comes only once every twenty-five years, lasting for no longer than twenty-eight days. He's been unsuccessful for hundreds of years. Why would this time be any different?

History lecturer Daniel Smith is still reeling from a broken marriage when he stumbles across a mysterious man. Frankie might be hiding something, but the connection between them is too strong to ignore. Can he unlock the mystery before it's too late?

Strange dreams. Dark forces. People who may not be what they seem. Time is not the only thing against them. And perhaps Daniel knows more than he thinks he does.

A sweet 82k MM paranormal romance featuring magic, witches, and a relationship that might just be able to endure anything.

Prologue

Time passes so slowly when you're trapped in a stone prison. Seasons endlessly cycle, so much changing year after year: fashions, language, culture, technology. While I stay exactly the same. I've seen wars. I've seen murders. I've seen first kisses, and I've seen marriage proposals. I've seen the best of people and the worst of people.

Inside my head, there's an entire history book. Only, I can never tell anyone what I know and how I know it. If I do, I condemn myself to an eternal lifetime inside this stone shell, a life even worse than the one I have already. You see, every twenty-five years, I get to escape. I get to spend an entire month living again. I get to breathe again. I get to feel the sun on my skin. I get to talk and laugh and experience everything I've missed during the last quarter of a century.

Did I deserve to end up where I am? I've had hundreds of years to ponder that question, and my answer still remains the same.

No, I didn't.

I made a mistake. A mistake that anyone who has ever fallen in love could make. My only crime was stupidity. Particularly the stupidity of ignoring those who tried to point out the dark path my actions could take me down. But deserve this cold, harsh prison, this life without living? No one, no matter how heinous their crime, deserves that.

My name is François Damont, and I still dream of a day when I will break the curse that led me to be where I am today. I have to believe that.

It's the only thing that keeps me sane.

Chapter One

Domme, Dordogne 1571

François

There were times when I hated the strip of land we farmed with a passion, when irrational hatred bubbled from me like water from a brook. Looking after the land in order to tease a bountiful harvest from it was worse than looking after a child. At least I assumed so. It wasn't like I had children. Not yet, anyway. Not unless my sixteen-year-old brother, Antoine, who was five years my junior counted.

I frequently had to remind myself that were it not for this piece of land that we rented from the lord, we wouldn't have enough money to eat. The land, together with the small number of livestock we had, was what bought my maman, my papa, Antoine, and me, the ability to make it through another winter.

Therefore, no matter how long the days were, and no matter how much my muscles complained at the labor, it was worth it. It didn't stop me dreaming of a better life though, a life where I wasn't a peasant, where I'd been born into French aristocracy and had nothing better to do than count money and drink wine.

I paused for a moment from the backbreaking work of plucking stubborn weeds from between the emerging stalks of barley to rub at the small of my back. As an effort to loosen the tight muscles that had locked into place from hours spent bent over, it was frustratingly insufficient. Squinting at the sun, I wiped the sweat from my brow. The temperature had barely dropped all day, and there'd been very little breeze. It was a day to be inside, not a day to be trapped in a field with no shade. It was good for the barley, but not so good for the people who had to tend it.

Antoine came to stand beside me, cupping his hand across his brow to shield his eyes from the worst of the sun's rays as his gaze followed mine to the sky. "Sun's starting to drop. We've only got about an hour of good daylight left."

I nodded. He looked just as exhausted as I felt. I took a moment to survey how much of the field we'd covered between the two of us; the realization that it was less than a quarter was depressing. There would normally have been three of us to do the work, sometimes four if Maman pitched in as well. But with my papa struck down by a mysterious illness, and Maman at home looking after him, it was down to Antoine and myself to do all the work. And we would get it done. It would just take longer, and other jobs would have to wait until it was done. The barley was our lifeblood. It took priority over everything else. I let out a weary sigh. "One more hour."

We returned to work, continuing for as long as we could until the sun had dropped so low in the sky that we were in danger of not being able to tell the weeds from the barley.

"François?"

I went still as I recognized the voice. It belonged to Madeleine Badeaux, the Badeaux family's smaller strip of farmland having neighbored ours for as long as I could remember. Antoine grabbed my arm as I went to move toward the boundary where her call had come from. "Don't!"

I shook him off. "I'm just going to talk to her, that's all. Go home and I'll see you soon."

The look in his eyes turned imploring. "Come home with me. You know what they say about that family. You've heard all the same stories I have."

I barked out a laugh. "I've heard them, but it doesn't mean I believe a word of it, and you shouldn't either. Or heaven knows what you will believe in next — unicorns and dragons perhaps? Is that why you don't like going down to the river? Are you scared a troll lives under the bridge?" It was a low blow, and I knew it. As a child, Antoine had almost drowned. Ever since then he'd been scared of any water deeper than a puddle. The expression on his face told me how much I'd hurt him by bringing up something we didn't talk about, and certainly not in such a mocking manner. I blamed the sun and exhaustion for me lashing out. I made a grab for Antoine's shoulder in an attempt to make amends for my thoughtless comment, but he slipped out of my grasp, turning on his heel and walking away.

"François?"

The call was more insistent this time. I stared at my brother's departing back. I should go after him, but I knew him. He'd sulk for at least an hour, and there would be no talking to him until he'd calmed down. It would be a waste of breath to approach him before then. Therefore, I went the opposite way, picking my way across the field and squeezing through the hedgerows until Madeleine came into view. Her long, red hair was fastened in its customary single plait, hanging over her left shoulder. The plait was long enough to reach her waist, and she fiddled with the end of it. Her lips curved up into a smile as she caught sight of me. I returned the smile, but I couldn't stop my gaze from straying over her shoulder, subconsciously seeking out a glimpse of her brother, Estienne, as I always did whenever he was in the vicinity. He was there, and what's more he was shirtless, sweat still glistening on his defined torso despite the evening rapidly starting to cool.

I forced my attention back to Madeleine as she spoke. "How has your day been, François? With just the two of you."

My gaze strayed back to Estienne, who hadn't so much as glanced our way. "There are only two of you."

Madeleine curled her plait around her finger in a way that I recognized as being flirtatious. "But our land is much smaller than yours." That was true. Their strip of land was barely half the size of ours. "And unlike your family, we have another source of income, the poultices and good luck charms that Mother makes to help the people of the village."

I shifted uncomfortably at the subject, my gaze dropping to the ground, the earth giving way beneath my boot as I scraped my toe through it. Antoine had been right. I would have been wise to have ignored Madeleine calling my name.

"How is your papa?"

Be polite. I lifted my head and forced myself to meet her gaze. "He was marginally better when I left this morning, thank you. We're hopeful he will be back to full strength soon."

Madeleine's eyelashes lowered to give her a distinctly coquettish look. "If you come home with me, I'm sure that Mother will have something to help your papa. If I explain to her that you are a friend, I'm sure she could see her way to waiving her usual price."

I couldn't help but take a step back, my throat drying up enough to make producing words difficult. "Th... thank you, that's very kind of you, but I am expected back for dinner. Maman and Papa will be worried if I tarry too long."

Madeleine tilted her head to one side, studying me as if there was something particularly interesting about me. She was definitely her mother's daughter. Cecile Badeaux had that same look. Although, that probably didn't feature high on the list of things which made people uncomfortable around the matriarch of the family. Whatever Madeleine gleaned from her scrutiny didn't seem to please her, her lips tightening. "Suit yourself, François." She tossed her head, her plait bouncing on her chest. "I was just trying to help."

I was left feeling like I'd wronged her in some way. I opened my mouth with the intention of apologizing, even though I wasn't sure what I was meant to have done, but Madeleine had already turned away before I could get the words out. I watched her as she made her way back across the field in the direction of her home.

The Badeaux family didn't reside in the village. They lived at the bottom of the hill, in an isolated spot that did absolutely nothing to help their reputation. Their need to live away from everybody else only made the whispers that much more pronounced, adding fuel to a fire that was already close to raging out of control.

Madeleine didn't pause to say anything to her brother, flouncing straight past him. I went to turn away, not wanting to be caught watching either of them.

"François?"

I stopped mid-turn, my breath catching in my throat. It was a male voice this time, the tone husky. *Walk away.* Just like with Madeleine, my brain didn't seem to want to listen to reason. It was probably sunstroke. Antoine had warned me not to take my hat off earlier in the day. I turned back to find Estienne striding across the field toward me. It was easy to tell that Madeleine and Estienne were brother and sister. They had the same red hair, the same emerald eyes, and the same smattering of freckles across the bridge of their nose. Only on him, they somehow seemed far more interesting.

Estienne came to a halt in front of me, one hand lifting to idly scratch the opposite shoulder, the position showing off the taut muscles of his biceps. "I'm going for a swim in the river to wash the sweat off. Would you be interested in accompanying me?"

My heart beat that little bit faster. We spoke sometimes, but it was usually about the weather or the crops. And we had never spent any time together away from the land. Yet, it seemed that he was seeking my company. What did that mean? Why now? When I didn't immediately respond to his question, he raised an eyebrow.

I found myself nodding, not trusting myself not to say something stupid if I spoke.

His smile was wide and gleaming, as if my agreement had made his day. "Great! Let me get my tunic and then we will go."

While he walked back across the field and retrieved his tunic from the ground, I had plenty of time to reconsider my choice. The path down to the river lay on the other side of the hill, which meant having to pass through the village in order to get there. That meant there was a possibility of being seen together, the knowledge sending a frisson of unease down my spine. But then Estienne was there in front of me, still smiling, and my doubts dissipated as quickly as if they had been nothing more than a leaf on the breeze.

We fell into step next to each other and when Estienne broke into a jog, I didn't hesitate to follow suit. Our pace meant that in no time at all we reached the village, our route taking us through the Place de la Halle. With day beginning to transition to night, the market square was empty. From there we traversed the Place de la Rode. As always, I averted my gaze from the breaker's wheel at its center, where all manner of criminal activities and acts of sin were punished. We passed the last house in the village, the moneyer's house, and from there it was just a case of making our way down the hill to where the river flowed through the forest.

I was relieved when Estienne slowed on the winding path that led down the hill. The last thing my family needed was for me to take a nasty tumble and suffer an injury that stopped me from being able to work. The path was uneven enough to prove treacherous during the day if you didn't watch where you were going, but with the light dwindling rapidly, another level of caution was needed. I reached out to grab Estienne's arm, his skin pleasantly warm beneath my fingertips where he hadn't bothered to put his tunic back on, slinging it over his shoulder instead. "I don't know if this is a good idea. It's going to be dark in the forest."

Estienne's teeth shone in the dim light as he grinned. "I didn't take you for someone so easily scared. I thought the Damonts were built of sterner stuff. Perhaps I chose foolishly in inviting you, and I should have asked Antoine instead. Perhaps he is the one with a spirit of adventure."

The accusation rankled and I increased my pace, my fingers dropping from Estienne's arm, where unbeknownst to me I'd let them rest for the entirety of his speech. "There is no need to mock me. I was only trying to exhibit a responsible amount of caution."

It was Estienne's turn to lay hands on me, the fingers that curled around my shoulder to bring me to a halt feeling like a hot brand through my tunic. "I apologize, François. You must forgive my lack of manners. Please come. I have a special place I'd like to show you if I may? Also, there will be a full moon tonight, so we will be perfectly safe. There will be enough light to see by, I promise."

How was I supposed to stay mad at him when he'd apologized so sincerely? And he was offering me something more than another evening spent with my family. "How do you know about the moon?"

"Mother knows all sorts of things. She teaches a lot of it to me and Madeleine."

The prickle of unease was back, but curiosity won out over the instinct to change the subject. "Like what?"

Estienne's eyes found mine. "Are you looking for horror stories and torrid tales? Would you like me to regale you with stories of ritual sacrifices and magical incantations performed in the dead of night?"

I was shocked that he would be so direct about it. "You are aware of what they say about your family?"

Estienne laughed, the sound deep and rich, and oh so beautiful to my ears. "Of course we know. But what you have to remember is that not everything you hear is necessarily true."

We'd reached the bottom of the hill, Estienne taking the lead down the small path that led into the forest. My heart began to pound as I considered asking the forbidden question hovering on my tongue, desperate to be answered.

"You can ask."

Even with his permission, it seemed wrong to voice it. Especially when we had never spent enough time together to be able to class the other as a friend. And I wanted to be Estienne's friend. I wanted it more than anything else in the world. Actually, that wasn't true. I wanted my papa to recover from whatever was ailing him so that we could be a proper family again. But being more friendly with Estienne came a close second to that. The closest thing I had to a friend in the village was my own brother, but it wasn't the same, not with the age gap between us and the usual sibling squabbling that our relationship entailed.

Whereas Estienne was twenty-three, a whole two years my senior. Therefore, it stood to reason that he was older and wiser. It was one of the reasons I'd assumed that he would have no time for me. But apparently that had changed today. For whatever reason, he'd noticed me. And not just noticed me but invited me on what he'd categorized as an adventure. He might have meant it as a joke, but to me it *was* an adventure. It was a respite from spending the evening watching my maman sewing by candlelight while my papa struggled to even sit upright without coughing.

I didn't ask the question. If we were going to be friends, there would be other opportunities. Instead, I gestured at the dark outline of the river, its gentle bubbling over the rocks a soothing ode to nature. "I thought we were going to swim."

Estienne pulled a face as he glanced toward the riverbank. "Not here. We go deeper. There is a better place."

While not entirely comfortable with traveling deeper into the forest, I'd come too far to balk at the notion now. Would Maman be worried? Where would she assume I'd gone? I supposed that depended on whether Antoine had informed her of my conversation with Madeleine, or whether he had decided it was more prudent to keep his own counsel.

Estienne pushed his way through the undergrowth, seeming to know exactly where he was going. The thicker it got, the more difficult it became to make out the outline of his broad shoulders. I concentrated on not lagging too far behind, lest I lose sight of him completely. And then we broke free into a clearing, the space open enough that the light of the moon broke through more easily. Estienne had been right about that.

I followed Estienne as he scrambled his way down the small incline that led to the river. "See! It is much nicer here."

I had to admit that it was. Surrounded by trees, the spot was secluded enough to make me feel like Estienne and I were the only two people in the world. Estienne had already kicked off his boots and was rolling his stockings down, his tunic draped over a rock by the water's edge. I quickly averted my gaze as more and more bare skin was revealed, turning in a slow circle as I pretended to examine our surroundings despite the fact that there was little to see apart from trees and rocks and soil. "It is nice. It's…" It was a relief when a splash of water told me that Estienne had waded into the river. "How did you find this place?" Feeling stupid talking to a tree, I turned slowly back to the river, relaxing when I found that Estienne had submerged up to his chest.

He made lazy splashing movements with his arms, the river apparently shallow enough where he was that his feet touched the bottom. "I've been coming to this forest since I was old enough to walk. I know every single inch of it. There are other places I could show you, if you were interested enough to want to see them?"

My heart skipped a beat. So we were to be friends, then. Something warm lit up my chest. I kept a tight hold on the emotion begging to break free, gracing him with no more than a shrug. "Maybe."

The moonlight was bright enough for me to be able to see his smile even at a distance. He splashed again, ripples spreading out from where his hands disturbed the surface of the water. "Are you going to stand there all night? Or are you coming in? The water is lovely. Just what is needed after a long day."

I was sure it was. The promise of refreshingly cool water only a few steps away made me that much more conscious of how my sweaty tunic and stockings clung to me. Yet, modesty held me immobile, Estienne's gaze fixed on me with an obvious intent to watch while I undressed. There was no alternative, though, save for refusing altogether, and how ridiculous would that look, that I had come all this way to bathe in the river without… well, actually bathing in the river.

Gaze fixed on the mossy ground, I did my best to shed my clothes as quickly as possible. I didn't look up as I entered the water, not stopping until it was deep enough to hide me from view. I'd picked a spot, a respectable distance away from Estienne, but he apparently had different ideas. He waded in my direction until we were face to face with very little space separating us. My heart thrummed in my chest and oxygen seemed to be in short supply. The moonlight accentuated his features, and I found it hard to tear my gaze away from him. It didn't help that he seemed just as fixated on me, the two of us staring at each other as if we were both searching for the answer to a question that hadn't been asked.

Estienne was the first to break the silence. "Do you think my sister is pretty?"

"Your sister?" My voice sounded unnaturally husky, and I was forced to clear my throat. "Yes, I think she is very pretty."

"Yet, you did not take her up on her invitation. Is it the red hair? You like blondes, perhaps? Or brunettes?" Estienne ran a hand through his own much shorter, but equally red hair, as if to illustrate his point.

I swallowed nervously, not liking the direction this conversation was taking. Was Estienne baiting me, or was there something else at play here? My mind was starting to go in directions I couldn't allow it to go. "I like red hair just fine."

"Are her breasts not big enough for you?"

There was a challenge in Estienne's eyes that filled me with fear, every nerve in my body going on screaming alert. He knew. Somehow, he knew. I must have been careless in the way that I'd looked at him, my glance lingering too long, or in the wrong place. I turned away from him and back to the bank, my clothes a dark promise of safety on the bank. "I think it's time I returned home."

Hands gripped my shoulders, the pressure too strong to resist as he turned me back to face him once again. We were close now. So close that our knees knocked together beneath the water. "François, I'm sorry, but I had to know. People like us can't be too careful."

"People like us?" I asked the question, even though I knew exactly what he meant. Wasn't that the reason I'd left behind any scrap of common sense I might have once had to come with him? I changed tack. "Why did you invite me here when we have barely spent any time together before tonight?"

Estienne's hands still rested on my shoulders, the warmth of his grip a strange contrast to the coolness of the water. "You turned my sister down."

I shook my head. "I didn't turn her down. She was just concerned about my papa, that's all."

Estienne's lips settled into a firm line. "You're not that naïve. No one your age is that naïve. I might have believed it of your brother, but not of you. You turned her down, but you barely had to consider my offer for longer than a second before agreeing to come with me."

"The river... I wanted to swim... I..." The words died in my throat, the look on Estienne's face saying he didn't believe a word of it.

Sure enough, his next words confirmed it and were particularly damning. "Do you think I don't see you looking at me?"

I stared at him. "I..."

"Shhh... don't be scared." Cool fingers lifted to rest on my cheek. "I've looked at you too. I'm looking at you now. And I think you're incredibly pretty, François." He lifted his gaze to the night sky. "Far prettier than any of the stars up there. They pale in comparison to you. I didn't dare to speak to you before in case you could see my desire written all over my face. I kept my distance for both of our sakes, but I don't want to keep my distance anymore. I can't."

The words were like something from a dream, the sorts of dreams I'd had for years but never dared to voice. Fear, though, still held me in its grip. "It's a sin. A man cannot lie with another man. It's an abomination in the eyes of God, the church says so. We would be struck down by lightning. We would—"

I didn't get any further, lips pressing against my own and silencing me more effectively than any words could have. For one long, suspended moment, there was nothing save for that single point of contact between the two of us, a rush of heat and longing enveloping me so fast that I forgot how to breathe, forgot how to do anything except stand there and accept the gift that Estienne was offering.

The kiss was over all too soon, Estienne's eyes glittering with suppressed emotion as he pulled back. There was the slightest curl to his lips as he raised a hand to the sky. "Do you see any lightning ready to strike us down?"

I tilted my head back and looked up. There was no lightning. In fact, there was nothing in the sky that hadn't already been there moments ago. Everything looked exactly the same as always, which was crazy when I felt like I'd been reborn as a completely different person. "No lightning." I lowered my gaze to find Estienne smiling at me, the moonlight caressing the sharp line of his jaw.

I smiled back at him, electricity thrumming through my body in a way it never had before. This was the moment I'd been waiting for all my life, the moment I'd convinced myself would never happen, *could* never happen. This time we moved as one, our heads bending toward each other and our lips meeting in a clinging acknowledgement of mutual desire. When Estienne's tongue made a polite enquiry at the seam of my lips, I opened up without hesitation, meeting it with a shy exploration of my own. The longer the kiss went on, the bolder we both grew, our bodies pressing together, our nakedness meaning that there was no disguising the mutual arousal of our bodies.

When our mouths finally separated, we were laughing. There were no words needed. We knew that in each other we'd found something we'd both desperately dreamed of but hadn't believed we would find. I wanted to stay there all night. I wanted to stay there forever.

Estienne seemed to read my mind, his face filling with a sudden regret. "We have to return home before we are missed and people start asking questions. But… this place. This can be where we meet. No one else comes here. It used to be my special place, but now it can be ours. Would you like that, François? Will you meet me here in secret?"

I didn't even need to think about it before nodding. I'd found my kindred spirit, my soulmate. My secret desire had been let out of its box once and for all, and now that I'd had a taste, there was no forcing it back in.

Chapter Two

Domme, Dordogne 1571

François

I lay with my head pillowed on Estienne's chest as I stared up at the starlit sky. Both of us were still naked and breathing hard from having just made love, our third or fourth rendezvous of the week. Despite the satiated buzz still pervading my body, there were a thousand questions all clamoring at my brain and begging to be addressed. Estienne's fingers stroked through my hair. "François, my love, I can hear you thinking from here. What is wrong?"

My heart melted the same way as it always did when he called me "his love." I had discovered that he was never shy when it came to giving out endearments. They seemed to roll off his tongue as easily as my name. Whereas I was getting better at them, but they certainly didn't come naturally. Perhaps there were times that I still lived in fear of that lightning bolt, that I believed that one wrong word would trigger God's retribution. I craned my neck so that I could look up at Estienne, his features as familiar and as perfect as ever, my heart swelling with love so much that it felt like my heart might burst. "It will be winter soon. What will happen to us then?"

Estienne cushioned my head as he maneuvered us so that we were facing, his fingers interlacing with mine to hold our joined hands against his chest. "What do you mean? We can still come here."

"We won't be able to lie like this. Not without losing valuable body parts to frostbite."

His lips curved into a gentle smile, a smile I'd come to adore more with every day that passed. "And there I was thinking that you wanted me for more than physical pleasure."

I shuffled forward until our noses touched and we were breathing the same air. "You know I do, but I'll miss this closeness. It won't be the same. Once the snow falls our families are not going to believe that we wish to take walks through the forest and bathe in the frozen river."

Estienne's sigh was long and heartfelt and imbued with the same sadness that filled my chest to the brim. "You raise a good point, my love." He turned his head slightly to drop a brief kiss on my lips, a tingling sensation following in its wake. "We will think of something. We will find a way to be together, François. Our love will always endure no matter what obstacle is put in our way. We were born to be together, trust me."

"I do trust you." I traced patterns on his chest, loving the way my touch evoked goosebumps on his skin. "I trust you with my life."

He bent his head forward so that our foreheads pressed together. "And I, you. Always and forever."

I couldn't help parroting the words back at him. "Always and forever." And then we just stared at each other like the pair of lovestruck fools we were.

* * * *

Winter brought many challenges. There was less work when we didn't have the fields to maintain, but that meant that we poured all our time into ensuring the livestock made it through the winter. We may have only had two cows, two sheep, two pigs, one horse, and a few chickens, but they all played their part in keeping us fed and clothed throughout the winter. It was a constant battle to patch up the barn from the ravages of the harsher weather, and to ensure the animals were kept safe from starvation and disease. At least with my papa back to full health from whatever had plagued him during the summer months, there were three of us to share the workload. Maman was left to sew and repair clothing, to make cloth, and to provide the meals that sustained us through the cold days where snow lay thick on the ground, and the wind howled so viciously that it was as if there were some sort of beast lying in wait outside the cottage.

I was sure my family must have noticed that this winter I was more taciturn than usual, irritation never far away from the surface. Today though, it was a struggle not to show my joy with such a bright spark on the horizon. During our last assignation in the forest, where Estienne and I had been unable to do more than huddle together under a tree and share a few kisses, he had imparted the news that his mother and sister were to be gone from the cottage for the entirety of a day.

In an excited whisper and with a quiver in his voice that had made my heart sing, he had suggested I visit. I hadn't hesitated in agreeing and had thought of little else for the past week, counting down the days until I could see him again, and the two of us could be alone in a place where warmth wasn't an alien concept. I could almost feel the ghostly impression of Estienne's hands on my skin, and his lips against my neck as he took me with a gentleness that never failed to take my breath away.

I'd been nervous the first time, but it had been just as perfect then as it had been every time since. There had been no lightning apart from the sizzling heat that our bodies had produced.

It wouldn't be an easy trip to the Badeaux cottage, but it would be worth it for what lay at the end—a few precious hours alone with Estienne, and the opportunity to lie with him for the first time in weeks. I had the cottage door half open when a hand appeared out of nowhere to slam it shut. I turned to find my brother, his expression one of concern. "Stay François, please."

Irritation rose up in me like a stem desperate to break the surface. Estienne and I would have too little time together as it was. Therefore, I had no wish to waste any of it talking to my brother. "The weather is not that bad. You do not need to worry."

His focus didn't shift from me, his concern not lessening in the slightest. "I am not worried about the weather." He leaned forward so that his words were for my ears alone. "Do you think I am stupid? Do you think I do not know what lies behind your sudden desire to bathe in the river and to go for long walks in the forest?"

A block of ice formed in my chest and all I could do was stare at him. If my secret was out, then… I didn't even want to think about the ramifications. Men were killed for less. It wouldn't just be the breaker's wheel for me. It would be execution. I would be labelled as a sinner, and my family would be forever tainted as a result.

Antoine's fingers trembled slightly as he lay a hand on my shoulder in what I assumed to be an attempt at brotherly compassion. "Madeleine is not worth it."

Madeleine! The ice in my chest eased, and it was all I could do not to laugh.

Of course that was the assumption Antoine would come to. His mind was far too pure to travel down any other path. He could never even begin to imagine the things that Estienne and I got up to. "I—"

Antoine didn't let me finish. "I hoped that winter would bring an end to you sneaking off to meet with her. The Badeaux family are trouble, François. You know that. If Cecile Badeaux finds out, there is no saying what she will do. She's a witch. She could do all manner of things to you. She could—"

"She's not a witch." Even as I said the words, though, there was that familiar trickle of unease, that strange sense of foreboding that sometimes hung in the air when I spent time with Estienne, the one that I had never admitted to him for fear of sounding stupid and having him laugh at me. During our many hours spent together, we'd talked about the rumors that circulated the village, and one thing always stood out. He laughed them off. He turned them into wildly exaggerated flights of fancy from people who should have known better. But he'd never actually denied any of them. He'd never actually said she wasn't a witch.

Antoine's fingers wrapped around my biceps to tug on my arm. "Please. Wherever you're intending to go today, don't. Stay here where you're safe. I have a bad feeling about today."

I did laugh then. "A bad feeling? Since when did you believe in such things? Perhaps you are the witch, Antoine."

A voice floated from the back of the cottage where my maman was stitching two furs together. "François, what are you and Antoine discussing? Is there a problem with the livestock? Something Papa hasn't told me?"

I raised my voice so she could hear me. "There is no problem, Maman. They are all hale and hearty. You do not need to worry." Giving my brother my best "now look what you've done" look, I shoved him away and slipped out of the door before he could make another attempt to stop me. I didn't look back as I trudged my way through the deep snow, pulling my sheepskin cape more closely around my body to keep out the worst of the wind as it tried to sink its icy teeth into me.

It took a long time to traverse the side of the hill in the perilous conditions, and at times I thought of turning back. Only the thought of Estienne kept me moving forward. He would be waiting for me. What would he think if I did not show? He might assume that I did not love him anymore, that my feelings for him were not strong enough to suffer a little hardship. The thought cut me to the quick and kept me half-skidding, half-stumbling down the hill until I finally reached the bottom and the cottage was in sight.

It looked like a perfectly ordinary cottage. There was no ring of melted snow around it to show that a weather spell had been cast. There were no winged demons nesting on the roof. There was nothing out of the ordinary apart from its location. Estienne had assured me that he would leave a sign if the coast was clear, and there it was—a dried flower the color of his hair in the window.

Despite the snow, I half-ran down the path, the door flying open long before I got to it, Estienne's smile almost stretching from ear to ear. I threw myself into his arms, the two of us stumbling backwards into the warmth of the cottage, our lips already glued together. We didn't talk. Everything we needed to say, we said using our eyes, our lips, and our hands. By the time Estienne led me over to a fur-draped cot in the corner of the cottage and undressed me as if I was something precious, I wasn't convinced I would last long enough not to embarrass myself. I needn't have worried. As always, Estienne was right there with me, our union brief and frenzied, but no less beautiful for the brevity of the act. He was beautiful. We were beautiful. The whole world was beautiful when we were together, as if in his presence everything took on a bright sheen that hadn't previously existed.

Afterwards, we lay buried in the furs, my head resting on Estienne's chest, where I could revel in the comforting *thud* of his heartbeat beneath my cheek. "I've missed you, François."

I lifted my head to find his green eyes full of an anguish that made me smile, not because I liked to see him hurt—nothing was further from the truth—but because it echoed my own feelings perfectly. It was another reminder that we were in this together, that somehow against all the odds we had found a love so pure that it defied description. We would make it work. Even if we had to run away together and live in the forest on a diet of rabbit and berries, we would make it work.

I stroked my fingers over his skin as I took my first look around the cottage. The only similarity to where I lived was the fire pit at its center. The rest was far more cluttered, things hanging from the ceiling, and shelves lining every wall of the cottage from floor to ceiling piled high with an assortment of jars. I'd never seen anything quite like it. "What's in the jars?"

Estienne turned my head back to face him, the two of us assuming our usual position of noses touching. "Nothing interesting. They're just things that Mother likes to collect. You don't need to worry about them."

The mention of Cecile Badeaux had my heart beating that little bit faster, especially coming so soon after my brother's warning. "Where are your mother and sister?"

Estienne stroked a finger over my lips, tracing the curve of the lower one. "They are gone for the day. We have hours before they will be back." His lips relaxed into a smile. "Plenty of time for me to have my fill of you."

I wanted to ask where they could possibly have gone on a day like today, but Estienne was already kissing my shoulder, his hand drifting down my body until his fingers encircled my manhood, teasing it back to full hardness in no time at all. I gave myself up to him as I always did.

* * * *

It was a noise that woke me, Estienne stirring beside me as I opened my eyes. We didn't normally fall asleep, but then we didn't usually have the luxury of a bed or blankets. There was definitely something to be said for the comfort of a cottage over a grassy bank open to the elements. "Estienne?" He made a sleepy sound against my shoulder, and I smiled at the vibration of his lips against my skin. I ached, but in that pleasant way that only came from spending time with the man I loved. "What's that noise?"

"What noise?"

We were both still, and then it came again, a scraping sound from outside the door. Estienne sat bolt upright, all the color draining from his face. "You have to go. Now."

I was already on my feet and tugging on my clothes, but we both knew it was a battle that had already been lost. The cottage only had one door. Was there somewhere I could hide? I hoped so. I trusted Estienne. He wouldn't let any harm befall me. The door flew open as I struggled into my tunic, my feet still bare.

Madeleine stepped inside, stamping snow from her boots, her long, red hair hanging loosely around her shoulders instead of being plaited, which gave her a look of wildness I had never seen on her before. She stopped short when she realized she wasn't alone, taking in my half-dressed state, her brother's nakedness, and the disarray of the cot where we'd lain together.

Wide-eyed, I stared back at her. It was Estienne who rose to his feet, one of the furs clutched in front of him to preserve his modesty. He motioned for me to continue dressing, and I quickly stepped into my boots before retrieving my fur from the floor. With his gaze still fixed on his sister, Estienne placed a finger on his lips, his eyes pleading with her not to say anything.

When she seemed frozen in place, Estienne caught my arm, tugging me closer to the door. Madeleine would stay quiet, and I would be able to sneak out. I would run home, and Estienne and I would laugh about how close we'd come to being discovered later. He'd swear his sister to secrecy. Maybe she would even become our ally. She could pass messages between the two of us so that our meetings were easier to arrange. Her discovery could turn out to be a good thing.

And then Madeleine opened her mouth, my dreams crumbling around my feet as effectively as an avalanche. "Mother? You need to come in here. You need to see what Estienne has been up to while we've been gone. He has not been ill at all. He lied to us. Mother?"

I shrank back as the door opened to reveal the tall figure I'd only ever glimpsed at a distance before. Cecile Badeaux was an intimidating woman if ever there was one. Her hair was just as fiery red as her children's, but it wasn't that that made her so fearsome. It was the look in her eyes. It was a look that shouldn't have belonged in the eyes of a woman in her forties. It was a look that screamed of hundreds of years of knowledge, a knowledge she shouldn't have possessed.

Stumbling backwards, my shoulder caught a shelf, the jar closest to the edge crashing to the floor and smashing at my feet. I looked down and something looked back at me, my stomach lurching at the sight of not just one eyeball, but a whole bunch of them.

My gaze flicked to the other jars, the ones that had remained on the shelf, their contents doing nothing to help settle my stomach. Some I could tell were parts of animals, but they weren't the worst. It was the ones containing elements that could only be human, the fingers floating in one taunting me with my own stupidity. Why hadn't I taken a moment to look around? If I had, my time in that cottage would have been very short, and I would never have set foot in there again. But I had had eyes only for Estienne.

Reality crashed down on me. Cecile Badeaux was indeed a witch, and I was trapped in her house with no means of escape. Love had blinded me to the truth. In that moment of clarity, I even felt animosity toward Estienne. He had known, and he'd let me come here. And even worse, he had let me fall asleep—had fallen asleep himself—when he was supposed to protect me.

Cecile still hadn't spoken, her gaze cool and assessing as it crawled down my body until it reached the broken jar at my feet.

It was Madeleine who spoke first as she came to stand next to her mother, tossing her red hair over her shoulder. "Mother, you said that I could have François. I told you I wanted him, and you said you would create a spell to bind him to me." She threw her brother a scathing look. "Why does Estienne get to have him? What they've been doing together is a sin."

Estienne finally seemed to find his voice. He ignored his sister in favor of speaking directly to his mother. "None of this is François's fault. Just let him go. Please. I should never have invited him here. We won't see each other anymore, I promise."

I opened my mouth with the intention of disputing that, but the look he shot me was more than enough to silence me. There was sheer panic in his eyes. He was scared. Scared for me. I began to edge toward the door, figuring that if I could at least get outside without Cecile noticing, it would buy me some time to get away.

I got as far as the door, my fingers mere tantalizing inches from the handle when something hit me on the back of the head. My knees gave way, and blackness stole over me, dragging me down into its depths.

Chapter Three

Domme, Dordogne 1571

François

Consciousness took a lot longer to take root than its more sinister cousin had. It was like trying to fight my way up from a deep, dark well and getting halfway, only to slip back down into the water, time after time. When I did finally rouse myself enough to be aware of my surroundings, it was to find myself face-down in hay, with a rope binding my wrists to a nearby fencepost. There was enough give in the rope that I could lever myself to a seated position, the movement sending a jolt of nausea through me, my head throbbing in time with my rapid heartbeat.

Madeleine was perched on a stool in the barn, her head tipping to one side as she watched me. A few steps away, Cecile Badeaux was leaning against the fence. As for Estienne, there was no sign of him. "Where's Estienne? I want to see him."

Cecile smiled, but it was a cruel smile full of loathing. "You will never see him again."

"You can't keep us apart. We love each other. You have no idea of the bond that exists between us. Ask him." Despite the lancing pain that accompanied any movement of my head, I made an effort to turn it. I'd hoped to find Estienne in the shadows, but the barn was empty of anyone except for the three of us. Why had he left me? Had they done something to him? She was his mother. She wouldn't hurt her own son, would she?

Cecile moved aside, and I caught my first glimpse of the strange array of items she'd arranged in front of her. She picked up the earthenware bowl and started to add things to it, her words strange and foreign-sounding. "What are you doing?"

She didn't answer, not even glancing my way as she continued the peculiar preparations for whatever would come next while Madeleine watched in glee. Did that mean that Madeleine was a witch too? What about Estienne? I couldn't believe it of him. Not the kind, sweet man who had openly adored me. But then, where was he?

The string of strange words came to a stop, the silence that followed all the more jarring until Cecile began to speak again, the language one I recognized this time. "You besmirched my son with your foul, perverted urges. For that, François Damont, you will be cursed."

Cursed? What did that mean? I wanted to ask, but the inside of my mouth had turned to ash. All I wanted was to go home. Back to the warmth and safety of my family. I would even put up with Antoine lecturing me, as if he was the older brother and I was the younger. He'd always thought he knew best. Although, perhaps in the case of staying away from the Badeux family he'd been right. I only hoped I got the opportunity to tell him that.

Cecile stepped forward, the light in her eyes something otherworldly and utterly terrifying. "You will be trapped in stone forevermore, your beauty hidden by a façade so ugly that people will not like to look upon it. You will feel, but you will not be able to speak. You will hear, but you will not be able to communicate. You will endure across the ages, a silent witness to the decades that go by."

She let out a laugh, the harsh maniacal tones sending a shiver down my spine. "I'm offering you eternal life, but not as a gift, as a penance for your sins, for the sins you inflicted upon my child. Every twenty-five years, you will walk upon the earth once more. You will experience everything you have lost, but only for twenty-eight days, and then you will be entombed once again. Only a love so pure that it is unmistakable will break the curse, and you will never find that."

The words she was uttering were grotesque, painting a picture of an eternal lifetime full of suffering. They were just the words of a madwoman, though. I had to hang on to that. She couldn't really do the things she was threatening. No one could do that.

Madeleine appeared next to her mother, a flame from kindling cupped in her hands. Cecile nodded, and Madeleine dropped it into the bowl. Cecile uttered a few more words, and then… Then there was nothing. Apart from three people all staring as fire consumed whatever materials that Cecile had placed in the bowl.

Laughter filled the barn, and it took me a while to work out from the edge of hysteria in it, that it was coming from me. I snapped my jaw shut and the sound stopped. Only now I could hear the wind. It had picked up, and it was inside the barn even though the door was closed, which didn't make any sense when it had been so still before. Where had it come from?

I tried to move. Maybe if I could stand, it would bring a halt to this ridiculous game. Cecile had set out to scare me and she'd succeeded, but I'd had enough. I couldn't move, though. Not even an inch. It was like my legs had become paralyzed. The full horror of what was happening became apparent as I glanced down. There was a gray film slowly stealing its way over my calves, like ice, but even colder. Harder as well. As I watched, it crept slowly higher until it reached mid-thigh.

My fingers shook as I reached out to touch it, snatching my hand back as whatever it was transferred itself to my fingers, spreading up my wrist and transforming my arm into the same cold, hard mass as my legs. "Please." I didn't even know what I was begging for. I just knew that I wanted it to stop, that I wanted to wake from this strange nightmare that couldn't possibly be true, and that they were the only people who could do that.

They weren't going to, though, not when they were both smiling. They were clearly pleased with whatever it was that was happening. And all the while, the coldness kept spreading, like an insidious and persistent mold that wouldn't stop until it had covered every inch of my skin. It spread to my chest, and I couldn't breathe, panic grasping hold of my nerve-endings. If I couldn't breathe, I would die.

There was a searing flash of light, and all I could think was that the lightning I'd been waiting for ever since the first touch of Estienne's lips against mine had finally arrived. I blacked out, Cecile's threats of a curse ringing in my ears. Death would be better than that. Death was peace, not suffering. I could handle death. Perhaps I'd even get to see Estienne again in the afterlife. The two of us would be reunited, free from censure, free from having to hide what we were from the rest of the world.

* * * *

When I awoke, nothing felt right. I opened my eyes, yet, the sensation was more mental than physical, as if I no longer had eyelids to lift. There wasn't a single part of my body I could move, no matter how hard I tried. What was it Cecile had said? *"You will feel, but you will not be able to speak. You will hear, but you will not be able to communicate."* Well, she'd made good on her promise. In an effort not to succumb to panic, I concentrated on what I could see, trying to piece together what was happening. I was no longer in the barn, the horizon moving in a gentle rise and fall. The sound of horse's hooves. Men's voices. I was on the back of a cart being taken somewhere. I strained to hear what the men were saying.

"Where are we taking this thing?"

"Not sure. We were simply told to take it as far as possible with no destination mentioned. I was thinking we could sell it and make some extra coin."

Far away. Far from my family. Far from Estienne. Did he even know what had been done to me?

The man let out a snort. "Sell it? Who is going to want to buy it? Have you not seen how ugly this thing is? It is a monstrosity."

"Someone might. Someone may be in need of something to keep the children away."

They both laughed before the first man spoke again. "We have to travel to Paris anyway. I say we transport it that far, and if we cannot find a buyer, we will find a place to leave it. What do you say?"

"I say that it is as good a plan as any."

The next couple of weeks were a voyage of discovery in more ways than one. I saw parts of France I'd never dreamed of seeing. As François Damont, it was doubtful I would ever have left Domme. I would have lived and died farming that same piece of land. But it was hard to see the experience as a blessing.

I also learned about my new existence. Although there was no physical need to do so, I discovered I could still sleep. Sleep made the time pass faster. And it seemed like there would be nothing but time in my future.

Cecile had said I would walk the earth again in twenty-five years, but twenty-five years seemed like a lifetime. Would Estienne still be alive? Could I get back to him in the twenty-eight days that Cecile had said I would have? He would be in his late forties. Would he have married and had children? And If I did make it back to him, would he even remember me? Would I age? Would Estienne be middle-aged while I stayed the same?

And what of my parents? What of Antoine? What would happen to them without me? Would they be able to manage the land and the livestock? Would they be able to pay the rent to keep the land? What about when my parents died? Hopefully, Antoine would have married by then. He'd have a family of his own to help him.

There were so many questions ricocheting around in my head, and I didn't have an answer to any of them, nor was I ever likely to. I had twenty-five years of nothing but my own company to look forward to. How would I stay sane? And what about when twenty-five years was up. What then? Where would I be? Would I be able to break the curse? Cecile had seemed sure that it wasn't possible. But to believe that would be to give up before I'd even tried. I willed down the panic threatening to rise up and overwhelm me.

I would break the curse, and I would see Estienne and my brother again. Cecile wouldn't win. She couldn't.

Chapter Four

Sheffield, England 2018

Daniel

A mixture of excitement and anticipation bubbled through my veins, the square box in my pocket feeling like it was burning a hole. I'd planned to pop the question at the restaurant. Only, nerves had gotten the better of me, and then a mutual friend had come over to our table and insisted on joining us, and I hadn't needed an audience.

I glanced over at Calvin, but either he was completely unaware of my agitated state, or he'd put it down to something else. There was a danger that if I didn't do it soon, it wouldn't happen at all tonight. And then I'd have to face the same cycle of anxiety all over again the following day. I wasn't sure my heart could take it if that was the case. Reaching out, I wrapped my fingers around Calvin's wrist and brought him to a stop. "I need to talk to you."

A furrow appeared on his brow, and he scanned the dark and almost empty lane. "Here? Can't it wait until we get out of the cold?"

Shaking my head, I slid my hand into my pocket and traced the outline of the box, my heart going a mile a minute, and my mouth dry. "I meant to do it at the restaurant. That was the plan." I looked around. "The venue shouldn't really matter, though, should it?"

Calvin's shrug said that he didn't have a clue what I was talking about. Eyeing the damp leaf-strewn pavement, I said goodbye to this particular pair of trousers and sank to one knee, the object of my focus just looking confused. *Oh, come on! I was down on one knee and nervous as hell. Did he really need any more of an indication what I was up to?* Apparently, he did. Well, he was going to get one, as soon as I could manage to maneuver the box out of my pocket, which due to my position seemed to be stuck. I should have put it in the opposite pocket or bent the other knee. It was too late now, though. I could only work with what I had.

Finally extracting the box with a vicious yank, my fingers shook as I worked it open. Thankfully, I managed it without dropping it, and without the ring pinging out to skitter down the nearest drain. I held it out to Calvin, my heart beating so fast I could feel it in my throat. "Will you marry me?"

The way he stared at the ring, and then at me, and then back to the ring said that he was still trying to make sense of what was happening. It was disconcerting, to say the least. Surely, he agreed that we'd been heading this way for the past year. I'd even thought that he might have been the one to propose on my birthday, but the day had passed without a proposal. So here I was grabbing the bull by the horns. Only it seemed the bull had wandered off to a different paddock. Calvin's lips formed into a circle. "Oh!"

That single word left me feeling like a complete idiot, a complete idiot kneeling in the dark, with damp slowly seeping through my trousers. I tried for levity, the crack in my voice meaning I didn't quite pull it off as well as I'd been hoping. "Oh, what? Oh, you're so happy that I chose a really nice ring?"

His gaze flicked back to the ring. "It is a really nice ring."

"But?"

He seemed to give himself a shake. "But nothing. It's just… it's a big decision that's all. You've really surprised me, Dan. I had no idea."

"Really?"

He smiled. "Really. I knew there was something bothering you, but I thought it was linked to work." He reached down to tug on my elbow. "Get up. Before a car comes by and splashes you, and I have to save you from drowning."

I resisted his attempts to pull me to my feet. "I was kind of hoping for an answer first."

"An answer, right." He scrubbed at his eyes with the heel of his hand. It was reminiscent of someone trying to decide whether they wanted to insert their penis or their testicles in a vise. "I need to think about it. Can I think about it?"

As romantic proposals went, it pretty much sucked. I'd had visions of tears and a breathless agreement, not a grimace and an "I need to think about it." I struggled to my feet, focusing my attention on the dirty patch on my trousers. What now?
Did I give him the ring? Or did I hang on to it? He hadn't accepted the proposal, though, had he? So I guessed that meant the ring was still mine.

I snapped the box shut and slid it back into my pocket, affecting a nonchalance I was a million miles away from feeling. "Of course you can think about it. There's no time limit."

We stood awkwardly for a few moments. I'd intended to spend the night at Calvin's place, but that suddenly seemed like worst idea in the world. Salvation came in the form of a perfectly timed cab appearing around the bend. I almost pushed Calvin out of the way in my rush to leap into the road and flag it down. Thankfully, the driver stopped, and I already had the door half open before turning to address Calvin. "I think it's probably better if I go home tonight. You know, give you a chance to do that thinking."

His nod was long and considering. He glanced down the road, his house only a five-minute walk away, and for a moment I thought he was going to argue with me, but then he nodded again. "You're probably right. I'll give you a call tomorrow after work."

I threw myself into the back of the cab, relaying my address to the driver even before I'd closed the door. I didn't look at Calvin as the cab pulled away from the curb. Only when I knew I was out of sight, did I allow myself to slide down in the seat and close my eyes. That definitely could have gone better. Was that a sign? We'd been together for over a year. We had fun. We were sexually compatible. We rarely argued over anything more serious than who was going to make the coffee. I'd thought we were perfect together and I couldn't wait to spend the rest of my life with him. Yes, there was an eleven-year age gap, but that shouldn't matter when it came to matters of the heart, should it? I just didn't know anymore. I couldn't shake the feeling that I'd just made a huge fool of myself.

* * * *

The next morning didn't find a huge improvement in my disposition. Even the three cups of coffee I'd drunk before leaving the house had done nothing to shift the feeling of gloom that had descended on me. At some point while tossing and turning during the night, I'd convinced myself that Calvin would say no to my proposal. Where would that leave us? What was the standard procedure for a relationship after a failed marriage proposal? Were we just supposed to carry on as if it had never happened, with me pretending I didn't care that I now knew that we were on the long road to nowhere? Were we supposed to split because we clearly weren't on the same page? Only, that seemed like a huge chasm in my mindset. How was I supposed to go from "I love you and I want to marry you," to "bye-bye, Calvin?"

There were no messages from him when I checked my phone, not even the customary goodnight message we normally sent when we weren't spending the night together. But then, I hadn't sent one either. I'd been too busy nursing my wounded pride.

I made it to the University of Sheffield with only ten minutes to spare before my first lecture was due to start. It wasn't a problem. It was a lecture I could do standing on one leg with my eyes closed. I was halfway down the corridor with the lecture hall in sight when a familiar strident tone rang out from behind me. "Mr. Smith, a moment of your time, if I may."

I stopped dead, turning as slowly as humanly possible to face the woman approaching me, her red hair pulled back severely from her face as always, and her high heels beating an ominous tattoo on the bare floor. Marjorie Rutherford — one of the deans of the university. I did my best to school my face into something that didn't resemble dread as she drew closer, but I probably failed miserably.

She came to a halt in front of me, her questing gaze giving me a once-over that said she was searching for faults. I suddenly became all too aware of the fact that I hadn't bothered to iron my shirt. The students didn't care if I wore a rumpled shirt. Marjorie Rutherford did, though. She was the poster girl for 'standards must be upheld at all times.' If there was a fault of any kind, she could usually sniff it out within seconds.

I often thought that she'd missed her true calling and would have been far better in the military. She had all the necessary attributes: the bearing, the watchful eye, the love of discipline, and the ability to turn even the bravest of men into a quivering wreck. I'd never quite gotten over the feeling that at any time she might ask me to drop and give her twenty. "You're late again,

Mr. Smith. That's the fourth time this month." She said it in a way that said my tardy timekeeping was a personal insult to her.

I glanced at my watch. Still five minutes to go before the first lecture was due to start. "Not really. It's not nine yet."

One eyebrow arched a fraction of an inch. She had very expressive eyebrows. "So… your slides are all ready to go, your notes are in order, and you are ready to greet the students as they start their first lecture of the day?"

We both knew that wasn't the case. I bit back on the urge to point out that by talking to me, all she was doing was delaying me further, that had she not waylaid me I might have been able to pull off that feat in the five minutes I had, as long as the IT equipment felt like playing ball today and didn't suddenly decide it wanted a day off.

I bit my tongue and inclined my head in a silent recognition of her point. "It won't take me long to set up. I had car trouble." More like boyfriend trouble. But she wasn't the type of woman who'd ever given any indication that she was remotely interested in listening to my — or anyone else's for that matter — relationship woes.

"Again?" The word was imbued with a great deal of disbelief.

I winced. I needed to manufacture a few more go-to excuses. "It's an old car."

"Perhaps it's time you invested in a new one."

Maybe when you give me a pay raise, I will. "Probably."

Her laser-sharp gaze released its hold on my face to settle on the doors of the lecture hall. "You had better go. I have no wish to make you later than you are already. We'll reconvene this conversation at 4p.m sharp in my office if that's agreeable to you."

It wasn't. It wasn't the slightest bit agreeable, but as it hadn't been phrased as a question, there was absolutely no other response I could give but to nod. As soon as she turned to leave, I hotfooted it to the lecture hall, the IT equipment thankfully deciding that I'd had enough shit already for one day.

For the next few hours, I got to lose myself in one of the things I loved most—history. Marjorie Rutherford might be a constant thorn in my side, but I did love my job, and while I was lecturing there was no Calvin, no sleepless night, and definitely no bungled marriage proposal.

One of the students on the front row raised his hand to ask a question. "So… what you're saying is… that there were no witches before the 16th century? Where did they all come from? Was there like a huge witch explosion one day and they all just popped out of the ground?"

A titter went round the lecture hall, and I waited until it had died down before speaking. "I didn't say they didn't have witches, just that there weren't as many witchcraft trials before the mid-1500s. That was the time when the authorities started to sit up and take notice of them. Mainly because that's when they started linking them to devil worship and other satanic rituals."

A girl in the third row with wavy blonde hair sat forward with a pensive look on her face. "But like… none of them were witches really, were they? They were just women who liked to experiment with things. They'd probably be hailed as scientists in this day and age."

"Some of them. And in a lot of cases, they were used simply as scapegoats, something to blame a bad crop on, or a convenient reason why a village had been struck down by a disease. But for each innocent woman, there were definitely cases of individuals dabbling with the occult in disturbing ways."

"Dude, are you saying witches are real?"

I smiled at the wide-eyed student in the back row, who was staring at me as if I'd just told him I'd spent the night drinking with Santa Claus, the Easter bunny, and the tooth fairy. "I'm saying that like with most things, you have to make your own mind up. I can only teach you about the European witch hunt and what happened to those women who the authorities decided were witches, I can't decide for you whether every woman burnt at the stake was innocent of any wrongdoing."

The student opened his mouth to say something, but whatever it was, was drowned out by the bell ringing to announce the end of the lecture. There was a flurry of motion as over a hundred students all packed up in unison, followed by a cacophony of footsteps as they hurried away for lunch, their enthusiasm for the subject matter drowned out by the need for food. I had to admit that they weren't the only ones eager for lunch. I'd been too busy feeling sorry for myself to eat breakfast that morning, and my stomach had started complaining about it an hour ago.

"Witches, hey?"

My head shot up to find my colleague and good friend, Richard, standing at the back of the lecture hall with his arms folded over his chest. I smiled at him. "How long have you been standing there?"

"Long enough to hear you suggesting to young, impressionable minds that witches might walk among us."

I rolled my eyes at him. "I did no such thing. I just suggested they should make their own minds up. You know, the power of independent thinking and all that."

"So you don't believe in witches?"

I took the stairs that bisected the lecture hall two at a time until I reached the place where he stood. "I have the same belief system as I have for ghosts. Until someone proves it or disproves it, I'll keep an open mind."

Richard deliberately dropped his gaze to my ass. "And how are the splinters?"

"Splinters?"

"From the fence you're determined to sit on."

I gave him a playful shove that had him stumbling backwards. "What are you doing here, anyway?"

Richard laughed. "I thought we could go for a walk and have lunch at the same time. You can tell me how last night worked out. Although, I'm guessing from the fact that you're not exactly bathed in a warm, sunny glow that it didn't go too well."

We made our way down the corridor and out to the campus lawn, the wall we eventually sat ourselves on offering a scenic view of the campus, a few students nodding at us in passing. I launched straight into relaying the events of the previous evening, Richard giving the requisite nods and grunts in the spaces where they were needed in between taking bites of his sandwich. Once I'd finished, I waited for him to share his thoughts. He was a typical scientist who liked to think things through carefully before offering an opinion. Finally, he spoke. "He didn't say no."

I let out a sigh. "He didn't say yes either. But it was the look on his face. You weren't there. It was like the thought of us getting married had never even occurred to him. I've been thinking about proposing to him for the last six months. How could I have gotten it so wrong?"

Richard arched an eyebrow. "So… what are you saying? That you don't want to marry him anymore?"

I shrugged. I knew I was wallowing in self-pity, but surely, I was within my rights to do that, for a short time anyway. I'd put my heart on the line and if it hadn't been rejected, then at the very least it had been found wanting. "I didn't say that."

"Well…" Richard rubbed a hand through his short, brown hair, leaving one bit sticking up at the front. "You better figure it out because there's still the possibility that he might say yes. I think you need to accept that he's not crazy for wanting to think about it first. It would be disastrous for the two of you to rush into something that's not right for both of you, especially considering the age gap."

I hated those two words. They always seemed to be casually dropped into any conversation concerning myself and Calvin. That, and the fact that he was an ex-student of the university. He'd never been my student, and our relationship hadn't started until he'd already left, but that never seemed to matter to anyone searching for a hint of scandal. "It's eleven years. It's not like I'm old enough to be his father."

A slight smile played on Richard's lips. "No Daddy games, then?"

I couldn't help the heat that rose to my cheeks. "No, definitely not. Both of us are strictly vanilla, thank you very much. Anyway, what do you know about being called Daddy? Something you're not telling me?"

Richard's smile grew wider. "Wouldn't you like to know?"

I was distracted from pointing out that I *would* like to know as the strident beeping sound of a vehicle reversing emanated across the campus. We watched in silence as the truck came to a stop, three men getting out and starting to manhandle a large, shrouded mass from the back of it until they'd gotten it on the ground. Given their level of exertion and the way they wiped their brows once the job was done, it was obviously something heavy. Two men stood back as the third cut the ropes and uncovered what turned out to be a statue.

Richard leaned forward to get a better look. "What the fuck is that?"

I smiled. "It's a gargoyle. Well… technically if you want to split hairs, it's a grotesque. To be a gargoyle, it has to have a waterspout, but most people would call it a gargoyle anyway."

Richard gave me an "alright Mr. History" look that I knew only too well. I climbed to my feet, pausing as Richard's hand landed on my forearm and he frowned at me. "What are you doing?"

"I want to take a closer look at it."

"I think you should stay the fuck away from it. It's quite possibly the ugliest thing I've ever seen."

I laughed, shrugging off his restraining arm and making my way across the lawn toward it, Richard eventually following, reluctance etched in his every step. I joined the small group of students gathered in front of it, most of their opinions in line with Richard's. The gargoyle—or grotesque—took the form of a winged demon complete with a hooked nose and horns. Its misshapen chin rested on its strangely human hands as if it was deep in thought about something. The group of students eventually drifted away, leaving just myself and Richard to contemplate it.

Richard snorted. "Well, someone's clearly lost all their marbles. I hope they didn't pay that much for it. I can't think why someone would decide to plonk that in the middle of campus. Maybe they're hoping it will help keep people off the lawn."

I trailed my gaze over it. It was clearly an original piece rather than a replica. I could tell from the unevenness of the stonework, and the fact that in several places, there were chips missing, as if over the years it had received more than its fair share of rough handling. The history buff in me couldn't help but marvel at it. I bet if it could speak, it would have some stories to tell. "I like it."

The look Richard shot me was reminiscent of someone deciding whether they should have me consigned to the local loony bin. "They ward off evil spirits, you know. People wrongly think that because of the way they look, they bring bad luck, but actually it's the other way round. It's good luck to have a gargoyle, or a grotesque, in the vicinity."

Richard turned his head to scan the campus. "Yeah, loads of evil spirits around here. Some of the students might be a pain in the ass, but I wouldn't go so far as to call them evil spirits. Although" — his lips twitched — "there is Marjorie of course, so perhaps it's not that far-fetched." He checked his watch and inclined his head toward the building. "Speaking of Marjorie, we better head back. Afternoon lectures start in ten minutes. I'd suggest not getting caught by our resident evil spirit twice in one day if you know what's good for you." He had a point. I reluctantly turned my back on the gargoyle and followed Richard back into the building.

The afternoon went smoothly, and the scheduled meeting with Marjorie proved to be less painful than expected, when she seemed distracted and did nothing more than lecture me on the importance of good timekeeping. I made the obligatory noises of agreement and left her office within ten minutes of getting there.

I found myself taking a detour on the way to my car, my steps taking me across the lawn and over to the gargoyle until I stood in front of it. It was strange, but I somehow felt drawn to it, as if it exuded some sort of mystical force that wanted me to take a closer look. Only once I was looking at it, it didn't seem enough, my fingers itching to touch.

I cast a covert glance around to check that no one was watching before reaching out and cautiously laying my hand on the rough surface of its wing. I immediately snatched my hand back as if my fingers had been burned. What the fuck! I could have sworn I'd felt some kind of strange energy emanating from it. I had to be imagining things. I reached out again, my fingers hovering in mid-air for a good thirty seconds before I finally plucked up enough courage to lower them. This time, I forced myself to leave them there and categorize the strange sensation. It was hard to explain, but it was like there was movement within the stone, a dull vibration which traveled all the way from my fingertips and up to my shoulder. The longer I touched it, the stronger it seemed to get. Even more peculiar was the feeling in my chest. It was like someone had gripped hold of my heart and was squeezing it tightly, an overwhelming and inexplicable feeling of sorrow engulfing me. And yet, I couldn't let go. It was like a storm I had to weather. Like the inanimate stone statue was trying to tell me something, only we were speaking different languages and I couldn't quite work out what it was.

A harsh ringing noise filled the air, and it took me a moment to work out that it was coming from my phone rather than the gargoyle. At least it broke the spell, and I was able to not only let go but to take a step back. I brought the phone to my ear without looking who it was, my voice sounding unnaturally husky as I said "hello."

"Dan?"

Calvin. I pressed my phone harder against my ear. "Yeah, it's me. Who did you think it was?"

"I don't know. You just sounded weird there for a moment."

I risked a glance back to the gargoyle, which looked like nothing more than a perfectly ordinary statue. I shoved the hand not holding the phone into my pocket, in case the strange urge to touch it overtook me again. "Did I? Sorry. I was probably thinking about… something."

"I owe you an apology."

My heart skipped a beat. "For what?"

Calvin's sigh echoed down the phone line. "It's really sweet that you would even question that. You know what for. You asked me to marry you and I was a dick."

"I'm not sure I would go that far, but I'll admit that it wasn't exactly the reaction I was hoping for."

"I know… and I'm sorry. You really did take me by surprise, but I've spent all day thinking about it, and it shouldn't have been a surprise, should it? Not unless I've got my head shoved so far up my ass that I've gone blind."

I laughed. "You said it, not me."

"Anyway…" There was a long pause and I imagined Calvin rubbing his neck, the same way he always did when he was nervous.

"You can say no, you know. I'll understand. It will hurt, but I'll understand."

"No, it's a… it's a yes. Unless you've taken your proposal back, that is."

A wave of euphoria filled me. "I haven't. Do you mean it?"

Calvin laughed, the sound just that little bit too high-pitched. "Yes! I'll keep saying the word if it makes you feel better."

"That's not necessary." I turned on my heel and started toward my car, the strange experience with the statue all but forgotten. "Are you still at work? A face to face yes would definitely help."

"I've just got home. I'll put the kettle on and see if I can rustle up something to eat that might be remotely celebratory. Although, it might be chocolate fingers artfully arranged on a plate."

"I'll be there in thirty minutes."

"See you soon, fiancé."

I imagined that the grin on my face as I hung up must have been ear to ear. It was a good thing that Richard wasn't around to mock me. Although, I doubted even he could have popped the bubble of happiness I was feeling.

Chapter Five

Daniel

I held my hand up in front of the gargoyle's face, its cold stone gaze as implacable as ever. "So, I'm a married man now. What do you think of the ring? Calvin chose it. It's probably a bit flashier than I would have chosen myself, but that's good because it makes me think of him, and marriage is all about compromise, right? I'm guessing we're going to have to do a lot of compromising when it comes to decorating the new house. He's got very different tastes to mine. He wants to get a dog as well, whereas I'm more of a cat person. I suppose we could get one of each. That seems like a better compromise than having neither. The wedding was good. Although, Richard got horrifically drunk and I'm pretty sure he propositioned at least three of the wedding guests, which wouldn't have been too bad, but one of them was Calvin's little sister, and he's understandably protective of her."

I trailed off. I was doing it again, telling all of my business to an inanimate object. I still felt that same vibration when I touched it, but it was nowhere near as powerful as that first time, and I'd never been assailed by that same inexplicable rush of sadness. Even knowing that it couldn't possibly have been anything more than the combination of lack of sleep and the emotional turmoil I'd felt about mine and Calvin's relationship at the time, I still pondered on my overactive imagination sometimes. And as for the vibration, that was obviously down to… Well, truth be told, I hadn't yet come up with an explanation that worked, but there had to be one. Something to do with stone and atmospheric pressure, maybe. I'd thought about asking Richard. He was a scientist, after all, but he would also mock me mercilessly.

* * * *

Even though dusk was rapidly approaching, I perched on the grass verge, the gargoyle staring back at me. "I know what you're thinking. You think I'm avoiding going home. You don't know Calvin, though. Its best to give him a bit of space after we've had a blow-up. He's got an awful lot going on at the moment, what with his sister being ill. They've done some tests at the hospital, but they don't seem any closer to finding out what's wrong with her. And no, I don't resent him spending time with her. I'd do the same for my family. That's what families do, right? They look after each other. I'll admit that it does bother me a bit when it's the whole weekend, though. With work, we don't get to see each other nearly enough as it is, which, I know, is the same for most couples. Marriage is never going to be one non-stop honeymoon. There's always going to be things that get in the way, storms you have to weather together. It's natural for there to be times where we don't quite see eye to eye on things."

I let out a sigh. I wasn't sure when the gargoyle had become my confidante, but I found myself unloading all my troubles onto it more and more. It was less judgmental than Richard, what with the fact that it couldn't speak. A lot less likely to shift some of the blame for my marriage not being a bed of roses at my own door as well. Whereas Richard was never shy about pointing out the flaws that had contributed to mine and Calvin's relationship not being smooth sailing.

I struggled to my feet as voices floated across the lawn and I recognized some of my own students. I didn't need them whispering behind my back about their poor sap of a lecturer getting caught relaying his marital difficulties to a statue. I walked away, struck by the feeling, not for the first time, that there was something behind its eyes looking back at me, as if it watched my retreat.

Jesus! Maybe I was losing my grip on reality. Calvin always told me that I spent so long thinking about the past that sometimes it was like I forgot to exist in the present. That was just one of the jibes he liked to throw my way when he was annoyed about something, which at the moment was the majority of the time. Maybe we needed to go on holiday. Yeah, that sounded good. Just the two of us with no work to distract us. Once Calvin's sister was better, we could book somewhere, somewhere hot. It could be a second honeymoon for the two of us and give us an opportunity to iron out the wrinkles in our marriage. I left campus feeling much more optimistic.

* * * *

Six months later

Okay, now it was getting ridiculous. It was one thing stopping for a chat with the gargoyle on the way into work or on the way home. It was another thing entirely to climb into my car late in the evening with the express purpose of coming here specially. And could you call it a chat when it was so one-sided? At least the lateness of the hour meant that campus was virtually empty; the students were either home or having fun in one of the many pubs and bars around the city.

I stopped in front of the gargoyle, feeling strangely tongue-tied. "Hi."

It continued to stare at me.

"You're probably wondering what I'm doing here so late."

No, it's not. It's not wondering anything because it's a chunk of stone. I sank down on the grass, glad that it hadn't rained recently. "Yeah, well, I guess I just needed someone to talk to, and you know, you're always here, and you're a good listener. By which I mean you never interrupt. According to Calvin, I do that a lot."

I picked idly at a few blades of grass. "Anyway, he's moved out. He's been really moody ever since his sister died. God, that sounds terrible. I mean, obviously, he's allowed to grieve. She was his little sister. But it's like I can't say anything right without him jumping down my throat. If I give him space, I'm ignoring him, and if I spend time with him, I'm smothering him. I just can't do anything right. And you know what he said today?" My voice cracked. "He said we should never have gotten married, that he knew when I asked him that it was a mistake, but that he'd gone ahead and done it anyway. I know, he's just trying to say stuff to hurt me, but the problem is that it does. It really hurts."

I took a deep breath, the night air just that side of too cold. "Anyway, to cut a long story short before I bore you to death, he packed his stuff today and he left. He reckons a trial separation will do us good." I pulled my knees in, wrapping my arms around them and resting my chin on top. "Between you and me, I don't think he's coming back. I think that's it for us." My breath was noisy as I let it out. "Two years of marriage!" The words were laced with bitterness. "That's all we managed. Pretty pathetic, huh? And if you want to be pedantic, it hasn't even been that long. I'm rounding it up. I feel like such a huge fucking failure, and I keep going over and over things. I can't stop thinking about what I could have done differently. I don't want to be thirty-four with a failed marriage. I keep thinking that maybe I can still fix things." I shook my head. "I just don't know anymore. I don't even know if I really want to."

* * * *

I plucked a cap that said *'Love'* in big letters, only there was a heart in place of the o, off the gargoyle's head. "No offense, but it doesn't really suit you." The students had a habit of dressing the gargoyle up whenever they fancied. I'd seen it in numerous items of clothing from a bra to a Liverpool football scarf. All the items now lived in a box in my office. I just hoped no one ever had a root around and started asking questions about why I had a bra in there. I wasn't sure any of the conclusions they might come to would do me any favors.

"So… the divorce papers came through last week. It's now official. I'm a single man once more, and I've got to tell you, I don't have a clue what I'm meant to do with that." I screwed my face up as I thought about it. "Am I meant to hit Grindr? Start touting myself as being up for a bit of no strings sex, because lord knows there was very little of that toward the end of my relationship with Calvin."

I quickly scanned my surroundings to make sure that none of my students were around to hear their teacher talk about hooking up with a bunch of strange men. Word would go straight to Marjorie, and I'd have her bearing down on me like a harbinger of doom. Any hope of her softening the longer she remained in the role had been dashed a long time ago. If anything, she had gotten worse. Nothing seemed to escape her beady eye, and I often felt like she had it in for me. I definitely seemed to attract her ire more than some of the other people in the department. I'd never seen her have a single issue with Chris and Rebecca. Mind, that might have had something to do with them being a married couple, who also happened to be a pair of goody-two-shoes. I was being mean. I was probably just jealous that their marriage of four years was still going strong.

I turned my attention back to the gargoyle. "I'm just feeling sorry for myself. I thought I was done with dating, but unless I'm happy to be alone forever, I'm going to have to get back onto the horse. Figuratively speaking, that is. I'm not trying to meet some sort of Yorkshire cowboy. Does that even exist?" I laughed to myself. The gargoyle didn't laugh.

Chapter Six

François

Time was something I never stopped thinking about. What time of day was it? How long until the next day started so that I was one step closer to twenty-five years being up? At first, I'd tried to keep some sort of record in my head. But it had proven impossible. Therefore, after the first century or so, I'd given up.

I couldn't even say how many times I'd lived over the years, only that every cycle ended in the same way, with the curse locking me back inside my stone prison. There'd been men — plenty of men — but no matter what I did, or what I said, no matter what I promised them, I'd never managed to find anyone who loved me enough to break the curse.

They'd said they loved me. I'd even believed it of some of them. There'd been Raphael, a free-spirited artist in eighteenth-century Paris, who'd looked at me like the sun rose and set in my eyes. Yet, once the month was up, I'd still found myself encased back in the gargoyle, my heart ceasing to beat and my lungs freezing in my chest.

There'd been Jeremy. I'd met Jeremy during my first taste of freedom after being transported to England. Jeremy couldn't have been more different than Raphael. He'd been a staid man, a man who played by the rules and took his role as an actuary extremely seriously. Despite our differences, we'd fitted together well, and he'd been nothing but patient with my faltering English at that time, teaching me more in those twenty-eight days than I could ever have learned on my own. In the short amount of time we'd had, we'd built an unmistakable connection. It hadn't made any difference, our relationship coming to a premature end the same way they always did. And now both men were dead, lost to the annals of time.

Just like Estienne.

Was it even possible to build the sort of love needed to break the curse in less than a month? I'd like to think that Estienne and I had, that our connection had been almost instantaneous. But we'd been special. There had only ever been one Estienne. One perfect moment in time. Ruined by the actions of his mother.

Sometimes I overthought things, but I had nothing else to do but think. I thought. I regretted. I made plans I could never implement. Anything to keep my mind busy because the thing I feared most of all was losing my grip on reality. If I lost my sanity, then the curse would never be broken. Sometimes I thought that might be better. I could slip into madness and all the pain and suffering would go away. Yet, I still clung on. I still couldn't let go of the flickering flame of hope that sustained me throughout the years.

I stared out across the university campus at the same view I'd had for a while. How long? Less than twenty-five years, I knew that. How many winters had passed since the last time I'd been freed? Definitely more than twenty, but I couldn't tell exactly how long. It was too difficult to keep track of. I had no idea why I'd been brought here, but I'd gotten used to being moved over the years. New scenery was good. It gave me new things to think about, extra stimulation for my brain. And the university campus was fairly busy, students going about their business at all times of the day and night—some silent and contemplative, while others had clearly consumed their own weight in alcohol, their raucous cheers and songs filling the lawns with noise and cheer. I didn't even care when they dressed me up. I preferred that to being invisible.

A familiar figure made his way across the lawn toward me, and if I'd still had lips with which to do it with, I would have smiled. Daniel. Daniel wasn't a student. He was a teacher. I'd learned that along with much of his life history. Daniel actually spoke to me. He often did it with the look of a man who feared he was going crazy, but he still did it. Sometimes he lay his hand on me as well, the strangest expression crossing his handsome face as he did so.

It was peculiar. When he spoke to me, I got the oddest feeling that he knew deep down that I was in there. I'd spent centuries being nothing more than a decorative ornament or an object of derision depending on the person's personal opinions, and Daniel was the first person who seemed to see me, or at least sense in some way that I was in here. Was it just wishful thinking on my part? Was it the beginnings of the madness that I'd worked so hard to keep at bay? Didn't they say that the person going mad was the last to know about it?

He looked tired today, and I wondered if he might pass by without stopping. It happened occasionally, if Daniel was late for work, or if he wasn't alone. He drew to a halt, his warm brown gaze falling on me in a way that only his could, and his lips curving into a smile. "Morning, my friend."

He'd only started calling me "friend" recently, and it had the same effect it always did, it made me feel slightly less cold, slightly less alone.

"You probably want to know how my date went?"

After his divorce, it had taken him a while to start dating again, and from the stories he'd been telling me, it hadn't been going all that well. Although, I suspected that Daniel's self-deprecating sense of humor led him to exaggerate.

"Well..." Daniel let out a little laugh, as if something had amused him. "It started well. He was my age, so that was a bonus. We chatted about films for a while and found that we had lots of favorites in common, so that was good. You can't find anything too contentious about films. Then, he slipped his dungeon into conversation. Yes, you heard that right. My date had a dungeon in his house. He seemed very disappointed when I didn't get excited enough to fall off my chair. Turned out that he was really into BDSM, and given that I barely even know what the letters stand for, things went downhill from there. In the end it was a complete bust. I don't get why he never mentioned that in his profile on the site. It strikes me as something quite important if you're looking for someone who'll stick you in a gimp mask and..." He trailed off. "And do whatever it is that people that are into that do. So, yeah! Back to the drawing board."

I hated to see him look so sad and defeated. *"You'll find someone."*

"I know I'll find someone eventually."

He had an unerring knack of sometimes saying things that corresponded exactly with the words in my head, almost like he could hear me.

"Richard thinks I'm trying too hard. He thinks I should just let things happen naturally."

"Richard is far too opinionated for his own good." In truth, I wasn't even sure who Richard was. I'd seen Daniel with a few different people, and I assumed that one of them was Richard, but I wasn't sure which one he was. I just knew that from everything Daniel had said he seemed to stick his nose into Daniel's business a lot.

Daniel pulled his sleeve back and grimaced as he checked his watch. "I better go, or Marjorie will be on the warpath. See you later, my friend."

"See you later. I'll be here." I pictured lifting my hand in an imaginary wave as I watched Daniel walk away. I couldn't understand why someone like him hadn't been snapped up, or why his husband hadn't been desperate to make things work between them. He was good-looking. He was kind. He was honest. He was funny, and he had the ability to laugh at himself.

The modern world was a strange one, where men didn't seem to realize how lucky they were that they were able to have relationships out in the open. It wasn't perfect. There was still homophobia. I saw it regularly, but it was nothing compared to the past. If only Estienne and I had lived in a time like today, we might have stood a chance. I dismissed the self-pitying thought. There was no point in dwelling on ifs and buts. Life — such as it was — was hard enough.

* * * *

It always started in the same way — with a gradual return to sensation, which quickly morphed into pain, like someone had shoved a hundred burning hot needles into limbs I didn't have. I awoke with a start. Had twenty-five years passed already? It seemed so because the experience of coming to life once again was unmistakable.

I never knew how the process actually happened. Only that soon after the pain started, I would find myself outside the gargoyle and choking for air. This time was no different. I fell to my knees, unable to enjoy the alien feel of the damp grass beneath my palms as I tried to remember how to breathe, each attempt feeling like a knife in my chest. My whole body was one big throbbing mass of hurt, as if beyond my lungs struggling, my heart didn't know how to circulate blood around it.

Lowering my forehead to the grass, I fought the overwhelming urge to pass out with every fiber of my being. It had happened once, and I'd awoken to a vagrant taking a piss on me. Even when the pain eased somewhat, pins and needles rendered my limbs completely useless to the point that even had I wanted to, I couldn't have risen to my feet. Not yet. I had to ride it out. I had to let my body remember how to be human. Only then would I be able to move.

I didn't know whether there were people around, but I'd learnt that the magic binding the curse seemed to provide protection from being seen at least for a little while. Thankfully, it also gave me clothes that matched the time period. I lifted my head enough to look down. I was dressed in blue jeans and a grey jumper that I'd heard the students refer to as a hoodie. I could have passed for one of them. If anyone could see me, they'd probably just assume I was drunk. I tried for a laugh, the sound alien in my throat. I would have to do all those things again that I hadn't done for twenty-five years: walk, talk, maybe even smile if I could find someone to do it with. I had twenty-eight days to find someone who could love me enough to break the curse. The notion was as overwhelming as it had always been, but I had to keep trying. To give in was to face a life of eternal incarceration. How many more centuries could I do this for?

Back in the nineteenth century, I'd thought I'd found a way to beat it, to be the one who came out victorious. Desperate and tired enough to bring an end to the curse with death, I'd jumped off the tallest building I could find. Instead of the blessed darkness I'd hoped for, I'd woken up back in the gargoyle, the twenty-eight days I should have lived cut short. Even death wouldn't break the curse. It seemed that Cecile Badeaux had thought of everything in her determination to create a curse that could never be broken. It had taken me years to realize that the periods of freedom had never really been a chance to break the curse. It had always been meant as punishment, a relentless cycle of hope that was dashed time and time again. Even so, I refused to give up.

Oxygen began to seep into my lungs a little easier, the rapid thrumming of my heart making way for a much steadier rhythm. Eventually, I struggled to my feet, my knees almost giving way beneath me. My first step was more of a stumble, but I managed to stay upright. I lifted my head and scanned the campus, able to see parts of it that I'd never been able to see before from my fixed position inside the gargoyle. Where was I supposed to go?

I turned in a slow circle, searching for some sort of clue as to the best direction to head in. It didn't really matter, though, did it? Not in an area that I didn't know.

I started the laborious process of putting one foot in front of the other, my arms wrapped around my middle in an effort to ward off the insidious cold that had absolutely nothing to do with the day's temperature and everything to do with my metamorphosis from stone to flesh.

My steps took me to a busy street filled with lights and cars and people and noise, the sights so overwhelming that I backed against the wall, sliding down it and putting my hands over my ears, my head bowed forward to block out the view. I should have stayed at the university. At least there, it had been quiet. Here, there was too much going on, too much movement, too much everything. It was always the same, and it never got any easier. I'd adjust, but it would take time, and time was in short supply in my human form. I needed to find someone and make them fall in love with me.

"Are you alright?"

The words held a note of caution, as if the speaker wasn't sure whether they should even have asked them. My head felt like it weighed a ton as I lifted it to look up. Daniel! I should have recognized his voice. Only it had sounded different without a wall of stone in the way. He was dressed in a way I'd never seen before, his clothes far more casual than the ones he wore to work. Did that mean it was the weekend? I wasn't sure. The evening? Was he even there? What If I'd dreamt him up and he was nothing more than a figment of my imagination? He shifted uncomfortably as I continued to stare at him without saying anything.

Chapter Seven

Daniel

The queue in the coffee shop was longer than it normally was at this time of day, mainly due to the person at the front of the queue fulfilling an order that seemed to be for half of Sheffield. I gave serious thought to abandoning my quest for a cinnamon latte. It wasn't a good idea to be drinking coffee at this late an hour anyway, not if I wanted to sleep tonight. But then, tomorrow was Saturday, and I was thirty-five, not ninety-five. I'd turned down Richard's invitation to go to the pub, citing the excuse that he and his fellow lecturers were going to talk science all evening, and this historian couldn't handle it.

But to be honest, I just wasn't feeling that social. The consensus seemed to be that six months was more than long enough to have recovered from the aftereffects of a divorce, especially when Calvin and I had been separated for seven months before that. But I wasn't. Not at all. I still couldn't shake the feeling that I could have done better, that I *should* have done better, and that if I had I might still be happily married. And then I wouldn't be returning to a marital home that seemed to grow increasingly cold and sterile, the longer Calvin was gone from it.

It was psychological. I knew it was. It wasn't like Calvin had even taken that much with him when he'd left. He'd been in so much of a hurry to move out that we'd skipped the conversation about what belonged to who. Apart from his personal effects, he'd seemed happy to leave everything else. The house itself was a different matter. We'd bought it together. Therefore, it needed to be sold so that we could both start again with a clean slate. So far though, we hadn't had any luck finding a buyer for the three-bedroom house in Crookes.

The woman at the front of the queue finally completed her mammoth order, struggling past me with a cardboard tray of coffees and a brown paper bag tucked under both arms. I gave momentary consideration to leaving the queue to open the door for her, but my chivalrous urge was quashed by concern for losing my place. Sometimes, you had to be selfish. I immediately felt guilty at the thought. Was that the sort of person I was turning into? One attempt at marriage that hadn't worked out, and I'd taken my first steps down the path of supporting a dog-eat-dog world where only the strong survive.

My turn at the front finally came, my latte delivered quickly. Stepping out onto the pavement, I found my gaze wandering in the opposite direction to the one I was going to be walking. There was a dark lump huddled in the doorway of the closed bakery. Even in the dim light, I could see they weren't in a good way, their whole body trembling so vigorously that they were almost vibrating.

I quickly averted my gaze. Sheffield was like any other city: you got your fair share of tramps and junkies. And whoever this person was couldn't have screamed withdrawal symptoms any more clearly if they'd been wearing a sign saying *'I'm desperate for a fix.'*

I'd left my car a couple of streets away, the road not willing to yield any parking spaces closer to the coffee shop. I turned in that direction. Five minutes in the car, ten-minute drive to get home assuming the traffic wasn't too bad, and then I could spend the rest of the evening... doing what? Staring at the TV? Raking over everything that had gone wrong in the last few years? Great! No change to the previous evening then. I should have gone to the pub and listened to them rattle on about things I didn't understand, after all.

I stole another glance at the shrouded figure. If anything, the shakes had gotten worse. It was a man. I could tell that much, the shoulders too broad and the hips too slim for it to be a girl. What if he wasn't a junkie? What if it was someone genuinely in need and I just ignored them? A few passers-by threw curious glances his way, but they seemed to share my instinct to move on, some of them even increasing their pace as if they were concerned that the wretched figure might make a lunge for them if they lingered too long in his vicinity.

He might even be a student at the university. Someone who'd taken drugs and had a bad reaction to them. It was my job to look after students. And that job didn't stop just because we weren't on campus and we were outside university hours. If I thought it did, it was way past time I took a long, hard look at myself and how emotionally embittered I was becoming.

Decision made, I turned on my heel, reaching the figure in a matter of seconds and looking down at him. The gray hood he wore meant that I couldn't see anything apart from the covered top of his head. This close, I could hear his teeth chattering as shivers wracked his frame. One thing was for sure, whether it was down to drugs or not, he wasn't in a good way, and someone needed to help him. Even though I was standing directly in front of him, he didn't seem aware of my presence. I cleared my throat. "Are you alright?"

It was a stupid question to ask when anyone with eyes could see he was far from being alright, but it was as good a lead-in to making conversation as any other.

There was no reaction, and I was just beginning to think he hadn't heard me when his head started to lift. It was a slow movement, a movement that said the action took a great deal of effort to accomplish. But finally, he was looking up at me.

Christ! I don't know what I'd expected, but it certainly wasn't the vision in front of me. The young man, who I wouldn't have put any older than twenty, had the face of an angel. He was so pretty that he took my breath away. He had one of those symmetrical faces that male models yearned for, each feature seeming to manage perfection on its own, from the perfectly shaped lips to the angular cheekbones. And then when you considered the effect of them all together, it was nothing short of stunning.

Most striking of all were his vivid blue eyes, though. They stared up at me, something in their depths making it impossible to tear my gaze away. There was pain in his eyes, but there was something else as well, something indefinable that made me want to know more about him. Who was he? Where had he come from? What had brought him to this very spot directly in my path?

"I…" He shook his head, the gray hood slipping back with the motion to reveal dark blond hair. He stopped, seemingly unable to say anything else.

I dropped to a crouch in front of him, wanting to make myself as unintimidating as possible. "Have you taken something?" He shook his head again. Not a bad reaction to drugs, then, which led me back down the path of it being linked to withdrawal. How did you ask that without accusing someone of being a junkie? I was way out of my depth. There was a drugs counsellor at the university—Susanne Brent. No doubt, she would have known exactly what to say, but given that we weren't close enough that I had her number, that wasn't going to help. "Do you need to take something?" Too vague. "Are you an addict?" Wow! I'd gone straight from not being clear enough to smacking him over the head with it. I might not know much about drugs, but I knew enough to know that most addicts wouldn't choose to use that word. "Sorry, I…"

"I don't do drugs."

He had a French accent, the lilt pleasing to the ear. "So, you're ill?" I scanned the street for sources of possible help, but what few passers-by there were still seemed intent on only seeing what they wanted to see. Unless I specifically asked for it, I wasn't going to get any assistance from those quarters, and even then, it was possible they'd refuse. They would have come to the same conclusions I had at first glance, that the young man was trouble, and that it was in their best interests to steer clear. Where was a passing doctor when you needed one? "I can take you to a hospital."

The young man shrank back, his expression one of fear. "No hospital."

Was he an illegal immigrant? That would explain his unwillingness to face the authorities. But where did that leave me? If I couldn't take him to a hospital, what was I supposed to do with him? I was no doctor. "What's your name?"

"François, but you can call me Frankie."

I pulled out my phone. "Can I call someone for you, Frankie? Your mum, maybe? Or your dad? Do you have any other family in this country?"

"There's no one."

No one in this country? Or no one at all? I didn't want to ask the question in case the answer was the latter. "Where do you live? My car is parked a couple of streets away. I can drive you home."

The blue eyes fastened on me without blinking, something in their depths telling me the answer even before he put it into words. "I don't have one."

Fuck! He was too young to be homeless. I wasn't stupid. I knew it could happen at any age, but that didn't make it any easier to witness first-hand. And he was far too pretty to be living on the streets. A pimp would snap him up in a heartbeat. That was assuming he didn't already have one. Nothing about him said male prostitute, but I was by no means an expert. Most of my knowledge was based on TV programs. They were supposed to be a lot more worldly than Frankie was, though, weren't they? Although, the air of innocence he wore could be nothing more than a front, a cleverly designed veneer to appeal to men. If so, he'd missed his calling. He should have been an actor.

I ran a hand through my hair. What was I supposed to do? I couldn't just leave him, not when he was still so pale, and the shaking hadn't subsided in the slightest. He didn't want to go to the hospital, and if I tried to take him, he'd probably run off. What other options were there? He was probably hungry. I could take him for something to eat, but given his poor physical condition, he'd be subjected to numerous stares. Something about the way he'd had his hood pulled up over his head told me that he wouldn't appreciate that. If nothing else, I could at least give him something hot to drink. I held out my coffee cup. "Here. Drink this. It'll warm you up." There was the slightest of hesitations before he took it.

You could take him home. It was the obvious solution. Yet, it was also the craziest one. He was a stranger. For all I knew, he'd rob me blind at the first opportunity. Mind, it wasn't like I had a house full of silver spoons and expensive jewelry, and if he wanted to try and run off with the large screen TV, well, good luck to him. That thing was heavy. I'd had to call Richard just to get it from the car to the living room.

Richard. He'd know what to do. He was always full of advice, whether I wanted it or not. Frankie was still staring at me. I offered him what I hoped was a reassuring smile. Lifting my phone, I pointed to a space on the street no more than a few feet away. "I'm just going to make a quick call, and then I'll be back." Alarm flashed across his face. He probably thought I was going to call the police. "I'm only ringing a friend, I promise."

He nodded and I clambered to my feet, retreating to the spot I'd pointed out. I figured it was far enough away that Frankie wouldn't be able to hear my conversation over the passing traffic. My first call went to voice mail. I hung up without leaving a message and tried again. If Richard was still in the pub, which given it wasn't that late, I'd bet my house that he was, it might take a few attempts before he heard it ring.

I cast a quick glance back to where I'd left Frankie to make sure he hadn't decided I was some sort of threat and pulled a disappearing act, but he was still there, his hands wrapped around the cardboard cup as he took cautious sips of the latte. It made me glad that I'd stayed in the queue. I might not get the coffee, but Frankie needed it far more than I did.

It took three attempts before Richard finally picked up. "Changed your mind about coming to the pub, have you? Want me to get you a beer?"

"No, I haven't changed my mind. Something has come up actually, and I need a bit of advice."

"Let me get somewhere a bit quieter or you'll have to shout at me. There's a hen night in here tonight, and it's about as close to wild as it ever gets."

"Sounds fun." It didn't. It sounded like my idea of hell. The last time I'd been in a pub with a hen night going on, I'd had to fight off one particularly over-amorous admirer who seemed to think that my claim of being gay was more an attempt to hide the fact that I was shy. Even flashing my wedding ring hadn't deterred her. In the end, I'd had to throw Richard at her.

Richard's voice came back on the line. "Right. I'm outside. Hit me with whatever your issue is. Has this got something to do with Calvin?"

"No! I do have problems that have nothing to do with Calvin, you know. We don't even talk anymore unless it's to discuss someone coming to view the house."

"Not Calvin. Got it. What's the issue? My beer's getting warm."

"There's this…" I didn't want to say kid, because I certainly didn't see a kid when I looked at Frankie, but it sounded far more innocuous, so I went with it anyway. "…kid. I think he's homeless. He's in a bad way, really pale, and he can't stop shaking. I thought he was on drugs, but he says he's not. I was going to take him to a hospital, but he says he doesn't want that. I think he might be an immigrant — illegal possibly. He's French, or at least he's got a French accent. I can't just leave him, but I don't know what else to do. What do you think?"

There was no answer. Thinking the call had been cut off, I lifted the phone away from my ear to check the screen, but the call was still connected, at least on my end anyway. "Richard?"

The silence continued, forcing me to repeat his name again.

"I'm here."

He sounded strange, something not sounding right about the way he'd said it. "Are you alright?"

"I'm fine. Why wouldn't I be?"

"You went silent on me."

"I apologize. What were we talking about?"

I frowned, wondering how much Richard had had to drink. He hadn't sounded that drunk, but maybe it had just hit him. I did remember a night on Tequila where he'd gone from perfectly sober to falling over drunk in the space of less than half an hour. "I was telling you about the man I found, the one who needs help. I was asking your advice about what I should do."

"Of course you were. How much time have you spent with him?"

Odd question. "Not long. I went to pick up a latte on Moore Street, and there he was. I was going to keep walking, but… yeah, I didn't, and now I feel like he's my responsibility. Like I said, I thought he was on drugs but he says he's not. I don't know what to do. I was thinking I could take him home and at least give him something to eat. He could have a hot shower as well. I—"

"Have you lost your mind?" Richard's outburst was so strident that I jumped. He was opinionated but he wasn't usually that aggressive. "Do not take him home! Are you crazy? Since when did you turn into such a pushover? Of course, he's going to tell you he's not on drugs. He's hardly likely to admit it, is he? He probably saw you coming a mile off. Don't be a mug, Dan. Don't let someone's bleeding heart routine get to you. This is what they do. It's probably a well-practiced routine and you're just his latest victim."

"You haven't seen him."

"I don't need to see him. His type is ten a penny on the streets of Sheffield, you know that. Walk away, Dan, while you still can. He's not your problem. You really don't need to get embroiled with some junkie prostitute who's an expert at knowing how to tweak lonely men's heartstrings."

"He's not like that." I was aware that I was basing my defense on absolutely nothing besides gut instinct. I'd known Frankie all of two minutes. And on some level, despite the unusually harsh way he'd phrased it, I knew Richard was right. I also knew that I should be taking exception to him referring to me as a lonely man, but I'd deal with that later. His warning about Frankie was nothing a hundred other people wouldn't also have said. Wasn't that why I'd been so intent on ignoring

Frankie in the first place? Only, I hadn't, and now he was a person, not a statistic.

Richard let out a long sigh. "I'm just being honest, Dan. I'm worried about you getting yourself involved in something stupid. If you're that concerned about him, call the police. Let them handle it. If he's not meant to be in the country, well, then that's his problem. It's not yours."

"You're right." I cast another glance back to Frankie. His head was down again, the coffee hanging limply between his fingers. Was he taking a turn for the worse? I needed to get off the phone and get back to him. "I'll do that. Thanks, Richard. I don't know where I'd be without you talking some sense into me."

His laugh was decidedly wry. "Probably in prison after doing something stupid. I'll call you later to find out what happened. Take care, Dan."

I said my goodbyes and hung up, retracing my steps back to Frankie. "Frankie?" He jerked upright, the latte slipping from his fingers and the lid flying off the cup as it hit the ground, the coffee spreading out across the tarmac in a wide puddle. Now, neither of us got to drink it.

Frankie's wide blue eyes met mine. "Sorry."

He looked so guilty that all I could do was smile. "It's just coffee. No harm done." I absently fingered my phone, willing myself to call 999. Except, it wasn't an emergency, was it? So… what number should I call? I'd need a local police station number, which I could get if I did an internet search. It seemed like such a long-winded process, though. Especially when Frankie would no doubt see them coming and be long gone before they got to him. He might look as if he was barely capable of walking at the moment, but adrenaline did strange things to people. And then he'd probably collapse, which again would be my fault.

I dropped to a crouch in front of him again, doing my best to avoid the rivulets of coffee. "My car is parked a couple of streets away and my house is only about ten minutes away. It's warm, and I can make you something to eat. Would you be up for coming back with me, Frankie?"

I held my breath as he stared at me. What did he see? Did he see a university lecturer who just wanted him to be safe? Or did he see something else? I hoped he saw someone he could trust. Because he could.

He gave a long, slow nod, and I tried not to look too relieved.

I held out my hand, and he stared at it for the longest moment before taking it. Richard wasn't going to be happy, but at the moment I couldn't give a fuck. I might be a gullible fool, but I would rather be a gullible fool who tried to help people than one who just kept walking. "I'm Daniel, by the way. I think I forgot to say that."

Chapter Eight

Frankie

The leather seat of the car squeaked as I shifted slightly to cast another surreptitious glance across to Daniel. It was hard to believe that him stumbling across me wasn't fate. There had to be millions of people living in this city, and of all the people it could have been, it had to be the one I'd seen daily for the past few years, the one person who'd taken the time to stop and speak to me. Well, not me — a gargoyle. It wasn't like there was any way he could have known that inside that stone shell lay a living person.

"Are you okay?"

I startled. I had to stop staring at him. He'd not only stopped when most people had walked on by, but he'd been nothing but kind. He'd even given me his coffee.
That kindness would stop if he decided I wasn't sane, and sane people didn't stare at other people without saying anything. I dropped my gaze to my hands and flexed my fingers. Hands and fingers. God, I missed them during the twenty-five years when I was nothing but a consciousness. And I could smell again. I might be able to see and hear when I was a gargoyle, but I missed being able to smell.

Even in the car, there were so many different scents: the leather of the seats, an air freshener in the shape of a tree hanging from the rearview mirror that gave off a pine scent, and fainter but definitely there, a spicy scent which could only be coming from Daniel. His cologne, perhaps? I wanted to get nearer. I wanted to bury my face in his neck and breathe more of it in, but of course I couldn't, or I'd be venturing down the road of coming across as a lunatic again. Sometimes, I wondered if I was, and I just didn't know it. How would I know when I crossed that invisible line?

"Frankie?"

I hadn't answered his question. Was I okay? I hadn't been okay for hundreds of years, but that wasn't an answer I could give. "*Je vais bien, merci.*" Oh, great. Now, I was talking in French.

To my surprise, Daniel smiled. "I knew you were French. I recognized the accent. "What brought you over to this country?"

A large container ship and a man with far too much money who wanted a strange decorative item to boast about to his friends. I lived in his garden for over fifty years. He was just one in a long line of people compelled by some strange urge to own the gargoyle, to own me. Luckily, I'd been asked the question before. I was practiced in answering it, my spiel already tested out on a number of people during my last period of freedom. "I wanted to see more of the world. France is beautiful, but there's so much more out there to see, to experience. Things didn't quite work out as I expected, though."

Daniel looked sad. "Are your family back in France? I could help you to get home, if that's what you need?"

Home! Fields and forests, the scent of barley after harvest, the sound of the river as it threatened to burst its banks after a particularly heavy rainfall. Maman and Papa talking to each other in soft voices, the way that only two people who were still very much in love after many years could. Antoine and myself bickering, two brothers who loved each other but sometimes found it nigh on impossible to like each other. And Estienne. Beautiful Estienne. His red hair catching the light, and his pale skin dotted with freckles. Freckles that covered his body as well, including the one I'd always liked to kiss on his inner thigh. Then there was the way he smiled. His touch when he'd run his hands over my body, no place safe from the questing exploration, just as no part of his body had remained safe from mine.

That was home.

Except… none of that existed anymore. It was all gone, all lost to time. "My family are all dead. I have nothing to go home for."

Daniel's fingers tightened reflexively around the steering wheel, and he seemed lost for words for a moment. "Oh! I'm sorry to hear that." He took his eyes off the road to turn his head and offer a smile. "We'll work something out."

Would we? I turned my head to stare out of the window, the blurred lights of the houses and streetlights we were passing more the result of the tears threatening to spill than the speed we were traveling at. If only Daniel could wave a magic wand and make everything okay, but the only way he could do that was to fall in love with me. Really fall, not just the empty promises of the many men whose names I could barely recall.

The car slowed, drawing to a halt outside a terraced house. I stared at it as Daniel switched the engine off and unfastened his seatbelt. I don't know what I'd expected — to be able to tell something about the man who owned it from the exterior, maybe? But it was just a house, a house almost identical to all the others on the street. The door next to me opened, Daniel standing there and waving his arm in an expansive gesture. "Here we are. Home sweet home." He cast a disparaging glance at the *'For Sale'* sign embedded in the lawn of his front garden. "For the moment anyway."

My limbs were still shaky as I got out of the car. It felt alien to walk, the feeling of movement giving me a sense of vertigo when I was so used to being rooted in one spot. I gingerly followed Daniel up the path, stopping behind him as he rooted around in his pocket, presumably for a key.

"Nice evening!"

Both Daniel and I jumped as the face of an elderly woman appeared over the fence of the next-door garden.

Daniel laughed, retrieving the key from where he'd dropped it on the ground. "You made me jump, Mrs. Featherstone. What are you doing outside at this time of night?"

Her gaze skated over me and I looked away, shrinking further into my hood in an attempt to become invisible. She sniffed. "Someone has to keep an eye on the neighborhood. Especially now that that nice boy Calvin is no longer around. Your house is empty all day while you're at work. I'd hate for you to be burgled while I was sitting around watching *Home and Away*."

Daniel's smile became decidedly strained. "Well, that's awfully thoughtful of you, but honestly, don't put yourself out. I have a burglar alarm. Now, if you'll excuse me."

"Who's your friend?"

Daniel had only gotten as far as putting the key in the lock. He paused, answering without looking Mrs. Featherstone's way. "This is Frankie."

I muttered a "hello," an awkward silence hanging in the air as the next-door-neighbor waited for more information, while Daniel clearly had no intention of giving it. Although, I supposed there wasn't a lot he could say. 'This is Frankie, I found him semi-comatose on the street, and I thought it would be a good idea to invite him into my home,' was hardly going to put anyone's mind at rest.

I was relieved when Daniel brought an end to the silent stand-off by pushing the door open and ushering me inside. I found myself in a hallway, Daniel closing the door and keying in the code on the burglar alarm to stop it from beeping before throwing his keys on a small table covered in mail and divesting himself of his coat. "Sorry about Mrs. Featherstone. She just likes to take an interest in the comings and goings of everyone on the street."

"It's fine."

Daniel stood for a moment as if unsure what to do next. Then he seemed to give himself a mental shake. He opened a door on the right, flicking on the light and gesturing for me to go inside. "Make yourself comfortable in the living room. I'm going to turn the heating up so that we can get you defrosted. I'll have a look at what culinary delights I can offer you to eat while I'm there."

He disappeared up the hallway and I fought the urge to follow him, walking into the living room that he'd indicated instead. It was a big room, tastefully decorated in differing shades of red and cream. My gaze was immediately drawn to the dark wood cabinet which took up almost the entire length of one wall. It wasn't the cabinet itself, though, that piqued my interest. It was all the photos it housed.

I walked over to stand in front of it, my attention caught by one where Daniel was embracing another man. They looked happy together, which seemed at odds with all the stories he'd relayed. But then, I guessed people didn't need to unload their happiness. And the bad times would never seem that bad unless they were in direct contrast to times that had been better. I picked another photo up. It was a wedding day photo, the pair of them in smart suits with matching button holes. Daniel's smile was huge, and he looked like he didn't have a care in the world.

"That's Calvin."

I jumped, nearly dropping the photo in my fright, the words "I know" very nearly slipping out. I needed to be careful. I knew things about Daniel that I should have no way of knowing. If I accidentally let anything slip, it would raise far too many questions. None of which I would be able to answer.

Daniel appeared next to me. "Sorry. I thought you'd heard me come in. I didn't mean to startle you."

"I'm just… jumpy." I held the photo up. "It should be me apologizing. I didn't mean to stick my nose into things that are none of my business."

Daniel's gaze dropped to the photo, his mouth twisting. "Calvin is my husband." He grimaced. "Ex-husband. I still haven't got used to saying that. That's who Mrs. Featherstone was referring to. She was a huge Calvin fan. I think she's disappointed that he moved out instead of me. That's why the house is up for sale. We bought it together, so we need to sell it and split the proceeds. Only the housing market isn't great at the moment, so we're stuck in this strange limbo where we can't really move on until it's sold."

I placed the photo back on the shelf. I felt bad for making Daniel relive it all over again when I'd heard it all before. "I'm sorry your marriage didn't work out."

Daniel's sigh was long and drawn-out. "So am I. Anyway"—he forced a smile—"I don't know why I've still got the photos on display." He ran his gaze over the shelf, his expression somewhat wistful. "I think I'm just a sucker for punishment. I obviously like to torture myself. And…" He gave an embarrassed laugh. "I'm still talking about it."

He walked across the room to draw the curtains. "I probably should have warned you that I was gay before you said yes to coming back here." His face was tight as he turned, and he didn't seem to know what to do with his hands. "In case you're worried, I didn't invite you back with any intentions other than for you to be able to get warm and to have something to eat. I promise."

"Do you think I'm a prostitute?"

He shook his head. "I…"

"You can be honest."

He took a deep breath. "All I know is that you needed help, and no one else seemed to be prepared to give it. It's none of my business what you do to survive."

"I'm not a prostitute, or a junkie." It was important to me that he knew that. I might not be able to tell him where I'd appeared from, or why I was in such a poor physical state, but I could tell him what I wasn't without there being any repercussions.

He stared at me, and I stared back. Finally, he nodded, a smile creeping back onto his face. "I believe you. You have an honest face."

I smiled back at him, something tantalizing that captured my breath hanging in the air between us.

The moment was broken as something dark launched itself onto the back of the sofa. I stumbled backwards, ready to run, and only Daniel's hands landing on my shoulders to steady me stopping me from doing that.

"It's just Napoleon. Don't be scared."

"Napoleon?"

Daniel turned me gently toward the sofa. "My cat. And he's even more of an arsehole than most cats. That's why I named him Napoleon. He's small, but he still manages to strut around like he owns the place."

I stared at the black cat, its green eyes staring back at me. He was indeed small, but he didn't seem remotely concerned by the fact that there was a stranger in the house. In fact, he seemed nothing but curious. "You never…" I stopped. I'd been going to say that Daniel had never told me he had a cat. He hadn't. He'd never mentioned it once in all those hours of talking to me. Was it his cat? Or was it another thing that he and Calvin had shared?

Daniel's brow furrowed. "I never… what?"

I shook my head, wrapping my arms around myself in a bid to get warm.

Concern dawned on Daniel's face. "Forget the shower. I'm going to run you a bath. Nothing beats a bath for getting warm."

Chapter Nine

Daniel

What were you supposed to do while a complete stranger was in your bath? I was fairly sure that the answer wasn't to pace around and constantly think about them, but that's exactly what I was doing. Whatever the circumstances that had brought Frankie to the situation I'd found him in — and from the look in his eye I didn't think he was going to tell me — that didn't change the fact that he was quite simply one of the most breathtaking men I'd ever seen.

That didn't mean I was going to take advantage of him in any way. I'd been one hundred percent honest when I'd told him that I hadn't brought him back for any other purpose but to help him. But I wasn't blind, and I was suddenly all too aware of just how long it had been since I'd been intimate with anyone. Divorces tended to kill your libido, or at least they had mine.

Only, my libido seemed to have perked up, spurred on by thoughts of the young man currently luxuriating in my bath. Napoleon butted his head against my calf in a bid for attention and I picked him up. "What do you think, Napoleon? Am I losing my marbles in bringing him back here? And what am I supposed to do with him once he's had a bath and something to eat? Am I meant to just throw him back out onto the street? Seems crazy when I've got a spare room, doesn't it? One night's not exactly going to hurt anything. I mean, it's late. I'd have to be a monster not to take that into account. Where's he going to sleep around here? Mrs. Featherstone will have him castrated if she finds him anywhere near her geraniums."

I stared at Napoleon, and he gave me a slow blink. I rolled my eyes at him. "Fat lot of help you are. When are you going to start talking so that you can give me some advice?"

I lowered him to the floor as quiet footsteps sounded on the stairs, Frankie appearing in the doorway a few moments later in the fluffy white bathrobe I'd left for him. He stopped in the doorway to peer around the kitchen. "Who were you talking to?"

Shit! He'd heard me. I just hoped he hadn't heard what I'd been saying. "No one."

Napoleon chose that moment to let out a plaintive meow, as if he was determined to call me out on being a liar. I resolved to take him down to the shelter and swap him for a silent cat, one that didn't argue with me. "Okay! I was talking to Napoleon. He can be very chatty at times. There's nothing wrong with talking to your cat, right? It would be rude not to. You should see me talking to the gargoyle on campus. That's when people think I've really lost it. Perhaps I just prefer talking to things that can't talk back." I was nervous, and I was doing what I always did when I felt self-conscious, I was letting my tongue get way ahead of my brain. Wiping my sweaty hands on the front of my trousers, I pulled the fridge door open and pretended to examine its contents. "Are you allergic to anything?"

"Not that I know of." There was a long pause. "You talk to a gargoyle?"

Fuck! Why had I told him that? I may as well have worn a hat with *"I'm halfway to crazy"* emblazoned across the front. "He's a very nice gargoyle." *Not any better, Daniel, you absolute idiot.*

"How can you tell?"

"Well..." I let the fridge door close, none the wiser about what it contained than when I'd opened it. Frankie had seated himself at the kitchen table, his chin resting on his hand. He looked far better after a bath, his pale skin now sporting a pinkish glow. "Most people judge gargoyles on the way they look. They think they're evil, but it's quite the opposite. One of their major roles is to ward off evil spirits. That's why they're often positioned outside churches and cathedrals."

"So... in your mind they're a good thing?"

Rather than thinking I was a freak, Frankie seemed genuinely interested in the subject. "Historically speaking, yes. People have always feared what they don't understand. That's why a lot of women in the Middle Ages were persecuted for being witches. Because they did things that the majority of the population didn't understand. Looking at it now from a modern perspective, a lot of them were attempts at early medicine. What we might think of these days as herbalism. I mean, they were pretty wacky and steeped in religion. Things like believing that wool soaked in olive oil from the Mount of Olives could staunch blood when it was combined with a story about Longinus, a man famously healed of his blindness by the blood of Christ. And then there were protective charms, sealskin to repel lightning and vulture body parts worn as an amulet."

Frankie's fingers gave a twitch where they rested on the table. "Do you believe that any witches were real?"

He was holding himself too still, almost as if something about my answer really mattered to him.

I answered honestly. "I don't know. I'm just a historian. There are certainly cases so famous that they're still talked about today. Take Mother Shipton, for example." I paused. I'd forgotten for a moment that Frankie was French. The name probably meant nothing to him. "Her real name was Ursula Southeil, and she was born in the 15th century. She was said to be so hideously ugly that you have to wonder if the title of witch wouldn't have been given to her anyway, even if she'd lived a pious life. Legend says that her mother had an affair with the Devil and conceived Ursula as a result. And of course, there are versions of the story that claim Ursula's mother was herself a witch who summoned the Devil for that specific purpose. Herbalism was just one of the strings to her bow. Prophesies were her big thing, and you have to assume that if her name lived on to this day that people believed in them at the time and for years after. Knaresborough has a whole tourist industry built up around her. Have you ever heard of the petrifying well?"

Frankie gave a shake of his head.

"It's a great example of how what was once thought to be witchcraft can actually be explained by science. Objects left in water with a high mineral content basically turn to stone through a process of evaporation and deposition. People hang all sorts of objects at the springs near Mother Shipton's cave where she used to live, teddy bears, socks, you name it. It's quite a sight if you ever get a chance to visit."

"Do you think she was a witch?"

I shrugged. "Who knows? Some say that the prophesies were actually made up after her death. But there has to be some reason why she was so famous at the time that even King Henry VIII was understood to know who she was. At least that's who he was assumed to be talking about when he wrote a letter to the Duke of Norfolk in 1537 and referred to the Witch of York."

I came to a sudden stop. What was I doing? I was meant to be offering Frankie food and shelter, not treating him like one of my students and giving him a full-blown history lecture. God knows how long it had been since he'd last eaten. He was probably starving.

Turning away to hide the heated flush that was no doubt lighting my cheeks up like a beacon, I opened up the fridge again. "I haven't been shopping this week, so I might have given you false hope of something decent when I offered to feed you. I can do an omelet, or I could order a pizza?"

"An omelet's fine."

"Yeah?" I turned to see Frankie's nod. "Mushrooms, onions, peppers, and cheese okay?"

Another nod. I set to work on making it, extracting all the ingredients I needed, beating the eggs, chopping the vegetables, and grating the cheese. At least an omelet was within my capabilities without me serving up something that wouldn't look out of place in a crematorium. It would also be easier to broach the subject I wanted to talk about while my hands were busy doing something else. "And I was thinking, with it being so late, that once you've eaten, you should probably stay for the night. What do you think?"

I cast a quick glance Frankie's way to discern his reaction, trusting that the eggs and vegetables I'd dropped into the frying pan wouldn't do anything too drastic in the few seconds I'd left them alone. The expression on his face sat halfway between discomfort and relief. "I don't want to put you out."

I turned my attention back to the pan, nothing having escaped. "It's no trouble. I've got a spare room and the bed is already made up, so…" There was nothing I could do if he insisted on leaving, and it really shouldn't matter so much, but for some reason it did. I didn't want him wandering the streets. Not tonight, anyway. I'd sleep better knowing that he was safe, which was a weird reaction to have to someone I'd only met just over an hour ago.

"Thank you. I would appreciate that."

Relief sat heavy in my chest. "I have to work early tomorrow." Now, why had I said that? That sounded like I was giving him his marching orders at dawn. But then, what was the alternative, to let him stay in my house all day—alone and without supervision? My mouth took care of it before my brain had even started to sift through the possible ramifications. "You can stay here tomorrow as well, if you want?"

"Can I?"

The note of caution in Frankie's voice had me turning around to face him. "Only if you want to? I understand if you don't. You might want to be on your way. If so, I can drop you where you want to go on my way to work. But, if not..." I suspected that my shrug was nowhere near as casual as I'd been aiming for. I gestured around the kitchen. "My house is at your disposal."

"That's very trusting of you."

I dumped the cheese on top of the omelet, letting it melt before folding the top over and sliding it onto a plate. It *was* trusting of me. Yet, it seemed the right thing to do. I picked up cutlery and delivered both to Frankie with a flourish that said cordon bleu cookery rather than heated up eggs, cheese, and vegetables. I'd expected him to dig right in, to eat like someone who didn't know where their next meal was coming from, but he ate slowly and deliberately, as if he was savoring each and every mouthful. I watched him until I became aware of what I was doing, my cheeks heating again.

Jumping up, I busied myself with putting my kitchen back to rights, not that there was that much to do. Even I couldn't make that much mess while preparing an omelet. Frankie still hadn't given me an answer about his plans for the following day. It would probably be for the best if he did decide to leave first thing in the morning. Things would only be more awkward if he'd spent the day in my house and then I kicked him out. "So... shall I wake you in the morning or not?"

Frankie paused with the fork halfway to his mouth. "Are you sure you don't mind if I stay here tomorrow?"

I flashed him a quick smile. "Least I can do when I rambled at you about witches. I promise I'm not always that weird."

Frankie gave a wan smile. "It's an interesting subject."

It was. As was he. He'd bathed and eaten in my house, but all I knew about him was his name, that he had no family, and that he was French. It was a strange basis on which to trust someone, but for some reason I did. Absolutely and completely.

Chapter Ten

Frankie

I always slept well when I was released from my stone coffin, no matter where that might be, whether it was a gutter, field, or loaned bed. I put it down to having a body again, to having an actual physiological need to sleep. I'd always wondered whether Cecile had known I would sleep within the confines of the gargoyle. It always seemed like an oversight on her part. Without sleep, without those hours passed in oblivion, I would have gone insane years ago. Perhaps she hadn't wanted that, though? Perhaps that wouldn't have been enough suffering for her. After all, a mad person would no longer care.

The house was silent, save for the odd creak that all houses had, those strange inexplicable noises that couldn't be linked to anything in particular. Did that mean Daniel had already gone to work? Daniel! The thought of him brought a smile to my face. It still seemed crazy that the same man who'd kept me going for the last few years by sharing aspects of his life with me had also been the one to sweep me off the pavement and give me a place to stay for the night.

He was a kind man. I'd always been able to tell that. A man who thought of others. He was handsome as well. In short, he was a man I could fall in love with. The smile died on my face. I

might be able to fall in love with him, but would he be able to fall in love with me? In twenty-seven days. The countdown to being entombed again was already in process, and I would be stupid to waste my time on
a man who for all intents and purposes still wasn't over his ex-husband. And all evidence seemed to point that way, given the wedding photos still on display and the way he talked about him.

I sat up in bed. I needed to leave. Daniel wasn't going to be the one to break the curse, so the more time I spent here, the less time it left to find someone who could, someone who would look at me and not give a damn about the secrets locked inside me that I could never share. I needed someone who could look past that and just see me. I jumped as the door creaked open, a black, furry body squeezing its way through the gap he'd just created. What had Daniel said his name was? Napoleon, that was it. How could I forget? The name of a French general.

Napoleon leapt on the bed as I climbed out of it, watching me as I dressed quickly in the only clothes I had. "I have to leave."

He stared at me in that implacable way that only cats can, as if they fully understand what you're saying but don't really give a damn about it. "He'll understand, right? Daniel, that is." No response, not even a twitch of a whisker.

Once dressed, I made my way downstairs, Napoleon falling into step behind me. "Why are you following me?"

He jumped onto the kitchen counter, his paw resting on the corner of a piece of paper that hadn't been there the night before. I stared at the words that were clearly meant for me, but they were nothing more than squiggles on a page. I couldn't read, had never been able to read. There hadn't been much call for it in the fields of Dordogne. People of my status weren't afforded the chance to receive any sort of education beyond that passed down from my maman and papa, and most of that had related to farming, or how to insulate your home in the winter when the weather was particularly cruel.

I might have learned to speak English over the long and lonely years incarcerated in stone when there was little else to think about besides the need to interpret the constant buzz of conversation going on around me, but reading it was another matter entirely. I'd actually been surprised how easily I'd picked up the language, given that my only chances to speak it were in my head or during my periods of freedom, but then what else had I had to think about.

I rested my palm on the paper, as if there was some chance of absorbing the words into my skin. But of course, I was no closer to understanding what Daniel had wanted to communicate to me. There were numbers on the paper, a 3 and a 5, and a longer string, but I didn't know what they linked to or why Daniel would have written them down. It would have to remain a mystery. There was about as much chance of Napoleon being able to read it as me.

The cat shoved his head against my arm, and I absently stroked the length of his back while I continued to stare at the paper. It was yet another reason why it was best that I left. Daniel would ask questions. I knew he would. He was far too curious not to. And most of the questions he asked would be questions I couldn't answer. Times had changed. I'd realized that during my last period of freedom, and where not being able to read hadn't been that unusual in times gone by, it would make me stand out like a sore thumb now. How was I meant to explain something like that away?

Pulling myself away from the words I had no chance of deciphering, I made myself some cereal and a cup of coffee and took them both through to the living room. Napoleon trailed after me again, as if the cat appreciated not being alone for once.

I didn't mind. I needed the company as much as he did. I flicked the TV on, the program that came on confusing in its rapid transition between wildly differing things. First, they were talking about fashion, and then there was a heartfelt conversation with someone whose son had been recently murdered. A competition. A cooking segment with lots of laughter. I couldn't keep up, but I watched it anyway with a strange sense of fascination. Napoleon decided to curl up on my lap, his body a warm and reassuring weight. Stay or go? Stay or go? The words kept reverberating through my skull, and I was no closer to coming up with an answer.

I managed to pass the whole day away on that sofa, only moving to make toast for lunch, and to use the bathroom. The last time I'd watched TV, there'd only been a few channels. Now, there seemed to be hundreds. I watched documentaries and comedies, dramas and quiz shows, my brain filling with hundreds of facts about modern life. It was fair to say that I lost track of time as I tried to take in as much as I could under the excuse of needing to fit in with modern culture when I left Daniel's house.

When the sound of a key turned in the front door, I jumped up, standing guiltily in the middle of Daniel's living room, as if I'd been caught doing something wrong. He appeared in the doorway, bulging plastic bags dangling from both hands. His face lit up when he saw me, something thudding in my chest at the genuinely pleased expression on his face. "Frankie, you're still here. I wasn't sure you would be, but I'm so glad you are. I'd hate for you to have disappeared without me even getting the chance to say goodbye. Thanks for waiting for me to get home from work."

I nodded, my attempt at words feeling thick in my throat. "I do need to leave, though."

A shadow passed across Daniel's face, the smile staying put but looking decidedly more forced than it had seconds before. "I understand." He hefted the bags up to chest height. "You can eat first though, right? I bought food. I thought we could have salmon. I couldn't find any snails or frog legs." His face fell. "Actually, that's quite rude of me, isn't it? To joke about stereotypes like that. I may as well have come in here on a bicycle, wearing a striped top and beret, with garlic around my neck."

He looked so crushed that I found myself smiling. "It's not quite the same. I think I can forgive you."

His smile returned. "Then you're far too generous." He waved the bags again. "I'll just go and unpack this lot."

I followed him to the kitchen. It seemed the polite thing to do, and more than that, it was what I wanted to do. There was something very calming about being in Daniel's presence, like goodness emanated from him. The last person I'd known like that was... Estienne. As always when I thought of my lost love, my chest clenched in a paroxysm of complete agony. It had been hundreds of years. Shouldn't it be easier to think of him by now? Or was that part of the curse? Had Cecile somehow made it so that my suffering would be as intense as if it had happened only yesterday?

"You look sad."

I jerked my head up to stare at Daniel, who had paused from laying the shopping items out on the kitchen table.

"I'm..."

His stare grew more intense when I didn't finish the sentence. In the end, it was him who changed the subject. "Did you feed Napoleon?"

Was I meant to? My eyes drifted over to where the note lay exactly where he'd left it. There could have been anything written on it. Daniel could have asked me to clean the house, and then come home to find that I'd done nothing but sit around and watch TV. I went for the truth, hoping I would get away it without elaborating. "No. He was either on my lap or outside."

Daniel nodded. "He was probably excited that someone was around all day." He paused, his smile cautious as his fingers curled reflexively around the bag of pasta he held. "Can I say something crazy without you running away screaming?"

My heart started to pound erratically. What was he going to say? "Sure."

His brown eyes were intent on my face, as if he wanted to gauge my reaction to whatever it was he was about to say. "It's really weird, but I keep getting this peculiar feeling like I already know you." He laughed, his cheeks flushing a deep red. "I told you it was crazy."

You've spent years talking to me. Through rain and snow, wind and blazing sun. You stopped and told me things about your life when everyone else just passed on by. Of course, you feel like you know me. Only I'm no longer made of stone. I'm real and I'm breathing, but only for twenty-six more days, and then I'll be back there. Will you still talk to me? Will you tell me about the person you met, who disappeared one day never to be seen again? Will you tell me that you miss him?

I was getting way ahead of myself, especially when I would be gone from his life once we'd eaten dinner. You couldn't miss someone who had been in your life for less than twenty-four hours. "It's not crazy." It was the best I could offer him.

Daniel resumed putting the shopping away, his cheeks still bearing a rosy flush.

"Well, it's very nice of you to say that to try and make me feel better. I probably shouldn't have said anything. There are some things that it's probably better to keep to yourself, but I've never been very good at that. Calvin used to say that I really didn't need to share my innermost thoughts with absolutely everyone I meet." He shrugged. "Guess I still haven't learned my lesson."

"You shouldn't need to change for anyone. If you do, then they were never right for you in the first place."

He went still for a few seconds before turning to face me with a slight frown on his face. "How old are you?"

I swallowed, nervous tension prickling along my spine. And so, the questions began, questions that left me with no other option but to lie or refuse to answer. For a moment, I pictured his face if I told him the truth, if I blurted out that I was four hundred and fifty years old. He'd probably think it was a joke, but I wasn't ready to test that theory. Besides, it wasn't the first time I'd been asked that question, so the lie was already there, ready to roll off my tongue. "Twenty-two." I'd been twenty-one when the curse had been bestowed upon me. Given how many years had passed, it had seemed natural to add another year onto my chronological age.

Daniel looked troubled by the answer. "Twenty-two! I'm thirty-five. You're the same age as the final year students I teach."

I wasn't sure why that fact would bother him so much, the frown not shifting as he finished putting away the last of the shopping, just the salmon, vegetables, and a bag of potatoes remaining in front of him.

"Why do you ask?"

He lifted his head, his brown eyes finding mine. "Because... you just seem wise beyond your years. You're giving me advice like you have far more years of experience than I do. And you can't have because you're only twenty-two. You've barely started to live."

There was nothing I could say to that, so I stayed silent. I needed to be more careful with what I said. Except, I was leaving before the night was up so what did it matter?

* * * *

We ate in the kitchen, enjoying a bottle of wine that Daniel opened to go with the food he'd cooked. There was a strange energy between us, and I was pretty sure he could feel it too. He was telling me about his day at work, but it wasn't his words I was interested in. Not that I wasn't listening to him, I was. It was just that other things kept capturing my attention. His broad shoulders. The way a lock of hair kept falling over his brow and he had to pause from speaking to push it back. The way his eyes crinkled at the corners when he laughed. The way his voice became ever so slightly more high-pitched when he became excited about something. His skin. His scent. The way he moved. The way his attention barely shifted from me, even when Napoleon wandered into the kitchen, his nose twitching at the smell of the salmon, and started begging for food.

It was like we were in our own little bubble where nothing and no one mattered. It made the relationships I'd forced myself into over the years pale into insignificance, and it made it plainly obvious why no one else had broken the curse. There had never been that connection there. Not since Estienne. I'd felt it with him too, that knowledge that two people were meant to belong together, that they were two halves of a whole. Did Daniel feel it too? He must. It explained why he'd said he felt he knew me. I'd put it down to him talking to me as a gargoyle, some sixth sense that we'd shared—if my muteness could be classed as sharing—conversation before. But it was more than that. After all, I'd always wondered what could possibly have drawn him to start conversing with a gargoyle in the first place. Had there been a connection between us even then? The thought was both scary and awe-inspiring.

"You've barely touched your wine."

I startled as Daniel's voice broke into my thoughts. I moistened my lips, Daniel's gaze immediately dropping to focus on the action. He was attracted to me too. I could see it in his eyes. "I…" I cleared my throat. "I don't really drink."

Guilt bloomed on his face, and he wasted no time in leaning across to swipe the glass away. "Oh God! You should have said. I don't normally force alcohol on people that don't want it, I promise."

"It's fine." I managed a weak smile. I needed to leave while I still could. Daniel might be attracted to me, but the problem of his ex-husband still remained. He'd been hurt, and hurt men weren't capable of letting go of the past and falling for someone else in the space of twenty-six days, no matter how much chemistry they might share with someone else. To stay would be to consign myself to the same fate for another twenty-five years. And when I came back, Daniel would be sixty. He would have married again, and I would have to stay away from him because he would have aged and I would look exactly the same as I did now. There could never be anything between us that didn't end in disappointment and pain.

I pushed my chair back and stood, the sound abnormally loud in the otherwise quiet kitchen. "I need to go!"

Daniel stood too, his face the picture of confusion. "Now?" He waved a hand at my half-eaten meal. "At least finish your food first."

I shook my head, turning on my heel and heading for the front door as fast as my legs would carry me. Only, when I reached the door and tried to open it, it refused to budge. I tugged at it furiously, putting all my weight into it, my fingers scrabbling uselessly against its surface. I needed it to open. I needed to get out of there. My chest burned with the desperate desire, nothing else mattering but escaping before it was too late. Why wouldn't it open? And then Daniel was there next to me, his confusion replaced by concern. "Frankie, what's wrong?"

I tugged at the door again. "Let me out!" My voice was almost a sob.

"Okay! Okay!" Daniel reached past me. "It's locked, see. You just need to turn the key and then it will open." He did it for me, his chest warm and solid where it pressed against my shoulder. The door swung open, a gust of wind blowing through the gap and stinging my cheeks where I hadn't even realized tears had fallen. One step and I would be outside. I could run and never look back.

Daniel moved into my eyeline. He didn't make any move to try and stop me. He was just there. "I'm sorry. Whatever I did, whatever I said that upset you, I'm truly sorry."

The words almost broke me. He hadn't done anything. He just didn't understand. And if I told him, if I tried to make him understand, I'd become one with the gargoyle again in the blink of an eye. I'd tried it once, doubting the terms of the curse could really be that rigid, that Cecile could have thought of everything. But she had. As soon as I'd spoken those words, as soon as I'd tried to share the truth of my existence, I'd found myself back there. It had only been day ten of my period of freedom and I'd condemned myself to spending another twenty-five years waiting and suffering. So... I couldn't tell him.

Therefore, the only way I could help Daniel was by leaving. Mine was a miserable existence, but that didn't mean I had to drag other people down with me.

And yet, I hesitated, something stopping me from taking that final step into the outside world and leaving him behind forever. It gave Daniel enough time to curl his fingers around my shoulders and turn me to face him.

We stared at each other, something electric passing between us. It was enough to confirm that whatever it was we shared was indeed mutual. The way Daniel was looking at me, it was if he could see beneath my skin. I recognized that look. It was the same way he used to look at the gargoyle.

"Stay."

It might have only been one word, but it packed such an emotional punch that I almost staggered backwards under the weight of it. I shook my head. "I can't. There are things you don't know about me, things I can't tell you, things that make it difficult."

Daniel's brow furrowed, his fingers tightening that little bit more on my shoulders. "Are you in trouble with the police? Is that what it is?"

I almost laughed. If only life were that simple. "No, not the police."

"Then"—he shook his head—"it can't be that bad. It must be something we can fix."

"You can't." Well, he could, but it would involve him falling head over heels in love with me in less than twenty-six days. "You'll keep asking questions, and I won't be able to answer them."

His expression was pained, and it didn't escape my attention that he didn't even try to deny it. "At least stay for tonight." He gestured to the outside world at my back. "It's dark… and cold. It even looks like it might rain. You don't need to be out on the streets in bad weather when there's a bed for you upstairs."

I knew that what he was saying was logical, but I also knew that this strange pull between us would only get stronger the longer I remained in his company. I barely had the strength of mind to leave now. How much worse would it be by the morning? But what if I was wrong? What if he was the one who could break the curse? Wasn't it worth the risk?

A hand curled around my cheek, the touch soft and exploratory, and in some ways almost apologetic, as if Daniel knew he wasn't supposed to be doing it. I didn't step back. I couldn't step back. Even when his lips descended toward mine, I did nothing to stop it from happening. The first touch was as soft as a feather, Daniel's lips barely grazing mine. Even so, something I could only describe as a feeling of rightness shot through me.

Daniel drew back, his lips still close enough that I could feel his breath against my skin. "I promised myself I wouldn't do that."

"*C'est bon.*" It said a lot that I had switched to French. I tried again. "It's fine."

It was fine. It was more than fine. He seemed to think so too, his head dipping for another taste. This kiss was longer, and sweeter, my hands lifting to clasp the back of his head as our mouths tasted and explored.

When he pulled back, he was breathing hard. Our gazes locked and I knew what was coming even before he spoke the word. "Stay."

I nodded, and his lips curled into a smile.

What was twenty-five more years as a gargoyle when I'd already endured more than four hundred? For once, this could be about Daniel instead of myself. I could fix him. I could prove to him that his husband hadn't been the right man for him, that there was someone else out there who would appreciate him for who he was.

Chapter Eleven

Daniel

The river was fierce, the current sweeping over the jutting rocks at its center containing a surprising amount of power. It was almost loud enough to drown out the birdsong from the surrounding trees. It was hot, the sun beating down on my bare shoulders. He was there, my heart rejoicing the same way it always did in his presence. Only, I couldn't see him. Where was he? I turned in a slow circle. Grass. Trees. Stones. He was there so why couldn't I see him. There was laughter. My laughter. What was I laughing at?

And then it all faded, as if the whole experience had been nothing more than an echo. He wasn't there anymore. The sun had gone, replaced by darkness. I was cold inside and out. And I was no longer laughing. It felt like I would never laugh again, my insides as frozen and desolate as my surroundings had become.

I awoke with a start, the strange dream still lingering in the recesses of my mind. What had that been about? I tried to place the river, but it didn't seem to fit any place I'd ever visited. How could I dream about a place where I'd never been? Was it somewhere I'd seen on a TV program? Or a film? It must have been. That was the only thing that made any sense.

My alarm forced me from my reverie, and I fumbled for my phone to turn it off. Work. Great! That was the last place I felt like spending the day. I wanted to stay home with Frankie. My lips curled into a smile at the mere thought of him, and I reached out to press my palm against the wall that separated my bedroom from where he'd slept in the spare room. Nothing else had happened between us after the kiss, but what a kiss it had been. My lips still tingled just from thinking about it.

When Frankie had announced he had to leave, I'd run the whole gamut of emotions from confusion to despair. Common sense had dictated that I let him go, but I'd been loath to lose that spark of connection without a fight. I'd never experienced it before, not even with Calvin, and I'd married him.

I pulled the covers back and swung my legs over the edge of the bed, unable to stop myself from grinning like a lunatic at the empty room. The whole thing was crazy. You didn't just meet someone one night and feel indescribably close to them the next. Especially when we hadn't even spent that much time together. But that's exactly what had happened. Frankie had wormed his way beneath my skin in a way that defied explanation. And it didn't matter what anyone else thought about it. They could scoff all they liked, but that didn't mean it wasn't real. And he could feel the connection too. I could tell. I'd seen the struggle on his face when I'd asked him to stay. It was written all over his face that he wanted to. If he hadn't, I wouldn't have pushed him on it.

Today was Friday, so once it was out of the way, we'd have the whole weekend together. The thought filled me with a sense of optimism I hadn't felt in a long time. Frankie might have his secrets. He'd admitted as much, but that didn't mean I couldn't get to know him.

I showered and dressed quickly, my trip downstairs delayed somewhat by the few moments I spent daydreaming outside the door to the spare room. What would Frankie look like while he was sleeping? I bet he'd look even more like an angel. There was no lock on the door, so it was oh so tempting to push it open just a crack and find out. Except, that would be intrusive, and I wasn't that sort of man.

Narrowly avoiding tripping over Napoleon and falling to my doom on the stairs, I made my way into the kitchen, feeding him and managing to grab a quick coffee before I left for work. I hadn't had time for breakfast, but I'd either get something on the way, or rely on the magic pastry fairy to fulfil their usual role and leave a high-in-sugar breakfast extravaganza in the recreation room shared by myself and the other historians in the department.

Pulling into my usual parking spot, I found my gaze drawn across the lawn to where the gargoyle stood. Something seemed different about it, and I couldn't put my finger on what it was. The feeling was strong enough that I changed direction and made my way toward it.

"Morning, Mr. Smith."

I gave a polite nod to the girl who'd greeted me. She was one of my students, one of the quiet ones who always sat at the back and looked interested but didn't ask any questions. I could have done with a few more like her. I slowed my steps, waiting until she'd disappeared around the corner before approaching the gargoyle. "Hi. Sorry, I've not been around for a couple of days. There's been a lot going on."

I frowned. Something definitely wasn't right. It looked the same. There weren't even any decorative additions to its stone surface. Either the students had been busy, or someone had already removed the evidence of their most recent drunken night out.

Whenever I'd spoken to the gargoyle, it had always felt like there was a presence, but now—insane as that sounded even in my own head—it was like that presence was no longer there. I really was losing it.

Casting a quick look around to make sure that no one was watching, I tentatively reached out and laid my hand over the curve of the gargoyle's shoulder. No vibration. Nothing. I kept my hand there, waiting to feel something, waiting for that familiar buzz to start up. But there was nothing, only cold stone beneath my fingertips, the rough granite not warming in the slightest to my touch.

I snatched my hand back. Perhaps it was time to book a session with a therapist. Divorces could be hard on people. One minute you were happily married, and the next you were moving mysterious young men into your home and begging them not to leave, and imagining that gargoyles were somehow less alive than they'd once been.

Shaking my head, I turned on my heel and hurried back across the lawn to the building, thankfully managing to bypass the disapproving eye of Marjorie as I made my way to the lecture hall to prepare for my first class of the day.

* * * *

I lifted my head from grading papers as my office door opened a crack and Richard stuck his head through the gap. He aimed a wink in my direction. "Hello stranger, so this is where you've been hiding. I looked for you at lunch, but you were doing a great impression of the Scarlet Pimpernel."

I rolled my eyes at him, gesturing at the large stack of papers in front of me. "Hardly hiding. I just had this lot to get through, so it was a working lunch for me." I straightened to stare at him as he stepped inside. "And I bet you don't even know who the Scarlet Pimpernel is?"

Richard shrugged. "Someone that was hard to find. Something about they seek him here, they seek him there. I presume it was some dude in history that had nothing better to do than be elusive. Probably hide and seek champion in 1812 or something."

I let out a sigh, fully prepared to deliver yet another history lesson. Although actually, it was more of a literature lesson. "He wasn't even real. It was originally a 1903 stage play about a chivalrous Englishman who rescued aristocrats from being sent to the guillotine during the French Revolution. Sir Percy Blakeney, aka the Scarlet Pimpernel, led a double life, a wealthy fop by day, and a master of disguise by night. The stage play was turned into a novel in 1905."

Richard smirked as he eased himself into the chair usually reserved for students wanting to discuss how they could get their grades up. He crossed his ankles in front of him and steepled his fingers together. "I stand corrected on my ignorance. I confess that I haven't read many novels from the early 20th century."

"You should. You might learn something."

He arched an eyebrow. "I'll pass, thanks. Anyway, I didn't seek you out to discuss literary classics. I'll save that for the next time I suffer from insomnia. I'll call you and you can lull me to sleep by telling me all about the top ten novels from 1901 through 1910." He sat forward. "I came to talk to you about tomorrow afternoon. Steve's organized a pool tournament at his local pub. I told him you'd be up for it. Few beers, few games of pool. Shall I pick you up? Or are you going to make your own way there?"

I stared at him. Any other time, I would have been up for it. Anything that got me out of the house on the weekend and stopped me from dwelling on things was usually a bonus, but I'd never had an intriguing young French man staying with me before. And I intended to spend every minute I could with him, exploring the strange connection that existed between us. "I can't."

Richard's brow furrowed. "What's your excuse this time? First, you couldn't come to the pub. Now, you're turning down the opportunity to humiliate Steve at pool? What's going on with you?"

I waved a hand at the papers again. "I've just got a lot of stuff to do."

Richard snorted. "Don't try and pull that one. There's no way you're turning down a pool tournament to grade papers when you never have before. What's going on? Has Marjorie managed to get some dirt on you? Did you accidentally send her a picture of you in the nude? And now, she's finally got enough ammunition to turn you into her work slave?"

I shook my head slowly. "Have I ever told you that I'm really concerned by the way your mind works? Why is *that* the first thing that comes into your head?"

Richard threw his head back and laughed. "You have told me that a time or two." He drummed his fingers on the desk. "Anyway, don't change the subject. What's this sudden reluctance to leave the house really about? The other day it was because you'd found a waif and stray and developed a social conscience…" A look of realization dawned on his face. "Please tell me that you did what we discussed, that you rang the police and left it to them, that you didn't do something stupid like take him home?"

I looked away, concentrating on a poster on my wall that an ex-colleague had put up as a joke, the lettering proclaiming, *'Warning. May spontaneously start talking about History.'*

"Daniel!"

The times where Richard referred to me by my full name were so rare that I could have counted them on the one hand. I reluctantly forced my gaze back to his. "He needed help, and he's not what you think. He's not some sort of opportunist who's just using me. He was going to leave last night, and I had to talk him into staying." It was better not to mention the kiss. "Listen, I'm a good judge of character. And he's got his secrets, but he's basically a good guy. I can tell."

Richard let out a weary sigh. It was a sigh that said he wasn't sure how he was supposed to deal with someone displaying this level of stupidity. "Have you left him alone in your house?"

I nodded. "If he was going to rob me, he would have done it yesterday, so…" I finished the sentence with a shrug. I knew where Richard was coming from. If the roles were reversed, I would probably have been saying the exact same things to him. But he hadn't met Frankie. He hadn't seen the sincerity and goodness that shone from him like a beacon. He hadn't seen him when he'd been shaking. If he had, he would know how lost and alone he'd looked huddled in a doorway. It was easy to judge when you were reacting to an idea. It wasn't so easy when it was a living, breathing person with feelings. I jutted my chin out in a mutinous fashion. Whatever Richard said he wasn't going to change my mind, so it was pointless for him to try.

"How old is this guy?"

"Twenty-two." I refused to break eye contact with Richard as I said it.

Richard's grimace said it all. "What is it with you and younger guys?"

"Oh, come on. That's not fair. You're only saying that because of Calvin. Before that, I always dated guys around my age. You're a scientist. Surely you of all people know that two is not a pattern. Besides"—I dipped my gaze to the table, unable to look him in the eye while I twisted the truth—"you're assuming something is going on between us."

"I'm not assuming anything." Richard's voice was strident. "I can see it in your face. Look me in the eye and tell me that nothing has happened between you."

I managed to meet his gaze, but I couldn't force the words out.

Richard nodded. "Exactly." He exhaled noisily. "I guess at least this one isn't an ex-student. Mind you, I can't see that making a lot of difference when Marjorie discovers you're shacked up with another man with a considerable age gap."

"It's none of her business what I do in my spare time."

Richard raised an eyebrow. "Or even who." He smoothed an invisible crease on his trousers. "I just don't want you to get hurt. What do you know about this guy?"

Not a lot. I needed to say something, though. Even if it meant telling a few white lies to put his mind at rest. "He's sweet and kind." No lies yet. I could tell that from our interactions so far. "He's a great conversationalist." That was probably pushing it a bit far. "We're still in the getting to know each other phase."

"Can he play pool? You should bring him to the pub so that I can meet him."

It was tempting. At least then Richard would be able to see that he was harmless and get off my back. But hard as I tried, I just couldn't see François in the middle of The Punch Bowl. It would be like sticking a carrot in the middle of a bunch of flowers and expecting it to blend in. "I don't think it's his sort of thing."

"Wow! Who is this paragon of virtue that doesn't do pubs? Are you sure he's not a runaway angel?"

I laughed. That would be one explanation for the air of mystery surrounding him. "Pretty sure. Listen, I know you're just being a good friend and I appreciate it, I really do, but trust me, its early days, and he's really not a threat. We're not at the meeting friends stage yet. But… I promise that if we get that far, you'll be the first person I introduce him to."

Richard leaned forward in his chair, the look on his face suddenly intense. "Some people seem harmless when they're really not. You shouldn't have strangers in your house, Daniel. It can only lead to trouble. You'll regret it."

It was such a change of tack that I was rendered speechless for a moment before something else snagged my attention. "You're bleeding."

Richard lifted a hand to his nose, turning his hand around to stare at the bright red blood covering his fingers. "So I am."

I quickly grabbed a handful of tissues and passed them across the table. Richard took them and pressed them to his nose.

"I didn't know you got nose bleeds."

He stood, the expression on his face somewhat confused. "Neither did I." He checked his watch and grimaced. "I better go. I've got a seminar at three. I need to explain to my student, Peter, in words that he might understand that setting fire to the lab on more than one occasion really is a problem." He paused for a moment with his hand on the door handle as if he wanted to say something else, but then left without so much as a backward glance.

I turned my attention back to the papers. I wanted to be able to spend the evening with Frankie. Therefore, the more I got done before I left the building, the less time I'd be forced to ignore him.

Chapter Twelve

Frankie

I sat quietly at the kitchen table while Daniel busied himself emptying various cupboards and preparing so much food that it might as well have been a banquet for a royal household, rather than what was meant to be a picnic lunch for the two of us. He glanced back over his shoulder, his smile lighting up his face. "I know what you're thinking. You're thinking that it's far too cold to be tramping around the Peak District, never mind eating a picnic, But there's this little pub in the middle of the walk, where they're happy for you to take your own food as long as you buy drinks and sit in the beer garden. They're used to hikers stopping there. And the beer garden has heaters in it, so it's not cold."

There was a lot to unpack from that. Chief among them was that I didn't even know what the "Peak District" was, or a "beer garden" come to that. And it wasn't a language thing. Although, there had been plenty of instances over the years where I'd realized that my command of English wasn't as good as I'd thought it was. But in this case, it was a twenty-five-years-culture-has-moved-on thing. For that reason, I couldn't ask him. Therefore, I just nodded.

Daniel paused from where he'd been shoveling the sandwiches he'd just made into a bag, his brow furrowing. "We don't have to go if you don't want to. We could do something else instead. We could… go to the cinema and watch a film. We could go to Meadowhall and do some shopping. Although, it'll be busy as anything today. It always is on a Saturday. It's not nicknamed Meadowhell for no reason. We could…"

"I'm happy to do whatever. It will be nice to get some fresh air."

Daniel's smile was blinding. "Well, the drive is always nice, anyway. And if it's too cold, we'll just eat in the car and then come back. That reminds me…" He left the kitchen, returning a few moments later with a thick gray coat in his hands. He held it out to me. "This is a spare one of mine. I thought you might want to borrow it." He glanced down at my hoodie and jeans, the same ones that I'd been wearing for the last couple of days. "You won't be warm enough, if not." I took it and put it on. It smelled like him. He stepped forward and fastened it for me, and I stared at his lips. We hadn't kissed again since the first time, and I didn't know why. I'd caught Daniel looking at me a few times while we'd watched TV together the previous evening, but he'd always averted his gaze when I'd caught him staring.

I'd wanted to kiss him, had even considered being the one to initiate it, but something had held me back. Whether it was fear of rejection or something else I wasn't sure. Daniel was probably trying to be a gentleman, but I didn't need that, and I didn't want that. I wanted his lips on mine. I wanted to lose myself in that magical connection again. I wanted to know that the alien feelings coursing through me were reciprocated, that I wasn't in this alone. I could kiss him now. What was the worst that could happen?

He stepped back with a smile, and the moment was lost. He put on his own coat and fastened it, and then picked up the bag with the food in it. "Are you ready?"

* * * *

The afternoon consisted of walking, stopping to admire the view, and then walking some more. I didn't mind. Huddled in Daniel's coat, I was plenty warm enough, my hands dug deep in the pockets to make up for the fact that I didn't have gloves. The scenery was truly beautiful, all the greenery reminding me somewhat of home. There weren't that many people around, and we spent the majority of the time in silent contemplation. I didn't mind that either. It was nice to be comfortable enough around each other that neither of us felt the need to fill the silence with meaningless drivel.

I was trailing behind Daniel so he had to stop to look back. "Are you warm enough?" I gave him a nod as we came to a stop at the side of a river. I stared into the bubbling waters, a rush of memories flooding back. It wasn't the first river I'd seen since Dordogne, and it was nothing like the one back there, but even so it still catapulted me back to stolen moments and a love so pure that I'd thought it could endure anything. It hadn't been able to survive Cecile finding out about us, though.

Had Estienne known she was a witch? He must have. He'd lived in the cottage, and I'd seen first-hand some of the grisly things that were in there. He would have had to be blind or stupid not to have known what was going on. And he'd been neither of those things. He'd invited me there anyway. Did I blame him? I'd tried to at one point, hoping it might make our separation easier to bear, but I'd known deep down that it was just a matter of him being so desperate to see me, to spend time with me that he'd thought it was a risk worth taking. He would never have put me in danger deliberately.

I roused myself from the past before Daniel started asking questions, turning my head to find to my surprise that he seemed just as lost in thought as I'd been as he stared into the water.

He laughed when he caught me watching him. "I had a strange dream about a river the other night. I was just thinking about it."

"What made it strange?"

He didn't respond for at least a minute, leading me to believe that either he didn't want to answer, or he wasn't sure how to. Finally, he spoke. "It was a river that I don't remember ever having seen, so it didn't make sense to be dreaming about it. You probably think that sounds crazy, that rivers mostly look the same. They are, after all, just water and rocks."

"I don't." I corrected myself when I realized my meaning wasn't clear. "Either of those I mean, I don't think that rivers all look the same or that you're crazy." I picked up a stone and threw it in the water. It bounced off a rock and then sank, never to be seen again. "Why do you think you dreamt about it?"

Daniel ran a hand through his hair. "I don't know. I've been asking myself the same question. That wasn't all either, the whole dream felt like it was important in some way, but I can't work out how." He laughed wryly. "I've probably been working too hard." He hoisted the backpack more firmly onto his back. "Which is why it's good that we're out here. I obviously need the fresh air and exercise." He pointed toward the opposite bank of the river. "We go that way, and then the pub I was telling you about is roughly a mile away. Are you hungry?"

I was. I'd grown used to eating again, my body starting to remind me that in my human form it needed sustenance. "I could definitely eat something. How do we cross the river?"

Daniel winked. "Can't you see the stepping stones? The ones jutting out from the water. We cross using those."

I could see them, but they looked to be an awfully long way from each other — and wet. I turned my head to scan the length of the river as far as I could see, first to the left, and then to the right. "Isn't there a bridge?"

"No bridge." Daniel seemed to be finding my reaction amusing, his eyes twinkling and those little lines around his eyes appearing again.

"What if I fall in?" It wasn't like I couldn't swim, but there was a huge difference between a dip in the river on a nice day and finding yourself submerged complete with a heavy coat determined to drag you down.

"Then I'll jump in and save you, and we'll both be wet."

"Promise?"

"I promise. Would it make you feel better if I go first and help you across?"

I gave a nod, and Daniel stepped up to the edge of the bank, gathering himself for a few seconds before executing a perfect leap that landed him right in the center of the first stone. It was large enough that he was able to move over to one side. We'd both fit on there, but it would be a bit of a squeeze. He held out a hand. "Come on."

I stepped up to the edge of the bank. "Can't we just go back the way we came?"

Daniel shook his head and wiggled his fingers at me. "Where's your sense of adventure?"

The words slammed into me. They were the same words Estienne had said to me on that fateful day when I'd first accompanied him into the forest. What would have happened if I'd turned and walked away at that point? Would I have discovered that my feelings for him were mutual at a later date, or would the moment have been lost forever? Would I have buried that part of myself and married a woman I wasn't capable of loving the way she deserved? Would we have had children? Or would events have eventually played out in the exact same way? I would never know.

"François?" My head snapped up to find Daniel staring at me with a look of concern. I was getting used to seeing that expression on his face when it came to me. "If you really want to go back, we can go back."

I shook my head. I was being stupid. I only got a month to live. I should be doing my best to live it as successfully as I could, to try new things and experience everything I could in the short amount of time I had. It was just a river. Even if I did fall in, Daniel wouldn't let me freeze to death. "No, I trust you."

A slow smile spread across Daniel's face, the slight flush on his cheeks seeming to signal that he couldn't quite decide whether to be pleased by my statement, or embarrassed. I dug my hands out of my pockets and shuffled closer to the bank, as close as I could get without falling in. There were five rocks spanning the width of the river. Five jumps, that's all I needed, and Daniel would be there to catch me. I launched myself at him before I could change my mind, laughing with a heady mix of relief and adrenaline as I crashed into his chest and he steadied me without either of us falling in.

He grinned at me. "There you go. That wasn't too bad, was it?" He slowly removed his hands from my shoulders. "You good? You balanced?"

I nodded, keeping my feet still and my arms outstretched to aid my balance as he turned away from me and executed another nimble leap to the next rock before holding his hand out again. "Just like the last one."

Sure it was. Except for the small matter of jumping from a slippery rock rather than the comforting grassiness of the riverbank. I shuffled forward so that I was as close to the edge of the stone as I could get. I focused on Daniel's face and his outstretched hand, trying not to overthink it. My jump was surprisingly sure, and he caught me again. We made it across the rest of the stones in the same way, Daniel always there to offer words of reassurance and encouragement.

The relief at once again finding myself on firm ground had me throwing myself into his arms. He didn't seem to mind, his arms closing around me to hold me tight. It made me regret the fact that we were both wearing thick coats. I wanted to feel his body heat. I wanted to feel the solidity of his chest pressing against mine. I also wanted him to kiss me again, so that I could know for sure that the kisses we'd shared before hadn't just been a byproduct of my heightened state of emotion.

Why was I waiting for him to initiate one? The one thing I didn't have was time. He was a gentleman. I could wait a week and we might not be any closer to what I wanted.

Before I could have second thoughts, I stood up on tiptoes and pressed my lips against his. There was a moment of frozen stillness. Just long enough for panic to surge through my body, but then he was kissing me back, a warm palm cupping my wind-chilled cheek as he leisurely explored my mouth. And it was just as good as the first time.

I don't know how long we stood there kissing, I only knew that the rest of the world ceased to exist. There was no river. No stepping stones. No cold wind. Nothing but the two of us beneath a wintry sky. How could I have ever thought I wouldn't cross a river for Daniel? I'd walk over hot coals for him. Except, I knew that made no sense when we'd only known each other a few days. That wasn't true, though, was it? At least not for me. Daniel had been talking to me for years. I knew everything about him. Well, nearly everything—Napoleon's existence had come as a bit of a surprise. When we finally unglued ourselves from each other, we were both rosy-cheeked and breathing hard in a way that had absolutely nothing to do with the cold weather. Daniel coughed. "Well, that was…"

"It was what?"

"Unexpected."

"I've been waiting for you to kiss me again since the first time. I was beginning to worry you'd never get there, so…"

His fingers flexed against my cheek where they still lay, and I had to fight the urge to turn my face into his touch like a flower seeking the sun. Daniel's lips curled up at the corners. "I didn't want to rush you. This thing between us is…" He shook his head as if it was impossible to put what he wanted to say into words that made any sense.

I knew exactly how he was feeling. I was right there with him. "Yeah, it is."

"It's crazy, right?"

I nodded. We stared at each other, all the words we couldn't say seeming to hang in the air between us. Whatever they were, they were bright and beautiful and larger than life — words that lasted a lifetime.

The charged moment was broken by voices carrying on the wind from the other side of the river. Daniel's hand dropped from my face as he stepped back and raised a hand in greeting. It was a young couple, and it was gratifying to see as we walked away in the opposite direction that they shared my earlier apprehension about crossing the river. I didn't complain when Daniel's hand slipped into mine, our fingers entwining as he tugged them both into his pocket. Could he break the curse? Maybe… just maybe. We still had three weeks.

* * * *

I'd been right about the amount of food Daniel had packed. I'd watched with growing amusement as he'd carefully laid it all out across the picnic table, the two of us sitting on either side. He'd been right about it being warm enough. In fact, the heater right next to our table was kicking out so much heat that I'd had to remove my coat. It was either that or end up drenched in sweat. And I didn't want to stink. I wanted Daniel to kiss me again.

Daniel had ordered a pint of beer while I'd stuck to orange juice. It wasn't that I didn't ever drink, but I couldn't run the risk of alcohol loosening my tongue to the point where I might let something slip that would have me back in the gargoyle before I could even blink. Therefore, it was always safer this way.

Finally satisfied with the layout, Daniel waved a hand over the food. "Dig in. It'll only go to waste if we don't eat it."

I pulled a paper plate in front of me, placing a sandwich on top of it. Cheese, by the looks of it. We ate in silence for a few moments, Daniel pausing every now and again to take a sip of his beer. He wanted to say something. I could tell. He had that awkward edginess that people got when they were trying too hard to act casual. "Just say it."

He startled, his brown eyes going wide as they met mine. "Just say what?"

I picked up another sandwich, the first one having gone down in record time. This one was tuna. "Whatever it is that you're thinking so hard about."

"You can tell that?"

I nibbled on the edge of the sandwich, nodding so that I didn't have to speak with my mouth full.

Daniel sighed. "It's just that... I don't know how I'm meant to not ask anything about you. I know I agreed not to ask questions, but it's hard because... I want to get to know you. And I don't know how to do that any other way."

The tuna turned to ash in my mouth and took far longer to swallow than it should have done. I should have known we couldn't live in the bubble the kiss by the river had created for that long, that reality would come crashing down on us eventually. I'd been here before. So many times. I usually handled it by lying, but I didn't want to lie to Daniel. He deserved better than that. He was already a man hurting from his divorce and I didn't want to make it any worse.

Add to that, the fact that in twenty-three days, I was going to disappear as quickly as I'd appeared, and we were on a one-way road to heartbreak. I searched for a compromise, something that would make it easier on him without risking breaking the conditions of the curse. "You can ask me questions. I just might not be able to answer them all."

He perked up, sitting up straighter as he dropped his sandwich onto his plate. "Yeah?"

I gave a slow nod. I just had to be careful.

"Where were you born?"

That was safe enough to answer. "In France. In a place called Domme." I knew it was still called that. Or at least it had been twenty-five years ago.

Daniel reached for his beer and took a long swallow. "And your family?" A shadow crossed his face. "If it's too painful to talk about, you don't have to. I know you said they weren't around anymore."

"I only had a small family. It was just me, my parents, and a younger brother." I swallowed past the lump in my throat threatening to turn the innocuous statement into an outpouring of grief at the loss that still burned so many years later.

Daniel looked thoughtful, his fingers tightening around the glass. "What happened to your younger brother?"

I reached across the table, using the action of transferring a piece of quiche to my plate as a distraction while I considered the best way to answer the question. The honest answer would be that I didn't know what had happened to him, but that he was dead. "He…" I shook my head, Daniel saving me from having to say anything else.

"Never mind. I can see that talking about him is going to upset you." He leaned his elbow on the table and rested his head on his hand. "What did you do back in France? For a job, I mean. I presume you had one."

I took a few seconds to consider my answer. "I worked on a farm. Harvesting the crops and tending the animals."

His brow furrowed as if something about the information didn't quite make sense. "And when did you come to England? Your English is very good."

"A while ago." That was as close I could get without it being an out-and-out lie.

Daniel's frown deepened. "You're only twenty-two, but you had time to work on a farm before coming to England, and you've been here so long that your accent isn't that strong."

I stood up from the table. It was the perfect example of why answering questions never worked. Eventually they always led me down a cul-de-sac that there was no escape from. "Shouldn't we get moving if we want to make it back before dark?"

Daniel blinked a couple of times before beginning to pack up the leftover food, which was most of it. I struggled back into my borrowed coat and then went to stand where I could see the view. It really was beautiful. I imagined in summer it would be even more stunning, but I would never get to see it. The timing of the curse had condemned me to a lifetime of winters.

A warmth at my shoulder told me that Daniel had joined me.

"I'm sorry."

There was so much sincerity in those two words that it hurt. He thought it was his fault, and he couldn't have been more wrong. It was my own damn secrets that were coming between us. "It's not you. It's—"

"Whoa!" Daniel reared back as if I'd slapped him. "Please don't use those words on me. Calvin said that when he... well, when he decided that our marriage was as dead as the proverbial dodo. It's what people say when they're trying to make the other person feel better."

Except, it was true. It wasn't him. I stayed silent, though. Any other words were just going to rub salt in the wounds. We needed to get back to where we were earlier, that sense of companionship where words weren't needed.

Chapter Thirteen

Daniel

I could hear the river, but I couldn't see it. Not yet. Excitement buzzed through me. He would be there. He usually got there first, even though my house was closer. The sun was just starting to set but it would still be light enough that we could snatch a couple of hours together. I would lose myself in him until we both smelled like the other, hating the point where we had to bathe in the river and lose that scent before heading home. Twigs crunched beneath my feet, the sound of the river getting louder, but not loud enough to drown out my footsteps. He would hear them too, would probably hide in that endearing way of his, where he found it impossible to believe that no one else would come this way despite the fact that we'd never so much as seen a single person in the forest in all the months we'd been coming here.

Sure enough, the clearing was empty when I walked into it. Definitely hiding. I opened my mouth to say his name, but the information wasn't there. Why couldn't I remember his name? Panic clawed at my chest. I couldn't remember what he looked like either. Why couldn't I remember his face or his name? He was everything to me, my heart clenching at the mere thought of him. Except how could that be true if I couldn't remember who he was?

A noise wrenched me from my dream and had me sitting bolt upright. The bedroom door was opening, the noise, the slight creak of its hinges that I never got around to oiling. I lay back down. It would be Napoleon. He'd disappeared out of the cat flap the same way he always did after I'd given him his supper. But there were some nights — especially in winter — where the lure of a warm bed outweighed the excitement of whatever it was he spent his nights doing. On those nights, he insisted on lying curled up against my chest, the rhythmic rattle of his purr sending me back to sleep in no time at all. I steeled myself not to jump when he launched himself onto the bed.

"Daniel?" The whisper was so quiet that had I not already been listening for noise, I doubt I would have heard it.

I sat up again, peering into the darkness. It was pointless, the thick black-out curtains doing the job they were supposed to and not letting even the slightest chink of light through from the streetlight right outside my window. I fumbled for the switch of the lamp but didn't turn it on, concerned it would be too jarring. "Frankie?"

"Can I come in?" The words were cautious and guarded, as if he was fully expecting me to say no.

"Yes." There. A slight movement in the darkness, my eyes adjusting enough as he came closer to the bed that I could make out a faint outline. "Are you okay? Did something happen? Do you need something?"

The dark shape halted at the side of the bed. "No, nothing happened. I just..." I waited, and he eventually finished his sentence. "I don't want to be on my own."

I swallowed nervously, a hundred reasons all popping into my head at the same time why it would be best to send him back to his own bed. I ignored them all as I reached over to pull the covers back on the other side of the bed. "Get in."

I lay down on my side, François mirroring my position so that we ended up face to face. He lifted his head slightly as if he was trying to search out my features in the darkness. "I didn't know if you'd be awake."

"I wasn't. I was dreaming, but then the sound of the door woke me."

"Sorry."

"It's fine." It was. There were no meaningless platitudes required when it came to Frankie. He brought raw honesty out of me. "It was a weird dream anyway."

"What was it about?"

That was an excellent question. What had it been about? A mysterious figure who'd made my heart sing, but whose name and face I hadn't been able to recall, even though the mere thought of him had roused so much emotion in me that it had felt like I could burst from it. But then, it was a dream. Dreams weren't meant to make sense. They were about dealing with emotions, sometimes positive, and sometimes negative. "Nothing important."

Frankie shuffled a bit closer, so close that I could feel the heat coming from his body. What was he wearing?

"Did you just want to sleep here?"

"No."

That single word was incredibly powerful, my heart immediately kicking into a faster rhythm, and goosebumps breaking out all over my skin. Because if he didn't want to sleep, that meant he'd come in here with the intention of something else happening, and it didn't take a genius to work out what. Could I really be that lucky?

Frankie's hand inched across the divide, plucking mine from where it was tucked under my head and pressing it to his chest — his bare chest. Well, that answered one question. Or part of it, at least. His skin was warm and silky-soft beneath my fingertips, and I could feel the steady beat of his heart, which wasn't much slower than mine. He removed his hand from mine, as if he wanted to make it clear that he wasn't forcing anything, that it was simply an invitation.

If so, it was an invitation I didn't hesitate to accept, my hand staying exactly where it was and my fingers starting a slow exploration. Smooth skin. Virtually hairless apart from a few around his nipples. Nipples that peaked beneath my touch. I went lower. Taut abdominal muscles. A treasure trail, which led down to... My fingers jerked spasmodically against the hard flesh that had risen to meet them. "You're naked." And aroused. If I'd had any doubt where this was going, that discovery had erased any lingering vestiges of it.

Frankie laughed, the sound soft and melodic. "What did you think I wore to bed? I don't have any clothes except for the ones I was wearing when you found me."

Fuck! The casually spoken statement floored me. I was such an idiot not to have thought of that. "I'm sorry. We can fix that tomorrow. We can go shopping, and we'll find you some stuff. We should have gone today instead of tramping around the countryside. I could have at least have given you something of mine. You must think I'm..." A finger landed on my lips, and I followed the silent instruction and stopped talking.

Another laugh. "I don't want to talk about clothes at the moment."

Neither did I. Not really. He took his finger away from my lips, and I became all too aware of my hand still resting on his lower abdomen, where there was the unmistakable springiness of pubic hair beneath my palm. Remove my hand or put it where I really wanted it? Temptation versus... versus what? Decorum? I had a naked man in my bed who'd put himself there willingly. It was clear what François wanted. The only choice was whether I was going to take him up on it or cut my nose off to spite my face and turn him down.

Shifting my hand slightly, I curled my fingers around his cock. It was long and thin, and felt just as elegant as the rest of him. If I could have seen it, I would have bet everything I owned on it being the prettiest cock in existence. I cursed myself for not having turned the light on, but then would we still be where we were? Or was it possible I might have scared him off?

I tightened my fingers around him, and he pushed his cock into my grip, a breathy moan that had my own cock throbbing escaped his lips. "Are you sure, François?" It was important to me that his consent was about more than what his body wanted. It had to be his mind too. He shifted closer still, lips close enough that I could feel his breath, but just far enough away that we weren't touching.

"I'm sure."

It was enough, any gentlemanly sense of restraint going out of the window. Why should we wait? We had something special, something indefinable – though if anyone else had said that to me, I would have laughed in their face. Letting go of Frankie's cock, I rolled him on top of me, so that he sprawled across my chest. This close, I could see the glitter of his eyes in the darkness. I traced his face with my fingers, searching out the perfect curve of his lips and the angular line of his jaw. His hands weren't idle either, questing fingers mapping my neck and chest.

I couldn't remember ever wanting anything more than I wanted Frankie. It wasn't even a need. It went beyond that, more like a fundamental and biological imperative, like breathing and eating. Something that I needed in order to survive.

When our lips met, it was different to the other times we'd kissed — more sensual, more heated, our bodies melting into each other until it was hard to say where one ended and the other began. Every brush of his skin against mine evoked a shiver, and every slide of his tongue sent a zing of sensation coursing down my spine. My cock was throbbing, but there was far more than a carnal need to sink it into a willing body. We'd get there. I was as certain of that as I was that the sun would rise in the morning.

There was no rush. There was only giving François pleasure. It would be our first time — one of many, I hoped — and I intended to make it special.

I wriggled out of the boxers I'd worn to bed, and he rubbed his cock against my hip. Swallowing his cries with my mouth, I slid my hands down the satiny smoothness of his back, muscles bunching beneath my palms. He was lean but perfect, his frame carrying very little body fat. Gripping his ass, I encouraged his movements. Harder. Faster. More friction.

When he came, it was with a gasp that reverberated right through my soul. We continued to kiss, and I released his ass to tangle my fingers in his hair, angling his head in just the right way to possess it completely. I could have kissed him forever. I could have stayed in this bed until we were nothing but skeletons, still kissing, eyes for no one but each other.

It was my turn to gasp as Frankie's hand stole to my cock, his palm enclosing the sensitive flesh but sensing that I was too close to the edge to stroke. "I want you, Daniel."

He didn't need to say more. I knew what he needed, what we both needed. I used the utmost gentleness to roll him onto his back before reaching over to the nightstand and seeking out condoms and lube by touch alone. My fingers hovered over the switch of the lamp. "François?"

"*Oui.*"

His voice was husky, and the switch to French made me smile.

"I'd really like to be able to see you."

"Yes!"

No hesitation. He hadn't even had to think about my request. I clicked the switch, soft light filling the room. When I turned back to him, it was enough to take my breath away. We'd lost the covers at some point, so Frankie lay sprawled on top of the sheet, one leg drawn up, and his cock — which was just as pretty as I'd imagined—still semi-hard. His skin was pale, but not an unhealthy pale, more the creamy paleness of someone who in years gone by would have been captured on canvas. And his face. God, it really was the face of an angel, the flush of arousal on his cheeks only accentuating it. There was amusement in the blue eyes that watched me as I scrutinized him.

My hands shook as I shifted position so that I was between his thighs and I tugged on his hips to pull him closer. "You're so beautiful."

Frankie's tongue darted out to moisten his lips, and I was torn between the need to kiss him, and the need to keep looking, to commit him to memory in case this was nothing but a dream and I woke in the morning with nothing but an empty bed and the realization that the whole experience had been nothing but a byproduct of my overactive imagination.

"So are you."

I laughed. "I'm really not. But you…" I trailed my fingers over his abdomen, tracing the defined muscles and watching with fascination as the skin contracted beneath my touch. "I could write poetry about you, about how perfect you are, about how blue your eyes are."

Frankie's lips curled into a smile. "I thought you taught history. Can you write poetry?"

I shook my head. "No, but I'd learn. For you."

"It's not necessary. And you are beautiful."

I wasn't, but reflected in Frankie's eyes, seeing the way his breath caught as his gaze roved down my body to settle on my cock, I could almost believe it. He was an enticing mixture of innocence and boldness all rolled up into one as he reached out to touch again. I arched into his hand, biting my lip as his palm slid over the sensitive head in a way that was absolutely perfect. I fumbled for the lube, almost dropping it in my haste to get the lid off. Once I had, I gave my fingers a generous coating. "Are you ready?"

Frankie gave a nod, and I used my non-lubed hand to pull him even closer, the way his thighs were splayed across mine tipping his hips up so that his tight, puckered hole was on display. It was just as pretty as his cock, and I said a silent prayer to whoever had given me the wherewithal to suggest putting the light on.

I stroked one lubed fingertip over the delicate skin, and Frankie sighed. He made the best noises. I didn't try to penetrate—not yet. I just concentrated on exploring and letting him know I was there. His thighs dropped open wider as I rubbed the pad of my thumb in a circular motion over the puckered skin. And all the time I watched his face. I watched the way his lips parted as his breathing sped up. I watched the way the flush on his cheeks grew gradually darker and his pupils dilated. If he was so beautifully responsive already, what would he be like once I got my cock inside him?

I introduced a finger up to the first knuckle, his hole gripping me so tightly that it made me wonder how long it had been for him. Unless… I froze with the tip of my finger still embedded inside him. "Are you a virgin?"

Frankie laughed. He actually laughed. "No, I'm not a virgin. You don't need to worry on that score."

There weren't enough words to describe the amount of relief I felt. Would I have stopped? I didn't know. Maybe. Maybe not. Was there a part of me that would have liked to have been Frankie's first? Quite possibly.

I slid my finger deeper, Frankie squirming in a way that had far more to do with pleasure than discomfort. Buoyed by his response, I withdrew it before reintroducing it. Only once he'd relaxed slightly did I introduce a second finger, finding a rhythm that had Frankie panting and muttering words in French that I didn't understand.

Frankie was the one to reach out to where I'd left the condom. He picked it up and flicked it at me, the foil square bouncing off my chest. "Daniel!"

I took the hint. Or was it an order? I wasn't too sure. Whatever it was, there was no doubt we were both ready. Ripping the condom wrapper open with my teeth, I smoothed it over my cock and added more lube. Frankie watched me with a languorous expression as I positioned us so that the tip of my sheathed cock pressed against his entrance. I pressed forward, another delightful noise spilling from Frankie's lips as I breached him. I took it as slow as I could, fighting the urge to bury myself deep inside him with every fiber of my being. We had all night. Hell, we had the rest of our lives, the knowledge filling me with a burst of euphoria the likes of which I couldn't remember ever having experienced before.

I pushed into him in that same slow, halting way until my cock was completely sheathed in his body and the two of us were as close as we could get. Leaning over him and supporting my weight on my elbows, I gazed into his face. There was a faint sheen of sweat on his forehead but apart from that there were no signs of any discomfort. "Are you okay?"

A slow smile spread across his face, and he nodded. "More than okay."

I kissed him, unable to resist the lure of his lips when they were so close. It was Frankie who started to move first, his hips pushing against mine in a silent plea to give him what he wanted. I gave in to it, starting slow and then gradually building the tempo, each slide of my cock into his body sending a ricochet of pleasure down my spine. This wasn't going to be any great demonstration of stamina. Everything was too perfect for that: the way he clutched at me, those noises that drove me crazy, his lips clinging to mine in a way that mirrored my own desperation.

Frankie's cock rubbed against my abdomen as I fucked him, the head slick with pre-cum. I went deeper, and faster, hoping to push him over the edge before I was forced to give in to the overwhelming pressure already gathering in my balls. We moved as one, both of us chasing the same thing.

When he came for the second time, it was with his head buried in the curve of my neck, his cock jerking between us. I wasn't far behind him, my muscles going rigid as I thrust one last time before coming, the world flashing white behind my eyelids.

I gathered him close, our bodies still interlocked as I maneuvered us into a
more comfortable position, cradling his head against my shoulder with one hand as I tugged the covers over us with the other. I couldn't stop myself from kissing him. Wherever my lips could reach became a target. Cheek. Shoulder. Forehead. I covered them all with soft kisses, Frankie laughing and squirming in my arms.

I got rid of the condom before reaching across and turning off the lamp so that we were back in darkness. Frankie's chest rose and fell against mine, his breath tickling my neck as we lay intertwined. We were both hot, our skin still slick from our earlier exertion, yet neither of us made any move to separate. There were more important things than a bit of discomfort.

Frankie eventually stirred against me, his hand finding mine beneath the cover. "I'm glad I made the decision to come in here."
"So am I." And I was. Left up to me to make the first move, months would probably have gone by. When something was right, it was right. Time shouldn't even be a factor. At least in an

ideal world, anyway. The only problem was that the world was usually far from ideal.

Chapter Fourteen

Frankie

Maybe.

That word wouldn't get out of my head. Maybe Daniel could love me. Maybe the curse could be broken this time. Maybe. Maybe. Maybe.

Three days had passed since the night I'd crept into his room and we'd made love. Because I refused to think of it as simply having sex. I'd done both—had sex, and made love. And what we'd shared was far closer to the latter.

The following two nights had followed a similar pattern, only without me having to sneak into his room. Instead, Daniel had simply taken my hand and led me in there, the silence and my lack of protest speaking volumes. We'd undressed and laid there in Daniel's bed, talking about nothing and no one. Eventually our bodies would move closer, and hands would stray. And then we would crash together like waves against a rock—an irresistible force building to a mutual orgasm.

During the day, Daniel worked, and I wandered around his house like a restless soul. I'd watch TV. I'd pick up a book and try to make sense of the strange squiggles that covered the pages. I'd pet Napoleon. I'd spend far longer in the shower or in the bath than I needed to. I'd clean the house. I'd stare out of the window. Nothing ever held my attention for long. Once I'd had enough of one activity, I'd move on to something else until that too couldn't hold my attention. The days were just a filler until Daniel came home from work.

Twenty-one days left. Three weeks. It wasn't long. It certainly wasn't long enough. But it was all I had, so it would have to be.

I unlocked the back door and let myself out into the small garden. It really was small—just a square of lawn and a few big pots that Daniel had referred to as planters. There were no bright buds. There never were in winter. The only flowers I saw were the ones from inside the gargoyle. I always wondered whether endless winters was another layer of suffering that Cecile had added, or just a happy accident. But then, it had been winter when I'd been imprisoned, so it stood to reason that it would be winter when I was released. I missed the sun, though. There was sun in England during the winter months, but it was the weak kind that barely warmed anything. I would have given anything to feel hot sun blazing on my skin once more.

It was cold outside, and I hadn't stopped to put on the coat Daniel had loaned to me, but I didn't mind. The cold helped to clear my mind. I startled as Napoleon hurtled out from the door, one mighty leap taking him to the top of the wooden fence that separated Daniel's property from the next-door neighbor's. His tail flicked in the air, and he paused to sniff something as he tight-roped his way along it. Why couldn't Cecile have turned me into a cat? I could have coped with that, even if I never got to speak to a single person again. At least I'd have been free. At least I'd have been able to feel.

The sound of a throat being cleared had me turning my head in that direction. The fence at the end of the garden wasn't as tall. It was at this part that Daniel's next-door-neighbor stood, staring directly at me. It took a few seconds to recall her name. "Good morning, Mrs. Featherstone."

Keen blue eyes raked over me. She might be old, but there was no mistaking that her mind was still sharp. She wasn't one of those harmless old dears who wouldn't say boo to a goose. "You're staying here? With Daniel?"

Merde! What would Daniel want me to say? Would he care if I confirmed it? I should have stayed in the house. But then I could hardly have anticipated Daniel's neighbor lying in wait for me in the garden. Although, from what Daniel had told me about her maybe I should have done. He'd said that she took a keen interest in *everything* that went on in the neighborhood.

She was still waiting for my answer, her gaze expectant. Daniel was at work and I was in his house, so denying it would probably be pointless. "He's letting me stay here for a while."

Her head tipped to one side as if she were weighing a few things up in her mind. "I see." She glanced back toward her house. "In that case, it just might be my lucky day. I need some boxes lifted down from the attic. What do you say? Can you help an old woman out?"

Go inside her house and spend time helping someone I didn't even know? I didn't want to. Daniel hadn't had anything complimentary to say about her, so had the question been aimed at him, I doubted he would have agreed. Was that why she'd liked Calvin more? Had he helped her out? I fidgeted on the spot, politeness warring with caution. It wasn't like I could plead being busy. She'd caught me standing in the yard, watching a cat. A cat who was sitting on the fence and watching the interaction between us with great interest. "I don't know. I…" I looked back at Daniel's house for inspiration, but nothing came to mind.

"I don't bite."

I was being stupid. All I had to do was move a few boxes. It would take what? Ten minutes? Fifteen at most.

I forced a smile. "Okay… I can move a few boxes." I gestured to the back door. "Should I go round that way?"

Mrs. Featherstone shook her head, already moving to unfasten a connecting panel in the fence that I hadn't even realized was there. It swung open and I stepped through to the other side. She led me into the house, and I politely wiped my feet on the mat meant for that purpose. Her house had the exact same layout as Daniel's, our route taking us through the kitchen. But where Daniel's was largely bare, hers bore a number of homely touches from a collection of teapots in the shape of buildings, to a bright collection of plates that seemed to be more for decoration than actual use.

She didn't stop in the kitchen, continuing on into the hallway and taking me up a flight of stairs, the dark blue carpet soft beneath my feet. At the top of the stairs, there was a stepladder positioned beneath a loft hatch. "It just slides across. You'll see the boxes on the left when you get to the top. Can you bring them all down to the kitchen?"

I nodded. It was strange that the stepladder was already set up. What would she have done if she hadn't stumbled across me in the garden? I hoped she hadn't been planning to go up there herself. That would have been a recipe for disaster. I might not know her, but I had no wish to hear that she'd fallen and hurt herself. It made me glad that I'd given in to her request. She turned to go back down the stairs. "I'll make us some tea. We can drink it when you've finished."

I waited until she'd reached the bottom of the stairs before I started the climb. Just as she'd said it would, the loft hatch slid straight across. I poked my shoulders through the hole, peering through the gloom to where she'd said the boxes would be. I'd expected two or three, but there had to be at least twenty there. So much for a few boxes. I sighed. They weren't going to move themselves so the longer I stared at them, the longer it would be before the job was done.

It took me the best part of half an hour to maneuver them all safely down the stepladder, and by the time I had, I was covered in dust and dirt, and sick of sneezing. Some of them had been heavy as well, and there was still the small matter of getting them down the stairs. I rubbed the small of my back before picking up the first one. It reminded me of the days I'd spent farming.

Mrs. Featherstone didn't turn as I carried the first box into the kitchen, even when another sneeze broke free as I placed it against the wall. By the time I'd navigated the stairs another nineteen times, my thighs were aching and my arms were complaining at the physical activity. I added the last box to the pile. "All done."

Mrs. Featherstone turned with a smile, waving a hand at the table where, while I'd been carrying boxes, she'd set up an elaborate display of biscuits, slices of cake, and various other tea-making things including a set of fancy cups and saucers. "Sit down."

I cast a quick glance toward the door. "I should get going. I left the back door open. I don't want Daniel to come home and discover he's been robbed."

Disappointment bloomed on her face. "Ten minutes."

Was she lonely? Had she really needed the boxes moving, or was it all an elaborate excuse for some company? And she had gone to a lot of trouble. It wouldn't kill me to drink her tea and eat her biscuits. I nodded, pulling out one of the chairs and seating myself at the table. She smiled as she seated herself opposite.

I watched as she proceeded to make us both tea in what had to be the grandest china I'd ever seen. I'd visited a museum once, and they seemed more like something from a bygone age. I guessed that meant that me and the cups were perfectly suited. Once I'd answered all the requisite questions about milk and sugar, the tea was stirred and the cup pushed in front of me.

I'd barely had time to take a sip before the plate full of cake was waved in front of my face. There were three types—chocolate, carrot, and what looked to be lemon. I chose the carrot cake, placing it on the plate in front of me that had been put there for that purpose. "Did you bake these?"

Mrs. Featherstone looked pleased at the assumption. "I did. There's not a lot to do when you get to my age, so I bake. But then I end up throwing most of it away because I can't eat it all."

She looked at me expectantly and I took the hint, picking it up and taking a small bite. "It's good." There was no lying required. It really was good—moist and full of flavor. Pleased by the compliment, she beamed at me, and I found myself smiling back. I relaxed back in the chair. There was no reason I couldn't spend some time keeping an old woman company. At least it was a change of scenery from Daniel's house. And his house didn't have cake. Although, he would probably fall over himself to get it should I mention it. I inclined my head toward the boxes. "What's in the boxes? Some of them were really heavy."

"Take a look."

I stared at her. "Are you sure?"

She nodded. It seemed invasive but, in the end, curiosity won out. The first box was full of photographs. I spread some of them out across the table, pointing at a young woman in one of the photos. "Is that you, Mrs. Featherstone?"

She leaned across to get a better look, her lips curving into a smile. "It is. And call me Gloria, please."

We chatted about the photos for a while, Gloria showing me pictures of her and her husband, Mike, who'd died ten years previously. She told me that they'd never had children with a faraway look in her eye that told me that it wasn't for want of trying.

Gloria pointed to the box on the far right. "Open that one."

I had to move some of the others out of the way before I could even get to it, and I had no idea how she could possibly know what was in each one when none of them were labeled, but she seemed to.

"Bring it here!"

She seemed particularly keen to get to the contents of this one. It was one of the lighter ones, so I had no problem lifting it onto the table once Gloria had cleared a space for it. She peeled the lid back and smiled, and my curiosity well and truly piqued. More photos? Something that had belonged to her husband? When she didn't make any move to lift anything out, my impatience grew. "What's in it?"

Her eyes were shining when she lifted her head. It made her look years younger.

"The answer to any question you could ask the universe." She waved a hand at the seat I'd vacated. "Sit, and I'll show you."

She waited until I'd done as she'd asked before starting to pull items out of the box and place them almost reverently on the table. With each new item that was unearthed, the breath became trapped in my chest that little bit more. I might have been able to pretend with the first few items that I was mistaken, but the evidence had become overwhelming. They were all items linked to witchcraft — candles, a chalice, runes, a pendulum, cards. It wasn't a jar full of fingers or eyeballs, but it may as well have been. It still catapulted me back to that cottage in Dordogne and a time I really didn't want to think about. I had to force myself to breathe, to think rationally. I knew that there were people in modern times who dabbled, who pretended they could use the items that were strewn in front of me. It was a hobby to them.

That's all this was. Gloria wasn't a witch. She just liked to think she was.

Even so, my instinct was to run. Only, my legs felt heavy, and I wasn't sure I'd even be capable. So, I stayed there, breathing and existing, watching as Gloria ran her hands over the items with a touch that spoke of a deep affection for the items. "Why…?" My voice cracked and faded away to nothing. I tried again. "Why did you lock them away in the attic?"

She smiled, but it was a sad smile, one full of memories and regret. "Mike didn't like it. It scared him, so for the good of our marriage — and it was a good marriage — I stopped. I made him a promise that I wouldn't use them. And I kept that promise. And then when he died…" Her gaze turned wistful. "I mourned him for a long time, so it never quite seemed like the right moment. Until today. I don't know… something told me I needed them again."

She reached across the table, grabbing my hand before I got the chance to pull it away, her gaze holding mine. "Palms were more my thing, anyway. And luckily, no one could ever take that away from me. I figured that what Mike didn't know, didn't hurt him." She turned my hand over, her gaze still fixed on my face. "May I?"

The desire to pull my hand away was almost overwhelming. All I had to do was say no, and then leave. Something stopped me, though. Perhaps it was the knowledge that all she was going to do was make stuff up. She'd tell me that I was going to be successful in the future, that I'd have three kids and live a long life — the usual stuff that people liked to hear. I could sit there and listen and make an old woman happy, give her something to fill the void the absence of her husband had clearly left behind in her life. So, I nodded.

She dropped her gaze to my palm. "Oh!" She was silent for a few moments before she lifted her head to stare at me, her brow furrowing. "You're not of this time."

I tried to yank my hand back, but she held firm, her grip surprisingly strong. I tried to quell the rapid beating of my heart by telling myself that it was nothing more than an open statement, one of those things that people could fit to any meaning they wanted to. Who didn't want to be mysterious?

Her gaze dropped again, and she leaned a little closer to my hand, studying it carefully. "I've never seen anything like this before." The cake I'd eaten turned into a lead weight in my stomach. She stroked a finger across my palm, tracing one of the lines. "Your life line…" She shook her head in a way that said she was struggling with something. "It should have ended years ago. And the future…" She blinked a few times.

I knew what the future held. I didn't need her to tell me. It entailed hundreds more years in the same stone prison where I'd already spent more than one lifetime, until I finally lost my grip on reality.

Gloria let go of my hand so suddenly that I almost reeled backward in my chair. "What's your name?"

I stared at her. I'd told her, hadn't I? Or Daniel had on that first night. But then, that had been a week ago. It was likely she couldn't remember. "Frankie."

She nodded as she reached across to pull the crystal ball in front of her. "Someone or something is telling me that I should leave well enough alone, but I need to know."

My mouth was dry, far too dry to speak. What if she wasn't full of shit and could actually see something in the crystal ball? Would it send me catapulting back into the gargoyle without being able to say goodbye to Daniel? Even after hundreds of years, the parameters of the curse still remained a mystery. But then, it wasn't me spilling secrets. I hadn't said a word. Would it matter?

And then it was too late, Gloria taking my silence for acceptance and smoothing her hands over the milky sphere in front of her. A hush fell across the kitchen as she scrutinized it.

"What do you see?" My voice was barely more than a whisper.

"You. You're in a field. There's another man there." She peered closer. "Your brother. He's younger than you, but you're very similar. You're arguing with him, telling him that you've done more work than he has, that he needs to pull his weight more, or the crops won't be harvested in time."

That sounded about right. In fact, it summed up my relationship with Antoine perfectly.

Gloria's eyes narrowed. "There's another man. He has red hair. You're not in the field any more. Oh!"

Her eyebrows arched, and my cheeks flamed at the thought of what she might be seeing.

"You love each other very much."

A lump settled in my throat, and I blinked back tears.

"But there's a constant shadow over him. There are dangerous forces at play, but you didn't know. You were blind to it. Too in love to see it. Even when people tried to warn you."

A look of anguish crossed her face. "And now you're so lost, so alone. Its dark and cold most of the time. And you're so invisible. It hurts, but at the same time you can't feel, not in the way you used to be able to."

I was holding my breath, my fingers gripping the edge of the table so hard that my knuckles had gone white. I knew that she wasn't talking about now, that she was reliving what had happened to me. Gloria suddenly shoved the crystal ball away from her so violently that I jumped. When she raised her head, there were unshed tears glittering in her eyes.

She'd seen it. She'd seen the truth, and I was still here. It was strange to look into the eyes of someone who saw the real me, who knew what had transpired. She might not know every detail, but she knew enough. And it was far more than anyone else had ever seen. Her hands trembled as she reached for her cup, the tea sloshing over the side of the cup and onto the saucer before she managed to gather herself enough to lift it to her lips and take a sip. "I'm so sorry, François."

I hadn't told her my full name. Neither had Daniel. I picked up a biscuit and placed it on the plate in front of me. I had no intention of eating it. I doubted I could have swallowed it even if I tried, but it was something to focus on. I squeezed it between my fingers, and it crumbled to dust. Dust! That's what I felt like sometimes, like a strong breeze might be enough to carry me away. *What about the future?*

The words hovered on the tip of my tongue. Did I really want to know? What if it wasn't something I wanted to hear? What if her words condemned me to hundreds of years of the same? What then? I couldn't do it. I'd go crazy. But maybe it was better to know? If she did confirm it, then it might be time to give up, to let myself slide into the abyss that I'd fought so hard to keep myself out of. Ignorance wasn't always bliss. I took a deep breath. "What about the future?"

Gloria took my hand again, her fingers curling around mine in a gesture clearly designed to give comfort. "I can see an end, but it's shadowy and indistinct. You're at a crossroads. There are things starting to slide into place, but they're…" She paused as if she was struggling for the right words to use. "It's like they're drifting on clouds, and the clouds might align correctly, or they might not, and they all need to be in the right place at the right time."

I clung on to the one thing she'd said that I could take comfort in. "But it will end? It won't stretch on for eternity?"

She nodded. "Yes."

"Is there a possibility that it could be soon?"

She smiled, but it was decidedly strained. "There's a possibility, but" — her expression became even more troubled — "don't assume that those same dark forces are gone. There are still obstacles in your path. You would be wise not to make the same mistakes twice."

What did she mean? The dark forces she'd spoken of before were Cecile, and possibly Madeleine. Although, I'd always felt like Estienne's sister had simply not known any better. But they were both long dead. Weren't they?

She squeezed my hand harder. "I can see that you're going to ask questions. I'm sorry, François, but I can't answer them. "This" — she waved a hand over the items on the table — "is not a science. The spirits will only show me what they want me to see. I could stare into that crystal ball all day long and still not see anything more. And there's always the possibility that what I've already told you could be damaging. That was why Mike had such an issue with it. He believed in my abilities, but he called it meddling, sticking my nose in where it had no business being. He always said it was dangerous, so…" Her gaze strayed toward the pile of boxes. "They were locked away for years, until a strange urge had me feeling the time was right to dig them out again." She patted the back of my hand. "At least I know why that was now. It was meeting you."

Gloria let go of my hand and let out a sigh. She stood from the table and started clearing the plates away. I guessed it was my cue to leave. I'd barely taken one step in the direction of the door when she spoke. "I can answer one question for you, though."

I stopped. "Yeah?"

She nodded. "You're torn between whether you should stay or go, aren't you? With Daniel, I mean."

I froze, my heart in my mouth. If she told me I needed to leave, I wasn't even sure that was something I was capable of doing, not now that we'd grown even closer. It would be like ripping off my own arm.

"Everything is telling me that you need to stay. But you should probably know that I'm not always right." She gave a wry smile. "Daniel is a good man."

Curiosity got the better of me. "I thought you didn't like him."

She laughed. "Have you met his ex-husband?"

I shook my head.

"They were so wrong together. They were never going to make each other happy. Calvin was a little like you. Not in looks, but he was a little lost too, and he thought that having an older man as a husband would somehow fix that. It was doomed from the start. I've no idea how they managed to stay married as long as they did. All I know was that Calvin grew more and more miserable, and Daniel didn't see it. And I didn't need the power of second sight to see that—just a pair of eyes in my head. Daniel can be very oblivious to what's going on around him."

"*Merci.* Thanks."

She turned from the sink, smoothing her wet hands over the front of her apron. "You'll have tea with me again, François, won't you?"

"Yes." There wasn't even a moment's hesitation in my response. I felt like I'd found an ally and I was going to cling onto that, even if she'd told me all she could.

"Good. I'll look forward to it."

I would too. I let myself out of the back door, Napoleon meeting me at Daniel's back door and following me into the house.

Chapter Fifteen

Daniel

The students were just packing away when Marjorie's voice rang out as clear as a bell across the lecture hall. "Mr. Smith? A word if I may?"

I was usually safe from her ire while I was teaching, which meant that whatever it was she was so keen to talk to me about, she deemed it urgent. I racked my brain to try and work out what I could possibly have done. Despite the mental effort it took to leave Frankie on his own, I'd been on time all week, so it wasn't that. I was up to date on my grading. I hadn't had a disagreement with anyone. My office was about as tidy as it ever got.

I kept one eye on her while the number of students thinned. She was like a little storm cloud at the back of the lecture hall. She only needed a dalmatian coat, and she could have been Cruella De Vil. Was that it? Did she want me to hand Napoleon over so that she could make him into a pair of gloves? I quelled the urge to smile at the ridiculous thought.

Finally, there was no delaying my date with the snow queen any longer, and I was forced to make my way toward the back of the lecture hall where Marjorie waited expectantly. What did she think would happen if she waited outside? Did she think I would climb out of the window in a bid to avoid her? I came to a halt in front of her and offered her a huge smile. To my surprise, she returned it. Well, that was weird. I couldn't remember ever seeing her smile before. And if she had, it certainly wouldn't have been directed my way. Was she ill? "You parked in one of the reserved spots this morning, Mr. Smith."

So, that was it. Crimes against parking. Except, she was still smiling at me. "All the other spots were taken."

She nodded. "They were, but one was just a delivery driver dropping off some packages."

Christ! Was there anything she didn't know? What did she do, spend the morning watching all the CCTV footage from around the university just on the off-chance that she might find some good blackmail material? "I didn't think it would make that much difference."

She gave another nod, her red hair catching the light. "I'm afraid it does. I'm going to have to ask you to move it, please."

Please! She never said please. It wasn't her style. I tamped down on the urge to press my palm to her forehead to find out if she was running a fever.

"Now?"

"Yes, please."

"Okay. It will only take me a couple of minutes." I slid my hand into my pocket and dug out my car keys, already pushing the lecture room door open to make my way to the faculty and staff car park. It soon became apparent that Marjorie was going to follow me. Did she have that little trust in me? It seemed she did. She stood and watched while I went through the rigmarole of moving the car about two meters to the right.

Slamming the car door shut and activating the alarm again, I made my way back over to her. She'd turned her face up to the weak winter sun, a smile playing on her lips. It was like looking at a stranger and it was very disconcerting. I'd watched *Invasion of the Body Snatchers* as a child and the film had stuck with me. I couldn't help but wonder if I searched Marjorie's office whether I would find a pod tucked away in a corner.

She turned to face me. "I hear your home circumstances have changed."

What had she heard? And more importantly from who? The only person who knew about Frankie was Richard. Had he been shooting his mouth off? And what exactly had he been saying? I guessed I was about to find out. I went for blind ignorance. If she wanted to talk to me about something, she could spit it out. I wasn't going to make it easy for her. "What do you mean?"

She looked momentarily confused, another look that I wasn't used to seeing on her face. She was normally far too self-assured to leak such human emotions. "I heard that you had met someone, that he had moved in with you."

I had a sneaky suspicion where this was going. This was where she reminded me of the furor that had followed my relationship with Calvin, no one wanting to accept that our relationship had only started once he was no longer a student. The idea of me carrying on a secret, tempestuous relationship had made me want to laugh. I was the world's worst person at subterfuge. Had I attempted something like that, I doubt it would have remained a secret for longer than a week. Of course, Marjorie had been one of the more vocal people about it, her eyebrows and pursed lips clearly displaying her thoughts on the matter even when she hadn't vocalized it. "I don't see that my home life is any of your business. And if you're going to mention the age gap, then neither is that."

"I wasn't."

"No?"

She shook her head. "I just wanted to…" She turned to stare across campus, her gaze unfocused. "We don't talk enough… Daniel. We should talk more."

Okay. This was getting weirder by the minute. I'd known her for years, and in all that time, I'd always been Mr. Smith, the name delivered with an icy superiority. Why had she suddenly decided to call me Daniel? Was this some sort of game? Whatever it was, I didn't want any part of it. I gestured toward the entrance. "I need to get back. I've got another lecture due to start soon."

When all she did was nod, I took the opportunity to make my escape, mulling over the strange conversation on the way back. One thing was clear from her comments. She knew about Frankie, and the only person she could have heard that from was Richard, which begged the question why he'd seen fit to open his big mouth and drop me in hot water? It wasn't what friends did, and the more I thought about it, the more it infuriated me. What had he been hoping to gain? Was he trying to win some brownie points with Marjorie? There'd been rumblings about the head of science looking for jobs elsewhere. Was Richard trying to ingratiate himself into the role of replacement even before it was confirmed? He'd never come across as being particularly ambitious before, but that was the only explanation I could think of. I needed to ask him a few questions.

Unfortunately, those questions would have to wait a few hours. I had a lecture hall full of waiting students, and another two back-to-back lectures after that.

* * * *

My irritation hadn't abated by the end of the afternoon. I just hoped that my acting skills had been good enough that none of the students had picked up on it. The last thing I needed was it getting back to Marjorie that Mr. Smith had seemed 'distracted.' She might have been unusually mild this afternoon but I doubted that would last.

I tried the scientists' recreation room first. No Richard. When he wasn't in his office either, I tried the lab. He looked up with a smile as I entered, his brow furrowing when I made no effort to return it. "What's up?"

I cut straight to the chase. "Why did you tell Marjorie about Frankie? What were you hoping to gain?"

He straightened from the bench he'd been leaning over, sliding his hands into the pockets of his lab coat. "Whoa! Back up a bit, would you? Marjorie knows about Frankie?"

I glared at him. "Yes, she knows. And she was so eager to make sure that I was aware of that fact that she couldn't even wait until lunch time. She popped up at the end of one of my lectures."

"What did she say?"

What had she said? Nothing really, but that didn't change the fact that the conversation should never have come up. I shrugged. "She was weird about it, and I could do without it."

"And you think I said something to her?"

My laugh was short on actual humor. "Well, I haven't told anyone else about him. I trusted you to keep it to yourself, Richard. I don't need her raking up the past in a bid to make life difficult for me. I didn't think you were the type to throw me under the bus just so you could ingratiate yourself with the ice queen. I thought we were friends, but I guess five years of friendship doesn't mean as much to you as it does to me."

Richard held up a hand. "Wait. Slow down. Before you say something you might regret."

I shook my head. "I already had Marjorie on my back. Now you've given her even more ammunition."

A muscle ticked in Richard's cheek. "I haven't given her anything. You might want to take a deep breath before you start throwing wild accusations around."

I crossed my arms over my chest. "You were the only one I told. I don't go around divulging personal information to all and sundry. You of all people should know that."

Richard's expression was decidedly belligerent. "I didn't say a word to her."

I laughed. "So… she just knew. Is that what you're saying? Maybe she's psychic. Maybe when she's not prowling the corridor looking for victims to lash with her tongue, she's in her office offering up sacrifices to the gods in order to summon demons to do her bidding."

"I'm saying… that there has to be another explanation. Was the door closed when we were talking?"

I frowned at him. "What?"

"Your office door… When you were telling me about Frankie, was it closed? Because you know as well as I do how easily sound carries down these corridors. Anyone could have been outside that door and overheard what we were saying. Maybe even Marjorie herself."

I tried to visualize that day in the office when Richard had come to talk to me. It had definitely been closed before his arrival, but could I honestly say with one hundred percent certainty that he'd closed it after his arrival? I'd thought he had. But I wouldn't stake my life on it. "You didn't tell her?"

He held my gaze and then shook his head. The pent-up frustration leached from me as quickly as if it had been water and someone had emptied a bath. Fuck! "I just assumed…"

Richard's mouth tightened. "Yeah, you made it really clear what you assumed, mate. And I have to say I'm hurt you'd think that. When have I ever dropped you in it before?"

There was nothing I could say to that. We both knew the answer was never. I'd been so sure that it must have been him, though. "I'm sorry."

"You're lucky I'm the forgiving type. Although…" A smile played on Richard's lips. "You're gonna need to buy me a pint before I can forgive you completely." He checked his watch. "I'll meet you in the pub at five. Don't be late."

I blinked at him. "Tonight? I can't…" The words dried up in my throat at the look on his face. I'd just come in here and accused him of doing something he hadn't done. Buying him a drink was the least I could do. One pint. It would only delay me by about an hour. I just wished Frankie had a phone so that I could let him know.

* * * *

I stared at the beer Richard had pushed in front of me when I'd thought he was just going to the toilet. I was only halfway through my first pint, the one that was meant to have been the one and only before I made my excuses and left. "I need to go home."

Richard eased himself back into the chair he'd vacated. "Oh, come on. One more's not going to hurt. Although" — he paused to take a sip of his own beer — "you owe me another now, because I bought this one, which makes us even, and you were meant to be buying."

"I really do need to go home."

"Why? What's he going to do, burn your house down?" Richard smirked. "I know he's young, but I didn't realize that he's so young he's not allowed to be left on his own. You should hire a nanny if that's the case."

"Fuck off!"

He laughed. "So… how are things going between the two of you? What have you found out about him?"

He was massaging his temple as he spoke and I frowned at him. "Are you alright?"

He shook off my question with a wave of his hand. "Just a headache. Nothing major."

"First a nosebleed. Now a headache. Maybe you should go do the doctor, get yourself checked out as a precaution."

"I'm fine. Now stop avoiding the question."

What question? Ah, right, what had I found out about Frankie? *Absolutely nothing.* I didn't say it, but my expression must have given me away, Richard grimacing. "Jesus! You haven't even asked, have you?" He took a gulp of beer, wiping the foam away from his top lip with the back of his hand. "It's a weird relationship if the two of you don't even talk. He could be hiding all sorts of things. The sex must be really good for you not to give a damn."

I shifted uncomfortably, heat rushing to my cheeks. I didn't want to discuss mine and Frankie's sex life. I especially didn't want to discuss it with Richard. Why was he so interested anyway? He was straight. He'd never been that eager for lurid details of my life with Calvin. I settled for a shrug, hoping he'd drop the subject.

"You have consummated your relationship, I assume?"

Consummated! Such a ridiculous word for what I'd shared with Frankie. It didn't help that Richard was grinning, as if he thought he'd said something hilarious. I lifted my glass to my mouth and took a few gulps. The quicker I finished it, the quicker I could get out of here.

"Have you?"

I lifted my head to stare at him. "Why does it matter?"

It was Richard's turn to shrug. "Just trying to work out what's so special about this guy that he has you acting so uncharacteristically. I want the old Dan back, the one that didn't fly off the handle at a moment's notice." He pulled a face. "It just strikes me that this guy might not be the right fit for you, if he's already changing you, that's all. I'm your friend. I'm allowed to be concerned about you, aren't I?"

I nodded, feeling guilty. "I've just had a strange day and I'm in a funny mood. That's got nothing to do with Frankie."

Richard gave a long, slow nod. "You're right. I've never even met the guy. I shouldn't be jumping to conclusions. But do me a favor, would you?"

I raised an eyebrow Marjorie would have been proud of in question.

"Stop checking your watch. You're making me feel like you'd rather be anywhere else but here."

I sat back and squashed the urge to sigh, my brow furrowing as Richard's nose started to bleed again and he was forced to rush off to the bathroom. He was right. I was being a terrible friend. I was lucky he still wanted to have anything to do with me after the accusations I'd thrown his way. I'd stay and I'd spend that time convincing him to see a doctor to get to the bottom of the nose bleeds.

Chapter Sixteen

Frankie

I pulled the curtain back an inch and scanned the street for what had to be at least the twentieth time. It was nearly nine, and there was still no sign of Daniel. Had something happened to him? *"There are still dark forces at work."* It had been difficult enough to get Gloria's voice out of my head all day, but with Daniel's absence it had become nigh on impossible.

With the street all but empty, I let the curtain drop and went back to pacing, Napoleon watching me with wide green eyes from one of his favorite perches on the back of the sofa. Daniel finished work at four. Even if he stayed late, he was normally home by six, but that had been three hours ago. Where was he?

There were a hundred things that could have happened to him. What if he'd been involved in some sort of traffic accident? What would I do then? I'd need to contact the hospitals. I couldn't contact the police because they'd want information from me that I couldn't give, and either my silence would have them asking questions I couldn't answer, or the holes in the scant information I provided would get me into trouble. Was it too late to speak to Gloria? She might know what to do. She might even talk to the police for me.

I whirled around at the sound of a key in the lock, my heart pounding. I reached the hallway just as the door opened and Daniel stepped inside. Relief hit me like a tidal wave. He was okay. The door closed behind him, and he stood there, something distinctly off about his posture and the way he seemed to be having trouble focusing on me. He took a step forward, the answer coming in his slight sway and the stench of alcohol. He was drunk.

Clumsy octopus arms wrapped around me, Daniel attempting to pull me close. I pushed him off and stepped back out of reach, fending off the hands that tried to come after me. "I was worried about you. And you were just... getting drunk."

"I'm not drunk." Had they been less slurred, the words might have been a little more convincing. The stagger as he said it was just the icing on the cake. He repeated the words, but slower this time, as if he was working on being able to say them convincingly.

I retreated to the kitchen, Daniel coming after me. "I didn't want to go to the pub, but I didn't have any choice, and then Richard kept buying drinks so I had to drink them. I only had..." He held up his hand, frowning as he tried to execute what seemed to be a painful counting exercise on his fingers. "I think I had four pints." He paused for a moment, his face twisting into an expression of regret. "I might be drunk. Sorry." He tripped over the leg of a chair, the kitchen table halting his progress. "I had a strange day."

Mine hadn't exactly been that joyful, but the worst thing was I couldn't tell him about any of it. Discussing what Gloria had said would be the same as telling him the truth about myself.

Daniel crowded me against the wall and this time I let him. He cupped my face and stared at me intently, emotion swimming in his brown eyes. "I wanted to come home. All I wanted all day was to see you. Is that insane?"

I shook my head.

"And now that I have seen you, you're annoyed at me." He frowned. "I don't like you being annoyed at me." He removed one of his hands from my face to rub at his chest. "It hurts. Right here."

I lay my hand over his. "I'm not annoyed at you. I just... I was worried. I started thinking that something bad might have happened to you, and I wouldn't have known what to do if it had, who to contact, or who to speak to. It scared me."

He nodded as if he understood, his eyes still on my face. "I'm sorry. I never meant to make you worry." His fingers stroked my cheek. "You're so beautiful, and I'm not just saying that because I'm drunk. I'm saying it because it's true. I've never met anyone like you before. You're..." He shook his head, as if he had no idea how to finish his sentence. "I want to kiss you."

I tipped my head back and stared at him. His pupils might have been more dilated than usual, and the stare less focused, but I still believed every word he said. Daniel didn't know how to lie. He was one of those people who oozed honesty and sincerity from every pore. "So what's stopping you?"

When he still didn't move, I made the decision for him, leaning into him and pressing our lips together until his relaxed. He tasted of beer, but he also tasted of heat, comfort, and safety. In my fear, I'd lashed out at him. I should have known better. After all, there was nothing new about being scared. I was used to it. I was scared more often than I wasn't. I wasn't scared now, though, not with Daniel pressed against me. Even drunk, he was a reassuring presence.

I made Daniel drink an entire pint of water, while he cast me surreptitious glances from beneath his lashes at my need to supervise him in order to make sure he drank it all. He'd thank me for it in the morning when he had to get up and go to work. We didn't speak as we both got ready for bed, brushing our teeth side by side at the sink, our reflections smiling when our gazes clashed in the mirror.

There was no discussion about sleeping in separate rooms. There hadn't been since that first night. If I'd had any things to move, I would have moved them into Daniel's room without hesitation. Instead, at his urging, I'd settled for helping myself to anything of his that took my fancy.

We both stripped to our underwear and slid beneath the sheets. His approaching sobriety had left him sleepy, so I knew that tonight was going to be about sleep rather than making love. I was fine with that. It was enough just to lay snuggled next to him, the two of us holding hands and sharing body heat.

It didn't take long for Daniel's breathing to even out as he slid into sleep, and it didn't take long for me to join him either.

I don't know what woke me, whether it was the frenzied movements Daniel was making, or the cries emanating from his mouth, but I went from being fast asleep one minute to wide awake the next. I sat up, reaching over Daniel's twitching body for the lamp switch and bathing us both in a soft light.

He was laid on his back with a pained expression on his face, his limbs jerking spasmodically. He let loose another cry, the sound full of anguish. He was dreaming, and whatever he was dreaming about was obviously far from pleasant. I laid a hand on his chest, the skin clammy and his heart beating a frantic rhythm beneath my palm.

The first gentle shake I gave him had no effect. I tried again, harder this time. It took four attempts and saying his name at the same time before Daniel's eyelids flew open. The way he was staring at me scared me. It was as if he didn't know who I was and what I was doing there. "It's me. It's Frankie." I kept my voice as soothing as possible. "You were having a bad dream, so I thought it was best to wake you."

Daniel swallowed, the action visible along the line of his throat. His breathing was still rapid, but as I waited it eventually slowed. Finally, he levered himself into a sitting position with his head resting against the wall. "François."

I smiled, my name from his lips feeling like some sort of victory. "Yeah, that's right. Can you remember what you were dreaming about?"

Daniel's eyes closed again, hiding his innermost thoughts from me. When he spoke, his voice was nothing more than a dry rasp. "I couldn't find him. I looked everywhere, but I couldn't find him. And I knew that something bad had happened. Something irreversible."

"Couldn't find who?"

He shook his head, his eyes opening again to find mine. "I don't know. And it's..." He screwed his face up. "It's so frustrating because it feels like it's right here." He lifted a hand to tap a finger against his forehead. "But I just... can't access it. I feel like I'm going mad."

His distress was genuine, and I found myself floundering around for what I was supposed to say to make it better. "It was just a dream. It probably doesn't mean anything. You said yourself that you'd had a bad day at work. It was probably brought on by that. Nothing else."

"I know, but..." He took in a shaky breath. "I just can't shake the feeling that there's something important that I'm missing, something I'm not understanding that I should be. Why am I dreaming about places I've never seen, and a person whose name and face I can't recall?"

There was no answer to that question, apart from that dreams were just dreams, but he already knew that. He'd convinced himself that there was something important about it, and I wasn't going to be able to dissuade him of that in the middle of the night. I stole a glance at the clock—it was past three in the morning. "You should go back to sleep. You've got to be up in a few hours."

Daniel gave a jerky nod. He eased himself back down and turned so that he had his back to me. "François?"

"Yeah?"

"Can you hold me?"

Now, that was something I could definitely do. I plastered myself to his back and tangled our legs together, throwing one arm across his chest.

Daniel gave a little sigh. "That feels good."

It did. "The light is still on. Want me to turn it off?"

He shook his head, grabbing my arm to hold me in place when I might have moved to do so. "No, leave it on. In case I have any more bad dreams. And thank you for waking me."

"You'd have done the same for me."

"What do you dream about?"

I got a bitter taste in my throat. *Stone and paralysis. Witches and spells. Pain and separation. And the never-ending failure of what my life has become.* The list was endless, and none of it was pleasant. "Just... normal stuff."

"You've got so many secrets."

He'd sensed my reticence, somehow. Perhaps in the rigidity of my body. Or maybe he just had some sort of sixth sense when it came to me. "I'm sorry." There was nothing else I could say.

We lapsed into silence, and I was beginning to think he'd fallen back asleep until he spoke. "Anyway, you've got the job."

"What job?"

"The job of being my guardian angel. You certainly look the part."

I didn't answer. What could I say? I couldn't tell him that the days were already ticking down far too rapidly to our inevitable separation. It was true, though, the knowledge making my heart beat faster and my arms tighten around Daniel even more. If I was capable of freezing time, it would have been the perfect moment to do so, but unfortunately, I wasn't.

Time would march on regardless.

Chapter Seventeen

Daniel

The more time I spent with François, the more I grew to adore him. He had an innate gentleness which seemed to come to him as naturally as breathing. His smile was enough to make my chest flutter, and his laugh made my heart sing. I'd known him for two weeks, and already I couldn't imagine life without him.

He was curled up next to me on the sofa, his legs tucked under his body, and his head resting on my shoulder. Work had been nothing but a hindrance for the past week — empty time that kept me from where I craved to be: glued to Frankie's side. We didn't even have plans, but then, with him I didn't need them. We were happy to do nothing as long as we got to do it together.

The TV was on, but I couldn't have said I was paying much attention to it. It was more for Frankie's benefit than mine. He seemed to be fascinated with everything from breakfast cereal adverts to political discussions about the EU. He watched them with rapt attention, firing out a million questions that I answered to the best of my ability.

He was like a sponge desperate to learn whatever he could. It made me wonder how long he'd been on the streets for. I'd assumed that it hadn't been that long, but maybe I was wrong. I wanted to ask him, but I was too scared that it would have him retreating back behind that carefully constructed wall. He'd tell me his secrets when he was good and ready. I just needed to be patient.

The strange chemistry we shared made it feel like we'd been together forever. To the point where I had to keep reminding myself that we were only at the beginning of our relationship. It was ironic considering I'd been accused by more than one person of moving too fast with Calvin. In retrospect, given how unsuccessful the marriage had turned out, and the relatively short amount of time it had taken to get to that point, there might have been more than a shred of truth in their musings. And here I was moving even faster with Frankie. Yet, no matter how hard I tried I just couldn't see it as being anything but right.

I wound my fingers through his, and he turned his face up to me with a ready smile. When I didn't say anything, a slight frown line appeared on his forehead. "What?"

My smile grew wider. "Nothing. I just like looking at you."

His lips quirked. "You should put me in a museum."

I barked out a laugh. "Really? Fancy being trapped behind a thick pane of glass all day, do you?"

Something flickered across Frankie's face, something which made me think I'd said something wrong. Despite not knowing what it was, I hastened to correct it. "Besides, that means lots of people get to stare at you. I prefer you to be for my eyes only." Wow! That had come out sounding a lot more possessive than I'd meant it to be.

Frankie's eyebrows rose slightly, but I could tell from the slight twitch of his lips that he didn't mind it one little bit. I eased myself away from him. When he went to sit up, I pressed my hand to his chest and pushed him back, shifting myself out of the way until there was enough space for him to lie back.

He stared up at me, a question in his beautiful blue eyes. "*Maintenant qu'est-ce que tu vas faire de moi?*"

I groaned. "You know I don't speak French. The only word I got from that was me."

His answering smile was so full of amused mischief that I wanted to kiss it off his lips. "I asked what you were going to do with me. You seemed pretty eager to get me on my back."

I picked up the remote control and muted the TV, the TV detective's smug speech about how he'd known who the murderer was all along silenced at the mid-way point. I could live without knowing who it was. I couldn't live without getting closer to Frankie. Carefully straddling him, I stared down at him. He looked like a rumpled angel, his hair sticking up in tufts and his borrowed T-shirt having ridden up to display a satisfying amount of bare skin.

A stronger man might have been able to resist touching, but I wasn't that man, my fingers sliding over the sleek, warm skin to push the T-shirt up higher. I was rewarded with the discovery of one of Frankie's pale nipples. Blue eyes followed my movements, the curve of his lips telling me that the exploration was very much welcomed.

I circled my thumb around his nipple, Frankie's sharp intake of breath going straight to my cock, which was already straining against the front of my trousers. I studied his face as I did it again. Arousal always looked so good on Frankie, his cheeks flushing and his lips parting as his teeth sank into his bottom lip. Sweeping my fingers up his chest, I removed his T-shirt altogether, Frankie twisting to help when it became snagged under his back.

"You are so damn beautiful! I know I keep saying it, but you really are." He was. He was all pale skin and lean muscles, the flickering light of the TV playing over his skin in a fascinating display of color that only accentuated the picture he made. I'd obviously been watching too much TV with Frankie, since the Skittles slogan of "Taste the Rainbow" popped into my head. I did, lowering my lips to Frankie's chest and following the patterns of light as they arced over his collarbone and down the center of his chest.

"What are you doing?"

"Tasting the light on your skin."

Frankie gave a small chuckle. "What does it taste like?"

"Like you. Like sugar and spice and all things nice."

"Is that the poetry you promised me?"

I snorted. I'd forgotten saying that. "It's probably the closest you'll get to it. Historians aren't exactly renowned for their ability to make pretty words."

"I don't need pretty words. I just need…"

Whatever it was he'd been going to say he didn't finish as I closed my lips around one of his nipples and sucked, my tongue tracing the stiffening bud.

He gave an exquisite shudder, the action reverberating through his entire body. Frankie was always so responsive—so open. Some men tried to hide their reactions, tried to act nonchalant even in bed. But not Frankie. Not with me. He might hide facts about himself, but his body he gave fully.

Needing him naked, I divested him of the rest of his clothes—or my clothes, if you wanted to split hairs. He was gorgeous from head to toe, his cock lying hard against his abdomen, the pale, slim length as perfectly formed as the rest of him. How had I ever gotten this lucky? I kept asking myself that question, and I still didn't have an answer.

Eager as I was to wrap my lips around his cock, I ignored it for now to concentrate on the rest of him. He let out a soft gasp as I turned my head into his inner thigh, my tongue tracing the flesh tantalizingly close to his balls but not close enough to touch. His thighs parted wider, and I took the silent offer, giving the other thigh the same attention.

"Daniel?"

His voice was full of want and need, and I hadn't even got to the good bit yet. Frankie's hands tugged at my clothes, questing fingers running through my hair, over my cheeks, and wherever else they could reach, the touch as light as a feather.

I raised my head to look at him, the languorous blue gaze that met mine almost desperate in its intensity. "What do you need?"

"You. Naked. Inside me. I need everything. Please."

He'd said the word please like there was a genuine doubt in his mind that I would give it to him. I'd give him whatever he wanted. Now and forever.

I leaned over to capture his lips, Frankie's parting beneath mine to return the kiss with equal fervor, our tongues doing a dance of their very own. When I pulled away, we were both breathing hard. I stroked the backs of my fingers down his cheek, the corners of his lips turning up in a beatific smile at the simple gesture. "Either we have to move to the bedroom, or I have to get… stuff." It seemed tacky to be talking about condoms and lube, when what we shared seemed to go far beyond such mundane practicalities. But Frankie deserved better than some oaf who let passion get the better of him.

His gaze held mine as he nodded.

I laughed. "Which one?"

"You go."

I sat back, trailing my fingers along the length of his torso and watching the way goosebumps followed in their wake. "I'm scared that if I let you out of my sight, you might… disappear, that I might discover you were nothing more than a dream conjured up by too many nights of late-night grading." Shit! Had I really said that out loud? I'd been doing my best to hide the fact that I was a neurotic mess from Frankie.

"I'll still be here."

Four simple words that I'd really needed to hear. "Promise?"

"Promise."

I scrambled off the sofa so quickly that I nearly tripped over my own feet, Frankie's laugh shadowing my departure from the room. Taking the stairs two at a time, I grabbed what I needed and hightailed it back in the direction I'd just come.

Frankie was still there. In fact, it didn't even look like he'd moved, except to link his fingers behind his head. He lay there like a sacrificial lamb, chest rising and falling gently. I halted at the side of the sofa, Frankie turning his head to look at me. "Clothes, Daniel."

Right! Only one of us was naked. I stripped quickly, Frankie's heated gaze on the bare skin I uncovered turning it into a far more erotic act than it usually was. But then he made everything better—even undressing. Once I was naked, his fingers curled around my thigh, their upward progress so slow that it was almost torturous, the wait before they finally wrapped around my cock feeling like forever. He held my gaze as he explored its length, those long fingers of his exerting just the right pressure to drive me crazy. It was his expression though, that snagged my attention. It was as open and as unguarded as ever, everything from desire to hope right there on his face.

"I…"

His gaze shot to my face, his fingers tightening. "What?"

I shook my head. I'd almost said I loved him. I'd known the words were right there on my tongue, begging to be released. He was already so deep under my skin that little else mattered, but there was a huge difference between knowing it and saying it out loud. It was too soon. It risked him slipping between my fingers like he was nothing but smoke. Because that's what it felt like a lot of the time, that I might wake one morning and find that Frankie was nothing but a memory. "Nothing."

His fingers fell away, an emotion that looked very much like disappointment present in his eyes. Or was I simply seeing what I wanted to see? Did he want me to say the words? Would he welcome them? Might he even say them back? The thought left me breathless.

I climbed on the sofa, Frankie parting his thighs to give me space between them. Bending over, I took him in my mouth, Frankie's back arching and a cry of ecstasy slipping from between his lips. So damn responsive. I lubed the fingers of my right hand, tracing his rim as I gave him a few good sucks.

He writhed against my fingers, a clear enticement to hurry the hell up. I wasn't going to be pushed. He might complain, but he was far too precious to risk hurting.
When I did finally breach him with my finger, his sigh of satisfaction had my cock throbbing urgently and it was almost enough to make me forget all my good intentions.

His hands fastened in my hair as I found my rhythm, combining the stroke of my finger over his prostate with the movement of my mouth on his cock. By the time I introduced another finger, his hips were bucking off the bed and his moans were all starting to run into each other. "*S'il te plaît*. Please. *J'ai besoin de...* Daniel."

I didn't think he was even aware that he kept switching from French to English, such was his need to come. I relinquished his cock with great reluctance and withdrew my fingers. Frankie panted beneath me as my fumbling fingers made hard work out of rolling the condom over my cock. "Are you ready?"

He studied me from beneath hooded eyes, the merest glint of blue showing, his body covered in a fine sheen of sweat that made the colors from the TV that much more enticing. I smiled at the stupidity of my own question. I could see he was ready. In fact, there was a danger of him coming before I even got inside him. "Don't answer that."

Smoothing my hands over his thighs, I pulled him closer, tipping his ass up so that I had the perfect angle of entry. "I like it when you speak French. I haven't got the slightest clue what you're saying, but I like it anyway."

Frankie's smile was slow and seductive. "*Alors, je le parlerai juste pour toi*. Which means, I'll speak it just for you."

I eased myself inside him so carefully that I was impressed with my own restraint. He was so tight… and hot, a groan escaping from both our lips. I paused, as despite my slow pace, his muscles grew taut, his body struggling to adjust to the invasion. I fought a battle against the desire to sink deeper, the molten heat enclosing my cock tempting me with the promise of ecstasy. Thankfully, I came out as the victor, only sinking in deeper once Frankie nodded.

From that point he opened to me like a flower unfurling for the sun, the image of his thighs splayed over mine and his body accepting my cock the most wondrous sight. Our gazes locked as I began to move, feasting on each and every moan I pulled from his lips. It wasn't long before he wrapped a hand around his cock and began to stroke it in time with my thrusts. We were both close. I changed the angle, supporting my weight on my elbows as I leaned over him to fuck him deeper, to give him every inch I could, my cock rubbing over that little nub that drove him crazy, his hand moving faster.

"Daniel." He repeated my name over and over again, each thrust of my hips bringing another repetition to his lips until they were no longer separate words but all ran into each other. I kissed him as I fucked him, tasting my name on his lips as we moved together. He was perfect. This was perfect. There was nothing in life that had ever compared to this before. There was nothing that could compare to this. He was mine, and I was his.

And then he was coming, his body convulsing around mine and sending me hurtling over the edge with him. My lips found his throat, his sweat tasting like nectar as I came down from my own orgasm. I withdrew carefully, gathering him in and tangling our limbs together, his arms squeezing me tightly like he never wanted to let go. I wanted to say those words again. I wanted it so badly even if they weren't reciprocated, but I didn't say them. Not yet. They would have to stay inside for me a bit longer.

Chapter Eighteen

Frankie

Daniel had warned me — with guilt written all over his face — about the open house viewing session organized by the estate agent. He'd even offered to call in sick so that he could be here, but it hadn't seemed fair to ask him to do that. It wasn't like I was a child that needed someone to stay home and look after me. So, I'd told him it was fine. After all, it was only for two hours and how many people could possibly turn up? Well, the answer to that had turned out to be quite a lot.

Whichever room I tried to go into, there was always someone wandering in and making comments about the amount of light, or that it had the wrong furniture for the space, and how they could make it better. I'd leave that room, only to encounter the same problem in the next one I went into. I'd long given up on the kitchen, the room seeming to provide a focal point for discussion, most of it not that complimentary. It was either too big or too small, too dark or too light, not enough cupboards, too many cupboards. It was like the people were desperate for an argument and I wasn't convinced that any of them were genuinely interested in the house. They seemed to be more interested in the tea and biscuits provided.

Napoleon was as unhappy as I was about the sudden influx of people into his house. He kept pacing restlessly from room to room, letting out the occasional plaintive little meow. And then he would stare at me as if he thought it was my responsibility to get rid of them. I picked him up, cuddling him to my chest and hoping that we could provide comfort to each other. I could have gone out. I *should* have gone out, but without Daniel's company the outside world didn't hold that much allure. Outside was all I ever saw when I was in the gargoyle. I was rethinking that decision and wondering whether it would be possible to take Napoleon with me, when someone stepped into the living room. He did a doubletake as he noticed me. "I'm afraid the cat doesn't come with the house."

Napoleon struggled free from my arms and ran over to him with a pleased little burbling sound, proceeding to wrap himself around the man's jean-clad legs. If I hadn't already recognized him from the photo, that would have been enough to clue me in to his identity. I was looking at Calvin—Daniel's ex-husband. I had to assume that had Daniel known he would be showing up, he would have told me. He was far too considerate not to have done. From the way Calvin was staring at me with a slight furrow on his brow, it was clear that he didn't have the slightest idea who I was.

His gaze narrowed as it dropped to my feet—my bare feet. I needed to say something, but the sheer awkwardness of the situation had stolen my voice away. What was the etiquette for introducing yourself to your lover's recently divorced husband? "I…"

Calvin beat me to it. "Are you staying here?"

I gave a reluctant nod.

He crouched to pet Napoleon, the cat obviously beside himself to see Calvin again. "Sorry. I didn't realize. I thought you were a visitor making yourself a little too much at home. Dan never mentioned that he's moved someone in." His tone was a mixture of accusation and curiosity. Before I could decide how to respond, he let out a snort. "Although, I should have realized." He gestured at my chest. "You're wearing his sweatshirt, and I should know... I was the one who bought it for him."

I fingered the fabric self-consciously, wishing that Daniel might have seen fit to mention that. If he had, I would have chosen something else. But then, he could hardly have foreseen past and present colliding quite so spectacularly. "Sorry." Apologizing seemed like the right thing to do. "I can take it off."

Calvin shook his head, a wry smile playing on his lips. "Not necessary." He straightened, brushing a few stray hairs that Napoleon had gifted him off the front of his jeans. "We should probably start again." He strode forward with his arm outstretched. "I'm Calvin. Pleased to meet you."

I took his hand, accepting the firm handshake. "François. Frankie."

He tipped his head to one side and appraised me. "French, I'm guessing?"

I nodded.

"And what brings you to these shores?"

I gave a shrug, already growing uneasy at the questions. "What normally brings people here?"

A faint furrow appeared on Calvin's brow, but he seemed to shake it off quickly, the smile returning. "Sorry, Dan always said that I stick my nose into other people's business far too much. I guess he was right. Don't tell him that, though, will you."

I could see what Daniel had seen in Calvin. He had an amiable air about him, which made him come across as simple and uncomplicated. Words that could never be used to describe me. I bet that Calvin didn't have any deep, hidden secrets. I fiddled with the sleeve of the sweatshirt, plucking at a loose thread. "It's complicated."

Calvin laughed. "Most things are these days." He looked thoughtful. "So... you and Daniel. How long has that been going on? And I know what you're thinking, that I've just apologized for sticking my nose in where it's not wanted and then gone and done it again, but this is different, this is about Dan. We might not be married anymore, but I still care about him."

I felt like a butterfly pinned on a board beneath Calvin's inquisitive gaze. "A few weeks."

Calvin's eyebrows shot up. "And you've already moved in?"

I picked at the thread with renewed vigor. "I needed somewhere to stay, and Daniel was kind enough to let me stay here."

Calvin took a moment to digest that piece of information. "But you are in a relationship?"

I shuffled my feet on the carpet, not sure what I was supposed to say. Would Daniel mind if I confirmed Calvin's suspicions? If it had been anyone else but his ex-husband, I was sure he would have been fine with me telling the truth, but this was the man he'd once loved, might even still be in love with. The need to not upset Daniel battled with the urge to stake my claim. I lifted my head and looked Calvin square in the eye. "Yes, we're in a relationship."

Calvin's nod was long and considered. He stared at me for a moment before giving a short, sharp laugh. "Sounds like Daniel."

I bristled on his behalf. "What's that supposed to mean?"

"Just that" — Calvin's head turned to the left, and I knew without following his gaze that he was staring at the wedding photo — "Daniel falls fast and hard." A smile wavered on his lips, the specter of past hurt shining in his eyes. "It's just the way he is. It didn't work out for us, but…" He didn't seem to know how to finish his sentence, his shoulders lifting in a shrug instead.

"Calvin."

The voice came from the hallway outside the door. Calvin grimaced as he turned his head in that direction. "I'm coming."

He fastened his attention back on me. "Well, it's been nice to meet you, Frankie. A surprise, but nice. But... duty calls. The quicker I answer all their questions, the quicker we'll all be out of your hair and you can get back to" — his gaze swept the room — "whatever it was that you were doing before we all tramped in here."

I nodded as he backed out of the room, the door closing behind him much to Napoleon's annoyance, who'd tried to follow him. I sank onto the sofa, Napoleon soon forgetting his preoccupation with the door to leap onto my lap and butt his head against mine. I stroked him, tickling him in that spot behind his ears that he particularly liked. "Well, that was..." I didn't really know what it was. Awkward, I guessed. But Calvin had been nothing but nice, especially considering he hadn't even known of my existence and I was living with his ex-husband in the house they'd once shared.

The living room remained blissfully untouched for the next hour, the inquisitive potential house buyers seeming to take the closed door as a hint. If I'd known it would have that effect, I'd have done it hours ago. The voices from outside the door eventually dwindled away to nothing, the estate agent finally poking his head around the door to announce they were done, and that he would call Daniel that evening to give him feedback on how it had gone.

I waited until I heard the front door close before venturing into the kitchen, Napoleon watching me as I made myself a cup of tea. His plaintive stare was enough to make me shake a few cat biscuits into his bowl, even though it was nowhere near feeding time. He pounced on them, the sound of loud crunching filling the kitchen. "Don't tell Daniel."

"Don't tell Daniel, what?"

I swung around, my heart pounding, and stared at the man framed in the doorway. He was tall with brown hair and brown eyes, nothing particularly remarkable about him apart from his presence. Where had he come from? The only explanation was that he must have been one of the people looking around the house, and the estate agent hadn't realized he hadn't left. I didn't remember seeing him earlier, but then, I hadn't looked that closely. I'd been more interested in avoiding them. "The tour of the house is over. You're meant to have left."

"Am I?" The man laughed, and there was something I didn't like about the sound, something I couldn't quite put my finger on, but that set my teeth on edge nonetheless.

I swallowed, my fingers curling into my palms. "I'll show you to the door."

"No need." The man stepped into the kitchen, seeming to fill the room, even though he wasn't particularly tall or bulky. I glanced across the room, my gaze snagging on the cutlery drawer, my instincts telling me to go for a knife. Which was ridiculous. He hadn't said or done anything remotely threatening unless stepping into the kitchen when I'd asked him to leave counted. But still, there was something about the way he was looking at me that made me feel uncomfortable. Perhaps it was the fact that despite us never having met, his expression was knowing—and smug, as if he had me exactly where he wanted me. "Who are you?"

His lips curved into a slow smile, as if I'd said something amusing. "A friend of Daniel's."

I leaned against the kitchen counter, trying to give off an air of nonchalance I was a long way from feeling. "He's not here. He's at work."

"I know. I don't want to speak to him. I want to speak to you."

"Me?"

"You are Frankie, right?"

There was something about the way he said my name, as if it was somehow distasteful and he couldn't quite believe that he was having to lower himself to have a conversation with me, that had my senses on high alert.

I settled for a nod, my throat too dry to force words out.

He crossed his arms over his chest. "Thought so." His gaze strayed around the kitchen, settling for a few seconds on Napoleon, who was still intent on emptying his dish, before focusing back on me with that same hard glint in his eyes.

He didn't like me. That much was obvious. What wasn't clear was why. Was he another of Daniel's exes? Had Daniel been seeing someone after his and Calvin's split that he hadn't mentioned? It was possible. It wasn't as if Daniel and I had talked about past relationships. The man took another step forward, and I automatically took a step back. "What do you want?"

He stopped at the edge of the kitchen table, his fingers tracing the outline of the placemat. "Just to talk."

"So… talk." I resisted the urge to add 'and then leave' to the end of my sentence. If he genuinely was a friend of Daniel's, Daniel wouldn't thank me for being rude to him. I found the possibility of someone as gentle as Daniel having such a creepy friend a little ludicrous, though.

The man tapped his fingers on the table. "How much has Daniel told you about his past history?"

His past history? "A fair amount." It was the truth. He didn't need to know that most of it had been gleaned from my time in the gargoyle.

Brown eyes held mine. "So you're aware of how much his relationship with Calvin was frowned upon by the university." When I neither agreed nor disputed his assumption, he continued. "Calvin was a student there. Student/teacher relationships are very much discouraged for obvious reasons.

And there were many who just didn't believe his steadfast declaration that they'd never met on campus. It's a big place, but it's not that big. Let's just say that he's been on unofficial probation ever since."

He lifted his hand to his nose, the back of it coming away stained red. He grimaced at the sight, his gaze finding mine again. "Now that he's moved a..." He paused to rake his gaze down the length of my body in a way that made me feel dirty. "... *another* younger man into his house, it's going to rake everything up again. It's going to have people asking questions about his tastes, about his ability to do his job without eyes and hands wandering where they shouldn't."

I frowned. I didn't know much about how things worked in a university, but it seemed like a fairly big leap. Surely, Daniel would have mentioned something if my presence in his house was making things difficult for him. The man was staring at me expectantly so it felt like I needed to say something. "I don't want to cause him any problems."

The stranger smiled, but it didn't reach his eyes. "I figured as much, which is why I wanted to help you both by having this conversation. Daniel likes you. But... it's like cake, isn't it? We don't always like the things that are good for us. In fact, sometimes we crave the very things that are damaging, like alcohol and cigarettes. We make stupid choices and then regret them later. It's for that reason that sometimes when we care about a person, we have to make personal sacrifices and make the difficult choices for them, so that they don't have to. We provide the strength that they're not capable of. Wouldn't you agree, Frankie?"

I didn't know if I agreed or not. I didn't really understand what he was trying to say. All I knew was that I couldn't look away from him, as if my gaze was being held captive by some irresistible force. "What are you saying?"

"That you should leave."

"Leave?"

He tilted his head to one side, his stare considering. I hadn't even realized that he'd been getting closer until his final step brought him to within a meter of me. He reached out, his fingers curling around my shoulder. I tried to take a step back, but it was like my feet had become rooted to the spot. He attempted another smile. "I'm just trying to help. I thought you'd want to know how your presence here could make life difficult for Daniel, that you'd want to find a solution." He pressed his free hand to his chest in a way that said he was sincere. "Maybe I'm wrong. Maybe you're in this for the long haul, and it will all be worth it in the end. Are you?"

A tight band wrapped itself around my chest. I had twelve more days before I returned to my stone prison. It was the opposite to a long haul. It was no time at all. Unless... Daniel could break the curse. I still couldn't quite shake the hope that he might be the one, using Gloria's words of comfort as evidence when my belief started to lag. "I..."

The man's eyebrows rose when I didn't get any further, his fingers tightening around my shoulder. "Because... if you can't promise Daniel that, then..." His gaze bored into me. "What's it all for? You'll leave, and poor Daniel will be left to pick up the pieces. He's only just weathered a broken relationship. He doesn't need another."

My head was swimming with noise, my thoughts lost beneath a foggy haze which made it difficult to examine them objectively. One day Daniel would wake up and I'd be gone without any explanation. Given that I couldn't write, I couldn't even leave him a note. Why would I do that to him?

"You should leave."

"I..."

"What are you going to do?"

I jerked my head up to meet the man's stare. "What did you say your name was?"

He gave a soft laugh, that same prickle of something materializing again. "I didn't. You don't need to know it. All you need to know is that I'm a concerned friend who's looking out for Daniel's best interests. Someone has to save him from himself, save him from blundering into another relationship that will cause him nothing but pain in the end." His fingers pressed harder and he leaned in, repeating the same words as earlier, but this time slower. "So... what... are... you... going... to... do?"

"I should leave." The words were out before I could stop them. But once I'd said them, I was filled with a sense of rightness. It was the only thing to do. I would be saving Daniel. I would be sacrificing my happiness for his. It was the least I could do.

The man's lips twitched, as if he was doing his best to hide how much I'd pleased him. "Good boy. I knew you really cared about Daniel."

He let go of my shoulder and I staggered backward as he strode over to the door, pausing with his hand on the handle to look back over his shoulder. "You're doing the right thing. You and him would never have worked."

"Why?"

The question was said to empty air, the stranger already having left the kitchen. As footsteps retreated and the front door opened and closed, I was left staring at the small puddle of blood on the kitchen floor. Strange. I hadn't noticed his nose continuing to bleed with his eyes holding me prisoner so successfully. Grabbing some kitchen towels, I cleaned up the mess. Once the floor was clean, I turned my head to look at the clock—four o'clock. The likelihood was that Daniel would be home by five. I needed to leave and I needed to do it now before he got back. I jogged out of the kitchen and up the stairs, swapping my clothes for those that I'd arrived in before the clock had even ticked through five minutes.

Thirty minutes later, I was back on the street where Daniel had first stumbled across me. I paused outside a busy café for a moment to contemplate where I was going. Only, the answer to that was simple—I had nowhere to go. Nothing and no one. Except for Daniel. There was Gloria, but given she lived right next door to Daniel, it wasn't a viable option. Would he look for me once he discovered my absence? Probably. Which meant that coming here was a stupid decision. It was probably the first place he'd look.

Pushing myself away from the window, I pulled my hood up and headed toward the nearby park. It was dark, which meant that it was almost empty except for a gang of youths, beer cans clutched in their hands and their loud, raucous banter ringing out across the space. I gave them a wide berth and headed in the opposite direction, not stopping until I found a bench under a tree. It was so tucked away that I wouldn't be noticed by anyone unless they were virtually on top of me. It was there that I let everything sink in. I was back where I'd started twelve days ago. No money. No food. I could have taken something from Daniel's kitchen, but it hadn't seemed right, and besides I'd been in such a rush to leave before he got back.

He would be devastated when he got home to find me gone. Feeling unbelievably weary, I let my head drop into my hands. Back in the kitchen, it had seemed like the only possible option. Almost as if the stranger's words had sunk so deeply into me, that they'd affected my thinking processes. But here—in the dark, with only the occasional rustle of some unidentified creature in the bushes for company, it seemed ludicrous that I'd just walked out.

Daniel had given me food and shelter. He'd given me his clothes to wear. And more importantly he'd looked at me like I meant something to him. He'd been nothing but patient, never pushing for me to disclose my secrets. He'd been gentle. He'd been considerate. He'd been… perfect.

Was I really going to pay him back for everything he'd done by deserting him? Except, I already had, hadn't I? I knew better than anyone that you couldn't turn back time. I was on my feet, even before I'd made a conscious decision. I needed to get back to Daniel. If he wanted me to leave, I'd leave, but not unless he asked me to. I owed him that. I might only have twelve days left, but that was better than nothing. I wasn't going to let some stranger's words come between us.

I broke into a run as I neared the gates of the park, one of the youths shouting something my way which I assumed was derogatory. I didn't care. I only cared about Daniel. He might not love me, but I loved him. He deserved better than for me to leave until there was absolutely no choice. That time would come, but it wasn't today. If he'd stayed late at work, I might even be able to make it back before he ever knew I'd been gone.

The lights were on in the house as I drew close, and I slowed to a walk. Had I left them on? I didn't think so. Which meant Daniel was home, and my absence would have been noted. Would he be angry? If I were in his shoes, I would be. Gloria's curtain twitched as I passed her house, but I didn't turn my head that way, intent on getting to Daniel.

The door swung open as I pushed the gate open, Daniel appearing in the doorway silhouetted by the light from the hallway. It was too dark to see his expression until I was only a couple of steps away from him. When I could, the mixture of relief and pain made something clench in my chest. I'd done that to him. And I'd do it again in just over a week. I launched myself at him, strong arms enfolding me in his embrace without even a moment's pause. I breathed him in, his warmth leaching into limbs I hadn't even registered were cold. He tugged me inside without letting go, my head tucked beneath his chin. It was a position I could have stayed in forever. We stood there, wrapped up in each other, neither of us making any move to separate.

"I thought you'd gone."

I jerked at the softly spoken words. "I'm sorry." It was all I could say. I couldn't even begin to try and explain what had been going on in my head when I didn't even understand it myself. It was like some force had convinced me to a course of action I'd never wanted to do. Pulling back from him, I stood up on my tiptoes and
kissed him instead, pouring everything I wanted to say — and couldn't — into the kiss instead, Daniel returning it just as hungrily.

How could I have ever thought I could walk away from this? Daniel was my sun, and I would orbit around him for as long as it was possible.

Chapter Nineteen

Daniel

Pressing the indicator to turn right, I cast a quick glance across to Frankie in the passenger seat. He'd been quiet all day, his mind God knows where. We'd never really addressed his disappearance of three nights ago. It had seemed safer just to let it go, to concentrate on the fact that he'd come back of his own accord. I'd been ready to search every inch of Sheffield if I needed to. And if that hadn't uncovered his hiding place, I would have thrown the net wider. But I hadn't had to. He'd come back. Whatever doubts, whatever anxieties had burrowed into his brain, he'd overcome them of his own accord. That was the important thing, right? And if I was honest, I hadn't wanted to risk ruining the happy buzz that had existed between us by asking questions that didn't really matter.

Our lovemaking that night had been the sweetest it had ever been, those three words almost forcing themselves up my throat in an overwhelming plea to be heard. Somehow, I'd managed to squash them, but I didn't know how much longer I could continue to do that.

"You had another dream last night."

I turned to find Frankie's eyes on me. "Did I?"

"You don't remember?"

I shook my head. It wasn't quite the truth. I didn't remember last night's dream, but the dreams were coming thick and fast now. And I couldn't shake the belief that there was some deeper meaning to them, that my subconscious was trying to tell me something. Only, I didn't know what that was.

They were all of a similar vein—fields, and rivers, and forests. Laughter and love with a boy I knew I loved more than life itself. Except he had neither a face nor a name. Sometimes that was all I dreamt. Those dreams were the happy ones, and I'd wake up with a real sense of peace. It was the ones that turned dark that were the problem, the ones centered around a sense of loss sharp enough to bring me to my knees. They were the dreams Frankie had to wake me up from, concern written all over his face as he shook me. On those nights, even with him holding me, it took forever to shed the sense of clawing terror and get back to sleep.

If he was mentioning it, it meant I'd had one of those dreams. Strange then, that I couldn't remember it. My fingers tightened reflexively around the steering wheel as I pretended a focus on the road ahead that wasn't really needed, the traffic fairly sparse. "They're just dreams."

"Have you always had them?"

I cleared my throat to try and shed the lump that had formed there. It wouldn't do any good to admit that they'd coincided with Frankie's appearance in my life. Not when it was just a coincidence. I didn't want him thinking that he was responsible in any way when the notion was ridiculous. I flashed him a quick smile. "Do you mind if we don't talk about them?"

"Sure."

The seat creaked as Frankie relaxed back into it. I concentrated on how we'd spent the day instead. I'd taken Frankie to Kelham Island, half expecting him to be bored. After all, the history of Sheffield's Industrial Revolution wasn't for everyone, but Frankie had seemed strangely fascinated, standing for at least ten minutes and staring in awe at the huge 12,000 horsepower steam engine that was their feature piece.

"I met Calvin the other day."

My foot almost slipped off the accelerator. "You did? When?"

"When the estate agent held the open house session. He came round to make sure that everything was running smoothly. He was… surprised to find me there."

I grimaced. *Shit!* Was that why Frankie had been so quiet all day? Had he been trying to find a way to broach the subject? Did he think I'd deliberately failed to mention that he'd be there? I hadn't. Nothing could be further from the truth. I hadn't spoken to Calvin for weeks. Our only communication had been the odd text, and that was almost always just about something linked to the house. Frankie's reveal probably went a long way to explaining why I'd had a couple of missed calls from Calvin yesterday, though. He hadn't left a message, and I hadn't called him back.

"Is that why you left? What did he say?" My words came out sharper than I'd intended, everything crystallizing in my brain to form a perfect explanation. Calvin had said something to upset Frankie, and Frankie had run. *Fucking Calvin!* I'd return his call and I'd give him a piece of my mind. He'd left me. He was the one who'd ended our marriage, the marriage I'd worked so hard to keep together even once he'd reached the point where he didn't seem to give a toss. He had absolutely no right to be sticking his nose into my new relationship.

"He didn't say anything. He was nice."

I forced myself to breathe evenly, surprised by the anger that had simmered so quickly. "Nice?"

"*Oui*. It was only a brief conversation, but he was nothing but friendly."

That sounded more like the Calvin I knew. Since when had I started jumping to ridiculous conclusions? It was one thing to be protective over Frankie, but it was another thing entirely to work myself into a state where I was ready to punch my ex-husband in the face for something he hadn't even done. "I didn't know he was going to be there, or I would have said something to you."

"I know."

I wasn't going to get a better opportunity. "So why did you leave?"

Frankie turned his head to stare out of the window. "Someone else said something."

Turning down a side street, I brought the car to a stop. This conversation was far too important to have to concentrate on driving. "Who?"

Frankie's shoulders lifted in a shrug. "I don't know. They didn't give me their name."

I undid my seatbelt and turned to face him. "What did they say?"

"They said some stuff."

"What stuff?"

"About you and Calvin. That he'd been a student at the university, that your relationship had caused a lot of problems because of that."

I let out a snort. "Some people are very narrow-minded. And he was never *my* student. I didn't meet him until after he'd already graduated."

A furrow appeared on Frankie's brow. "They said that, but they seemed to think that me staying with you would rake up the past, that it wasn't a good idea for you to be involved with someone else where there was an age gap."

I let out a snort. "There's always going to be narrow-minded people. They're unavoidable, unfortunately. My personal life has got nothing to do with them, though, and I'll be quite happy to tell them that."

"I don't want to make life difficult for you."

Reaching across, I grabbed Frankie's hand and entwined my fingers with his. "You're not. You're making life so much better. In every way. There is absolutely no reason why I can't have a relationship with you."

He tipped his head back, a question in those wide blue eyes. Eyes the color of the Mediterranean Sea. "Really?"

I squeezed his hand. "Really. My work at the university is just a job. I like the students, but there are other jobs, other universities. I can always move."

Frankie blinked. "Would you do that?"

To be honest, I'd never given much thought to it. But if it was a question of him or my job, I knew the answer. There was no competition. "Sure."

He nodded, and my heart skipped a beat. Did that mean he'd consider moving somewhere else with me? I forced myself to slow down, to not blurt out something stupid that would have us going one step forward and two steps back. Besides, there were far more important things to concentrate on, such as the identity of the stranger falling over themselves to discuss my personal details with Frankie.

Calvin must have brought someone with him, one of his friends, maybe? There were definitely a couple I'd never seen eye to eye with. Ross immediately came to mind. He'd always thought I was a stick in the mud. We'd done our best to avoid each other during my marriage to Calvin, keeping the peace for his benefit. I certainly wouldn't put it past him to stick the knife in one last time. "What did he look like, this man that was so eager to discuss all my personal business with you?"

Frankie's brow furrowed. "I don't know, just normal. Brown hair, brown eyes. Taller than me."

The description fitted Ross. Everything seemed to point toward him being the most likely culprit. I'd return Calvin's call and tell him to keep his friends away from the house, and more importantly away from Frankie.

"Are you okay?"

I looked down to find that I was gripping Frankie's hand far too tightly. I relaxed my hold. "Sorry. I was just thinking."

Frankie's smile was tinged with regret. "I came back."

"Yeah, you did." That was the main thing, the shining light in all the meddling. Whether it had been Ross or another of Calvin's friends. I raised my head to take in where my impromptu stop had left us. "I'm going to be in such trouble with my mum."

"Your mum?"

"She lives a few streets from here. I usually drop in when I'm passing through."

"Then you should do that."

I studied Frankie's face, searching for signs of it being nothing but the expected politeness. "You wouldn't mind?"

"Not if you don't?"

I shook my head. I had absolutely no problem with introducing Frankie to my parents. In fact, the thought filled me with a giddy excitement. It made the whole thing more real, more permanent. Which was why I was surprised that Frankie hadn't been more resistant to it. Maybe introducing your parents to your boyfriend didn't have the same significance in France. Whatever it was, I wasn't about to look a gift horse in the mouth.

* * * *

We were all gathered around the kitchen table, Frankie, my mum and dad, and myself. My mum had performed her usual magic to produce a cake out of nowhere, and to serve up tea in the blink of an eye. To give my parents their due, they'd gotten over their initial surprise at being introduced to someone I'd never even mentioned fairly quickly, or at least they were covering it well.

My mum seemed fascinated by Frankie, her eyes barely leaving his face. "So... you two are... together."

I barely resisted rolling my eyes. "Yes, Mum. Frankie is my boyfriend."

My dad coughed. "Since when?"

I hadn't thought this through, had I? It was natural for them to question how short-lived our relationship had been. And I hadn't even disclosed the fact that we were living together yet.

"A while." Vagueness seemed to be the best way to go. "Frankie moved in a few weeks ago." It was better to get it over with. I'd brought him here without thinking it through, so I should be prepared to suffer the consequences.

"Moved in!" My mother's eyebrows shot up, but she still didn't look away from Frankie. "That's... sudden."

I reached for Frankie's thigh beneath the table and gave it a squeeze. "When you know, you know."

"You said that with Calvin."

I aimed a hard stare at my dad. He'd just had to go and bring Calvin into it. "I was married, and it didn't work out. It's hardly the crime of the century. Thousands of people get divorced every year. We can't all be lucky enough to find our soulmate at the first try."

My dad ran a hand through the brown hair that was so similar to mine. It was starting to thin slightly, but I doubted a stranger would have been able to tell. "Your mother and I are just concerned, that's all. We don't want you rushing into things. You were so miserable during the divorce. We don't want you having to go through that again. Maybe..." He cast a quick glance Frankie's way. "You should take things a bit more slowly."

I sat back in my chair and regarded them both steadily. "While I appreciate your concern, it's not needed."

My father's nod of acceptance was tinged with a distinct air of sheepishness.

I shook my head. The conversation was one thing, but for them to be having it in front of Frankie bordered on rude. He was skittish enough as it was. I didn't want him feeling like my family didn't welcome him. He was uncomfortable. I could tell from the way he was focusing on his plate, his fingers crumbling the last remnants of the cake.

"Anyway… we were talking this afternoon about the possibility of moving somewhere else. Then you wouldn't need to worry about me dragging everyone down with my inevitable misery."

My mother looked like someone had slapped her in the face. "What do you mean, move? You've got a good job here. You were hoping to make professor one day. That will be harder if you start afresh somewhere else. Where would you go?"

I met her stare. "I don't know. There's a whole wide world out there. Frankie's French. Maybe we'll go to France." We wouldn't. It wasn't like I could teach history in French, and I doubted there was much call for a history lecturer over there who could only speak English. But it had seemed as good a place to name as any. My mother opened her mouth, probably to point out the exact same thing, but I got in there first. "And if not France, then somewhere else. A fresh start. Somewhere I won't be judged just because I had a failed marriage."

My mother finally managed to tug her gaze away from Frankie. "I'm sorry, sweetheart. You're right. You're a grown man. You know your own heart, and we support you wholeheartedly."

My dad offered a grunt, which was about as close as he ever got to agreeing.

When my mum changed the subject, I gladly went along with it, Frankie joining in as we conversed on far safer subjects, managing to bypass too many personal questions about Frankie, questions that even I didn't know the answer to.

* * * *

I rubbed the back of my neck as I threw my car keys in the middle of the kitchen table. "I'm sorry about today. I should have realized that producing a new boyfriend out of nowhere would come as a bit of a shock to them. I should have had the good sense to speak to them first, prepare the ground, so to speak. They worry, but they had no right to make you feel uncomfortable by voicing their concerns in front of you."

When Frankie didn't answer, I turned to find him staring down at the table, his face devoid of expression. "Frankie, are you okay?"

He lifted his head to meet my gaze, the haunted look in his eyes enough to send a bolt of alarm through my chest. "We need to talk."

Four words guaranteed to send a chill down anyone's spine. "Okay."

Frankie waved a hand at the chair closest to me, waiting until I'd taken a seat before seating himself opposite me. "I don't want to hurt you."

"You won't." I searched his face, but he was as impassive as I'd ever seen him. I barely recognized him. He looked like someone else wearing Frankie's face, and that scared me a great deal.

"I will." There was a quiet assurance in Frankie's voice that I didn't like the sound of one little bit. "You don't get it, Daniel.

There are things going on that you don't understand, that you could never in a million years understand."

I reached out to him, but no sooner had my fingers grazed the tips of his than he retracted his hand, and I was left with nothing but the cool surface of the table to keep my hand company. "So… tell me. Tell me what's going on with you, and then whatever it is, we can face it together. I can help, if you just let me in."

Frankie smiled, but it was a sad smile. "You can't. No one can. I did something years ago, and I've been paying for it ever since. And I'll keep paying for it, for a long time to come."

I tapped my fingers on the table, attempting to make the tight muscles in my shoulders relax. "It can't be that bad. Is there someone after you, is that it? Are you on the run from the authorities? Frankie, I—"

"I can't tell you. I wish I could."

I stared at him. "Can't or won't?"

"Can't. And if I did try and tell you, you'd think I was crazy, and then I'd be gone."

He was speaking in riddles. I couldn't think of any scenario which would require this level of secrecy. "What do you mean you'd be gone?"

Another sad smile. "I've been doing my best to ignore it, but then you sat there this afternoon, and you told your parents about all these plans for the future, plans that involved both of us, and I felt sick because none of that can happen."

"Why?"

Frankie's gaze turned distant. "I want you to know something, Daniel. I *need* you to know something."

"What?"

"When I do leave, it's not because I want to, it will be because I have to. Because I have no other choice."

My breath froze in my chest. "Don't talk about leaving! You're not going anywhere."

Frankie's exhale was noisy. "But I will. And I probably won't get to say goodbye. It's the way it usually works."

I got up from the table in an explosion of movement, no longer able to sit still and just listen. I started to pace. "You're not making any sense. How can you sit there and just calmly tell me that one day you're going to walk out on me, and you won't even say goodbye? That's just cruel. I've done nothing to deserve that."

"I know."

I might have thought from the calmness of his tone that he was completely unaffected, if it wasn't for the single tear that slid down his cheek. Despite everything he'd just said, I couldn't bear to see him cry. I pulled him up from the chair and into my arms, wiping the tear away with the pad of my thumb. "Oh God, don't cry."

Frankie sniffed. "Please don't hate me."

I tipped his chin back and stared into his face, the usually clear blue eyes brimming with unshed tears. "I could never hate you. I…" Fuck! There was no denying it anymore. There never had been, really. I'd known it for quite some time, maybe even since that first moment when our eyes had met and I'd found myself unable to walk away. "I love you." There was a release in being able to say it. So much so, that I said it again, my lips curving into a smile as I repeated it. "I love you, François. And I could never hate you, no matter what you did."

The expression on Frankie's face changed to something that looked remarkably like hope. He took a shaky breath in, one of the tears spilling over to trace a path down his cheek. "I love you too."

A million emotions all exploded in my chest. I loved him and he loved me, so surely nothing else mattered. I wiped the tear away with my thumb, laying my forehead against his so that the two of us breathed together. We would be okay. Whatever demons were driving him, we would slay together. No matter what he said, there was no problem that couldn't be overcome. He wouldn't leave me. He couldn't. And if it came down to it, and there was no other choice, we'd run together. Wherever he went, I would follow. There was nothing in the world that could keep us apart.

Chapter Twenty

Frankie

The process had already started. You see, twenty-eight days had always been a lie, really. It always happened the same way. It wasn't that I hit day twenty-eight and I was slammed back into the gargoyle, in the space of time it would take someone to click their fingers. It was a gradual slow-down, a gradual decline of physical condition until I could no more resist returning to the gargoyle than I could manage not to eat and drink while I was human. By rights, I should have still had four days. But they wouldn't be four days full of fun. They would be days where my body would start turning back to stone, bit by slow bit. Four days of torture.

And worst of all, Daniel telling me he loved me hadn't stopped it from happening. It wasn't like the other times. They hadn't been the empty words of someone trying to get me into bed, or the glib words of someone trotting them out simply because they were expected. He'd meant them. He'd really meant them. But they still weren't enough. Cecile had known what she was doing when she set the parameters of the curse. I wish I knew where her grave was so that I could piss on it.

I raised my head from the pillow as the bedroom door creaked open, Daniel entering with a hot water bottle clutched in his hands. He smiled, and I did my best to return it. Although, I doubted it was convincing enough to fool anyone, especially not him. "Are you feeling any better?"

It was tempting to lie, but he'd no doubt know I was lying through my teeth. "Not really."

He lay a hand on my forehead, his face creasing with concern. "You're so cold."

Not as cold as I will be in a few days. He held out the hot water bottle. "I thought this might help." I took it from him and hugged it to me. He could strap a hundred of them to my body and it wouldn't cure the problem when the cold came from within, but it was a sweet gesture nonetheless.

I glanced over at the clock. "You're going to be late for work."

Daniel let out a snort. "You really think I'm going to leave you alone like this? I rang in sick."

"You shouldn't have done that."

He perched on the edge of the bed, his gaze raking over me. "I haven't rung in sick for years. I think they can cancel my lectures just this once. Marjorie won't be pleased, but then that's nothing new. I've never pleased her in the five years I've known her, so…" He shrugged. "I'll go back tomorrow when you're feeling better."

Except, I wouldn't be feeling better the next day. Or the day after that. My only hope was that it wouldn't progress that fast this time. Some times were slower than others. I hugged the hot water bottle tighter to me, Daniel tucking the duvet in around my neck so that there were no gaps for cold air to get in. "There's an extra blanket in the top of the wardrobe. I'll get it for you. And I'll stick the heating on high."

I managed a grateful smile. He bent over and dropped a gentle kiss to my forehead. "Try and get some sleep. I'll wake you for lunch. We have to keep your strength up."

I closed my eyes obediently and was surprised when sleep crept over me.

*　*　*　*

When I awoke, Daniel was lying on the opposite side of the bed. As promised, he'd draped another blanket over me. I rolled over so that I was facing him. "How long have I been asleep?"

He lifted an arm to check his watch. "Couple of hours. Did it help?"

I ignored the question. "You should have gone to work. What's the point in you being here just to watch me sleep?"

Daniel's smile was decidedly wry. "This may come as a bit of a shock to you, but I don't love my job enough not to appreciate taking a day away from it. The building isn't going to fall to pieces just because I'm not there. I doubt anyone will even miss me. Richard, maybe. Oh, and Marjorie might have to find herself someone else to gripe at, but I'm sure she's got a list of candidates as long as her arm. I can't be that special. As for the students, they'll be perfectly happy to spend a day getting away with doing very little. They're probably flicking paper balls around the lecture hall as we speak. So…" Daniel's smile grew wider. "You're stuck with me, I'm afraid."

"I can cope with that."

Daniel searched my face, in a way that said he wasn't quite sure whether I was being one hundred percent honest. He cleared his throat. "Besides, I've had a lovely morning. Ask me what I've been up to."

"What have you been up to?"

He shifted closer on the pillow until there was only about half a meter of space between us. "I watered all the plants. I read the newspaper, which I never get time to do. I watched some morning TV, which I have to say was quite eye-opening. I could have probably done without the in-depth report on people who drink their own urine. Apparently, it's really good for you, but I think I'll remain my usual unhealthy self if that's what's required. Luckily, I had the distraction of Napoleon on my lap, who expected to be told he was a beautiful boy at least once every five minutes. At least until he got bored with all the adoration and went outside to shout at the birds."

I had to smile at that one. Napoleon did get very frustrated by the fact that the birds wouldn't simply surrender to him. "You've packed a lot in."

"Exactly. And I would only be on my third lecture if I was at work. Oh, and I almost forgot, I spoke to your new best friend and told her that you couldn't come out to play today."

"Gloria?"

Daniel nodded. "I had no idea the two of you had been spending so much time together. She seemed quite concerned when I told her that you weren't feeling well. She's probably wondering how she's going to clear her cake surplus without you eating it."

It was more likely that she knew exactly what was happening. "Did she say anything else?"

Daniel's forehead creased. "Like what?"

"Nothing."

Daniel reached across the space to run his fingers through my hair, the touch achingly affectionate. "Should I be worried about you and Gloria becoming so close?"

Despite the teasing note in his voice, there was also a note of concern, my secrets hanging between us, always unspoken, but still very much there. "No, you shouldn't be worried. I'm not leaving you for her."

"Glad to hear it." Daniel shifted again, so that his nose pressed against mine.

Everything within me froze, memories of how often Estienne and I had lain the same way rising up to torment me. It was too much. Too similar. I'd thought after Estienne I would never truly love again. But that was before Daniel. And I felt the same as I had back then. It might be a bed rather than a riverbank, and I might have been hundreds of miles away from Domme, but the feelings were unmistakable. And it was so cruel when time was so short.

Unable to bear the achingly familiar position for even a second longer, I rolled away from him, untangling myself from all of the covers and fending off the hands which were doing their best to stall my retreat. "Don't. I need to…"

Daniel let go. "What did I do? Frankie, I'm sorry. Just tell me what I did, and I won't do it again. You don't have to run away. I—"

I didn't hear the end of the sentence as I stumbled into the bathroom, closing the door and locking it before leaning heavily against the sink. Dragging in air greedily, I tried to get myself under control as tears pricked my eyes. I refused to give in to self-pity. It had never gotten me anywhere before, and it wouldn't now. It took a few minutes of slow, deep breathing before I was able to lift my head and stare at my reflection in the mirror. I turned my head to one side, and then the other. I looked normal, perhaps a little pale, but otherwise normal.

I gingerly lifted my hand to my cheek, my fingers much warmer than the skin of my face. It was almost as if I could feel the ridges of stone starting to form beneath the surface. I couldn't. It was nothing more than my over-active imagination. That wasn't how it worked, but even so, I couldn't shake the feeling.

"Frankie?" It sounded like Daniel was pressed up against the door. He tried the handle, letting out a little grunt of frustration at the discovery that I'd locked it. "Let me in, please."

"I'm fine, Daniel." It was easier to lie when he couldn't see my face. "I just need a bit of time on my own, that's all."

"What did I do? You were fine one minute, and then the next…"

I continued to stare at my reflection in the mirror. A reflection that had remained unchanged for hundreds of years. I was staring at the same face that Estienne had once told me he could look at forever and never get bored. I closed my eyes against the pain. "You reminded me of something, that's all. Something… that's painful to remember."

"I'm sorry."

Daniel sounded so crushed that I almost smiled. "You don't need to be sorry."

"But I am. What can I say to make it better?"

"Nothing. I mean… you don't need to."

There was a long pause before Daniel spoke again, so long that I'd begun to think he'd walked away.

"I think I should call a doctor and get him to take a look at you."

My eyes snapped open as I spun around to press a hand against the door. "No doctor. Promise me, Daniel, that you won't call a doctor."

"You're not well."

I'd been talked into seeing a doctor once. They'd admitted me to a hospital to run tests, tests that had all proved inconclusive and had given zero explanation for the fact that my body temperature and pulse rate were slowly dropping. All it had meant was that I'd spent my last days of freedom confined to a bed being poked and prodded. Technology and medical know-how might have moved on since then, but I doubted the results would be any different. Unless they had a pill that could reverse a curse, it would prove useless, nothing but a waste of time. "Promise me!"

Daniel's sigh could be heard even through the door. "Fine. I promise. Not unless you get worse." There was a long pause. "I'm going to go and make lunch. Do you think you could come downstairs to eat it?"

I rested my head against the door, the wood cool against my forehead. Things would be much easier if I could hide the worst effects of what was happening.
That way Daniel would go back to work, and I wouldn't have him watching me so closely. "Yeah, I can come downstairs. I'm feeling a bit better. I must have needed to sleep."

"Yeah?" There was a note of pleasure in Daniel's voice. "That's good. It must have been a bug or something."

"*Oui!* Just a bug."

I returned to studying myself in the mirror as footsteps announced Daniel's departure from the door. It had been stupid to freak out just because Daniel's actions had reminded me so much of Estienne. It wasn't like there was any way Daniel could have known. Coincidences happened. He would have enough to deal with in a few days when I disappeared, without me making the last few days difficult as well.

It was a few more minutes before I'd gathered myself sufficiently to open the bathroom door a crack, only leaving the safety of the bathroom when I found the bedroom empty. I dressed quickly, steeling myself to put on the performance of a lifetime.

* * * *

It was time.

And it wasn't just the calendar telling me that. It was the deep pull in my chest, the sensation akin to an elastic band having been stretched taut, urging me back to where I belonged. I'd tried everything over the years in my efforts to fight it. I'd drunk so much that I'd passed out. I'd gotten someone to lock me in a room that I had no way of getting out of. I'd tied myself down. Whatever I did, it always ended the same way. The magic preferred me to make my own way back to the gargoyle, but it had no problem bypassing it if that wasn't possible.

Therefore, it was time to go. I'd already put it off as long as I could, the pull becoming more painful with every minute that passed. I took one last look around Daniel's house, committing everything to memory, which was stupid when it was just a house and not the man himself.

It had taken all the acting skills I possessed to pretend I was asleep while he'd readied himself for work this morning. When he'd hovered over me and pressed a kiss to my forehead, I'd kept my eyes squeezed tightly shut, too scared to open them in case the truth was written all over my face. Besides, it was easier to say goodbye when I didn't have to speak. Once Daniel had gone, I'd dressed quickly in the clothes I'd arrived in, leaving the clothes I'd borrowed from Daniel neatly folded on the bed.

A wave of overwhelming dizziness had me pausing to lean against the wall as I tried to make my way to the front door. My pulse was already beginning to slow dramatically, making even the simplest of movements feel like a marathon. I calculated that I had a few hours at most before I turned back to stone.

Something brushed my calf. I looked down to find Napoleon winding his way around my legs. "I've got to go." The cat stared up at me with wide, green eyes almost like he understood. Animals sensed things. Maybe in some strange way he did understand. "You'll look after Daniel, right?"

Napoleon opened his mouth to meow, and I crouched to pet him before standing and wrenching the door open. Every step required a superhuman effort. I should have returned earlier. What had I been waiting for? Had I hoped Daniel might forget something and return, so that I could have seen him one last time? Quite possibly. I would see him again, but it would be from behind the cold, stone eyes of the gargoyle, where he could speak to me, but I could never say another word to him. Would he still speak to me? I hoped so. The only thing more painful than seeing him would be not seeing him. For a moment, anger ripped at my chest and I was consumed by how unfair it was to have to live this half-life full of cruelty and torment where others were impacted by my all-consuming need to escape from it.

Fixing my gaze on the gate as a target, I tripped, almost falling. My head was fuzzy, and I could barely see. And the tug in my chest had become so insistent that it was like a fist squeezing my heart. The magic wanted me back there, and it wanted me back there five minutes ago. It didn't understand that it was the thing stopping me. It only knew how to demand, how to take, how to complete the cycle of life that it had me trapped in.

And then suddenly there was a presence next to me, fingers wrapping around my elbow in a gesture of support. Daniel? No, not Daniel, Gloria. I slowly blinked her back into focus, her lips downturned and her eyes sad. "Is it time?"

I nodded, words suddenly seeming far too difficult to muster.

Her fingers tightened around my arm. "Will you let me help you?"

Nobody had ever offered before, but then nobody had ever known the truth. She was the first. And she would probably be the last. I swallowed, tears springing to my eyes at the sweetness of the gesture. I gave another nod and she smiled, the slight tremble in her lips belying the otherwise stoic exterior.

Gloria guided me down the path and through the gate, and I was ashamed to have to lean on her quite so heavily. She brought us to a stop at the side of a lime green Mini. It had been parked there ever since the first night I'd arrived, but I'd never given much thought to it. "This is your car?" My voice sounded like it was being forced out between two sheets of metal.

She gave the roof an affectionate pat. "It is. It might not look like much, but it gets me from A to B."

Gloria opened the door and I squeezed myself into the passenger seat as she rounded the car to climb in the driver's seat. I didn't fasten my seat belt. Why bother? If something happened and I flew through the windscreen, I wouldn't die. I'd just find myself back in the gargoyle sooner. For a moment, Gloria just sat there, her stare distant. Then she seemed to come to, giving a startled little jerk before turning the keys in the ignition, the engine flaring to life.

I settled my head back against the headrest as she pulled away from the curb. "Do you know where we need to go?"

"Yes. I saw it."

I nodded, closing my eyes and trusting her to get me there.

"I'm sorry, Frankie. I thought…"

"You thought what?"

"That Daniel might be the one, that it might end for you."

I rubbed at my chest, the pain easing more with every mile that we grew closer to campus. "He told me he loved me, and I believe him."

"Then why is it still happening?" There was a sharp frustration in Gloria's voice, and I loved her for it.

"People… men have said it before. It's never enough. I don't know what it wants." It seemed strange to call the magic binding me to the gargoyle "it" but that's what it felt like, a living, breathing entity capable of changing the rules when it felt like it. I knew deep down that the blame lay firmly at Cecile's door, but she'd been dead for hundreds of years, so blaming her seemed pointless. A hand closed over mine and gave it a squeeze. I wanted to squeeze back, but that required physical reserves that were rapidly dwindling.

"You're so cold."

My head felt too heavy for my neck. It was reaching the point where being back in the gargoyle and being unable to feel would be somewhat of a blessing. At least for the first day or so, anyway. "I'm turning back into stone. That's the way it happens."

"Oh, Frankie!" There was so much emotion in those two words—sorrow, empathy, anger. "I did see an end to it. I wasn't lying to you."

"I know. I guess, it's just not this time. I'll be okay." I would. It was nothing I hadn't been through before. Even the emotional wrench at leaving Daniel wasn't new. I hadn't died from the grief of losing Estienne. I'd survived that, and I would again. How would Daniel cope? He didn't have memories of the past to fall back on the same way I did. He did have a failed marriage, though. Hopefully, he could use that experience to see that things would get better in time.

Even so, concern nibbled at me like a persistent mouse. I forced my eyes open and looked across to Gloria. "Will you look after Daniel for me? Please. He's not going to take it well. I tried to warn him, but he didn't understand. How could he?"

Gloria reached across to give my hand another pat. "I'll look after him for you. I'll… force feed him cake and pretend that I've got odd jobs I need doing around the house so that he has to visit frequently." I smiled at the memory of how easily I'd fallen for that one. "And if that doesn't work, I'll… I don't know… I'll stage a fall or something. I've got a few tricks up my sleeve." Gloria let out a sigh. "Or I could just tell him the truth?"

I blinked at her. It had never even occurred to me that while I couldn't speak the words, Gloria had always been able to. Or had she? Would it have mattered who spoke them? It was possible that it would have had the same effect, that I would have found myself back beneath a layer of stone before Gloria had even finished her first sentence. That wouldn't matter, though, would it? Not once I was back in the gargoyle. There could be no repercussions beyond what had already happened. I thought about it. "He wouldn't believe you. He'd just think you were mad."

Besides, even if he did believe Gloria, he might know the truth, but it wouldn't give him any peace. If anything, it would probably make things worse. It would leave him as trapped as I was, just in a different way.

Gloria took the next left-hand turn. We were only a few streets away from the campus now. "Are you sure?"

"*Oui*. I'm sure. Telling him won't help him." The car drew to a stop, and I turned my head to stare out of the window at the lawn. In the distance, I could just make out the familiar shape of the gargoyle. Home. Sort of. If home was a prison.

I leaned across the space and pressed a quick kiss to Gloria's cheek. She was boiling hot. Except, it wasn't her that was abnormally hot. It was me that was turning to ice. "Thank you."

"I could come with you?"

I shook my head. "No. This bit I have to do alone. Besides, you wouldn't see anything. One minute I would be there and the next I'd be gone. It's shrouded from sight somehow." I fumbled for the door handle before she could argue, refusing to look back as I closed the car door and took my first few faltering steps in the direction I needed to go. I didn't know what time it was, but there were a few students milling around, one or two giving me a curious look as I staggered past. Given what I'd seen during my silent scrutiny of campus life, they probably assumed I was drunk.

The tug in my chest was like a second pulse, thrumming with a greater intensity, the closer my steps brought me. The magic seemed happy at my return, as if for those twenty-eight days it resented having to let me roam free and was relieved that

I would soon be back in its clutches. The gargoyle, when I came to a stop in front of it, looked the same as it always had. Cold. Inanimate. Untouched by time. The opposite of me. It begged me to reach out, to touch it, to become one with it once again.

I resisted it, turning my head in the direction of the building instead. Daniel was in there somewhere. What was he doing? Was he looking forward to returning home and seeing me again? What would he do when he found the house cold and empty? Would he search for me? I hated to think of him traipsing the streets for hours on end when I would be right here.

A whisper started up in my head, a whisper that told me that my time was up, that I could either give in or that they would take me anyway. I turned back to face the gargoyle, its expressionless, demonic face staring right back at me. I lifted my hand, but I didn't make contact. Not yet. I just held it there as I filled my lungs with air, trying to hold on to what the sensation felt like. I concentrated on the way the wind ruffled my hair. I breathed in the scent of flowers from the nearby flowerbeds. I listened to the noises around me, without them being muffled by a surrounding layer of stone—birdsong and voices, a car in the distance, and the faint chime of church bells somewhere. What would the world be like in twenty-five years? Would I still be in the same place, or would I have been moved again?

As soon as I lowered my hand and made contact, the blue light came. Just like the first time—bright and overwhelming. I closed my eyes against it and kept them closed. If I didn't open them, I could believe for a bit longer that there was still grass under my feet, that I could feel the slight warmth of a winter sun on my back. Except, it was impossible when breath no longer flowed through my lungs, and I could no longer feel.

I opened my eyes, greeting the same view that I'd known for so many years. Another twenty-eight days had passed. I'd fallen in love, and he'd loved me back, but it still wasn't enough.

Inside, I screamed, but of course I couldn't make a sound. I could only stare. I could only watch. I could only wait.

It was hours later when Daniel left the building. He had a little smile on his face that almost broke my heart.

He didn't so much as glance my way.

Chapter Twenty-one

Daniel

Huddled on the sofa under a blanket, I ignored the knock at the door. Whoever it was would go away. It had been a week since Frankie had left me. There'd been no note, no nothing. No indication that he'd been anything apart from a figment of my imagination, except for the pile of neatly folded clothes that smelt faintly of him. And I should know. I'd sat with them pressed to my nose for long enough, trying to convince myself that he would come back, that it would be like the other time, where he'd realized his mistake and returned of his own accord.

When that hadn't happened, I'd searched for him. I'd combed the streets of Sheffield, looking into every doorway and into every nook and cranny where a human could possibly be. I'd questioned everyone I could, but I'd drawn a complete blank. No one had seen him. No one knew where he was. Frankie had become a ghost.

It had been seven days since he'd disappeared. Seven long days, in which I hadn't been to work, and after giving up on the search I'd done little else apart from lie on the sofa and stare at the TV. This was worse than when my marriage had broken down. Frankie had wormed his way into a part of my heart that Calvin hadn't been able to touch, and the pain of losing him was indescribable.

When the knocking didn't stop, I levered myself off the sofa and stumbled to the door, opening it to find the slightly stooped figure of Gloria standing there. Fucking marvelous! Just what I needed. She usually only came around if she wanted to complain about something. Napoleon had probably been crapping in her hydrangeas again. She seemed to think I had some way of controlling my cat's bowels.

Her gaze raked over me, and it didn't take a genius to work out what she was thinking. I hadn't shaved or showered in days, and I wasn't sure whether the jumper I'd put on had even been clean at that point. It certainly wasn't now, the front of it displaying a rather large stain from the tomato soup I'd managed to force down. I leaned weakly against the doorjamb. "Whatever I've done, I'll fix it, just… not today, okay."

"Are you alright?"

No, I wasn't alright. I was a long way from being alright. I was heartbroken. Or maybe I was angry. I couldn't even decide which. My emotions were all over the place. Could you be both at the same time? "I'm fine."

"Can I come in?"

I stared at her. Gloria and I had never been anything more than acquaintances that fate had placed next door to each other. We had nothing in common, nothing to talk about. Therefore, I couldn't think of any possible reason for her wanting to step over the threshold. "I'm not really feeling up to entertaining."

She smiled, and I wondered whether I'd ever seen her do that before. Maybe at Calvin, but never at me. It made her look less formidable and far more approachable. "I'll make you a cup of tea."

I didn't have the energy to fight her, so I stepped back from the door with a shrug. "Knock yourself out." She wasted no time in squeezing past me and making her way into the kitchen, letting out a tut as she was faced with a sink piled high with dirty plates, some of them spilling onto the countertop when I'd been faced with there being no room left. "Yeah, good luck finding a clean cup."

She rolled up her sleeves, and I watched in disbelief as she carefully removed the dishes before filling the sink with hot water and attacking the dishes with gusto. "You don't need to do that."

She cast a glance back over her shoulder. "Well, as you pointed out, I can't make a cup of tea without any clean cups, so the obvious solution is to clean the cups."

I took a seat at the kitchen table. "You haven't asked about him, which makes me think you knew he was leaving."

She went still. "Let's have a cup of tea first, shall we?"

Gloria had insisted on putting my kitchen back to rights before she finally served up the promised cup of tea. I wrapped my hands around it, the action reminding me of Frankie, but then everything reminded me of Frankie. I'd have to move houses… Hell, I'd have to move cities to rid myself of the memories we'd shared. I took a sip of the tea, Gloria watching me as if she was expecting marks out of ten. I cleared my throat. "You still haven't said why you're here. We've never exactly hung out and had tea together before."

There was a clatter of the cat flap, Napoleon running into the kitchen at a speed which indicated he'd caught wind of the German Shepherd that lived at the house on the corner. Gloria pulled her gaze from the cat and back to me. "I just wanted to check if you were alright. I noticed you hadn't been going to work since…"

Since Frankie left. I hadn't done a lot of things since Frankie left. The world outside my door had ceased to be of much importance. "I've taken some time off."

Gloria nodded. My next gulp of tea burned my mouth. "Did you see him…? before he left… I mean? Did he say goodbye to you?" *And not to me.* Gloria seemed torn about what to say, which meant she knew something. Hope flared in my chest, and I leaned forward, my gaze firmly fixed on her face. "Tell me. Whatever you know, tell me. Please. I don't care what he's gotten himself involved in, what he's mixed up in. All I care about is getting him back."

She folded her hands together in front of her in a prim and proper fashion. "It's not that simple, Daniel. And if you look deep within yourself, you know that, don't you?"

I frowned at her, not having a clue what she was talking about. "Just tell me where he is."

Her gaze held mine. "You need to work that out yourself. I consulted the cards last night, and that's what they told me."

"The cards?"

"Tarot cards. I never did Frankie's because, well… I just never did them."

I didn't need this. She might have done my washing up, but that didn't mean I had to sit there and listen to a load of mystic bullshit. That wasn't going to help me find Frankie. I stood, the action so abrupt that the table wobbled. "Thank you for the tea, and for locating the cups, but I think it's probably time you left."

Gloria was much slower to rise. I tried to temper my impatience as she pushed the chair beneath the table, her cup of tea only half empty. Well, wasn't I the asshole to be throwing out the little old lady before she'd even drunk the tea that she'd gone to the trouble of making? I might find it within me to feel guilty once she'd gone. Or maybe not.

I walked her to the door, her frustratingly slow gait forcing me to take only half steps. It was a relief when I finally got to wrench the door open. Next time, I would know better than to let her in in the first place. However, she made no move to step outside, turning to face me instead. "Why do you think you and Calvin weren't right for each other?"

Oh, it got better. Now, she wanted to talk about Calvin. Maybe I should tell her about the boy who'd dumped me for my best friend when I was seventeen. She could poke her nose into that as well and tell me why my best friend had been a far better match for him. "I don't know. Some things just run their course, I guess."

She looked disappointed by my answer as she tipped her head back to look me in the eye. "You have all the answers, Daniel. You're just not letting yourself be open to them. Stop fighting the dreams. Let them in, and everything will be become clear."

My mouth dropped open. "How do you know about the dreams? Did Frankie tell you? What did he say? And more importantly, what do you mean by not fighting them?"

She placed a hand on my shoulder, the grip stronger than I would have expected it to be. "Frankie didn't tell me anything. You're scared of what the dreams are trying to tell you. Instead of running away from it, embrace the knowledge. They're the key to finding Frankie before it's too late."

"Too late? What the hell do you mean by that?"

But she'd already turned away and was halfway down the path before I could stop her, her ability to walk fast apparently having returned in the last few minutes. I was left staring after her with a million questions battering at my brain. She'd always been a bit of a busybody, but I'd never thought of her as mad. Was she going senile? That was the only thing I could think of that would explain her cryptic comments. And if she wasn't mad, then… If she knew where Frankie was, why didn't she just tell me? And how the hell were the dreams going to help?

I closed the door and returned to my vigil on the sofa, pulling the blanket over my knees and switching the TV on. When it wasn't enough to distract me, I turned the volume up until it was far louder than I usually had it. I doubted Gloria was going to come round and complain. And if she did, she could damn well answer my questions.

I'd done my best to ignore my phone for the last few days, but for some reason I reached for it. There were two missed calls from Marjorie, four from Richard, and one from my mother. Richard had also sent me a long string of messages.

Richard: *Hey, what's this I hear about you taking a holiday. That's a bit sudden, isn't it? Where are you going? Hope everything's okay?*

Richard: *I came round last night, but all the curtains were drawn. Were you in? Answer your phone. I'm beginning to worry that something might have happened to you.*

Richard: *This has got something to do with that guy, right? I warned you he was going to hurt you.*

Richard: *Mate, just send me a text, would you? Just so I know you're okay. No man is worth shutting yourself away from the world. When are you coming back to work?*

Richard: *Still haven't heard from you. It's been four days. Give me a ring.*

Richard: *Earth to Daniel. Come in, Daniel.*

Richard: *Alright, I give up. I'm here if you need anything. I'll even promise not to say I told you so. Just tell me what you need.*

I dropped the phone back on the table without bothering to reply to any of the messages. I would have to call my mum back, though. There'd be hell to pay if I ignored her. No doubt she and my father would be overjoyed when they discovered that Frankie was no longer a part of my life.

The rest of the evening passed in something of a blur, where I did my best to concentrate on nothing but the flickering images on the screen, immersing myself in anything that could keep my attention for longer than five minutes. The hours passed until the clock crawled closer to midnight, and I finally admitted defeat and made my way to the bathroom.

I brushed my teeth and filled a glass with water before reaching for the sleeping pills that I'd started taking. They helped me not to lie awake for hours. I shook two into my hand and got as far as bringing them to my mouth before pausing. They helped me get to sleep, but I never dreamed when I took them. I laughed at myself, the reflection staring back at me from the bathroom mirror joining in, more grimace than amusement. Was I really going to listen to the mad ramblings of an old woman?

I dropped the pills in the sink and switched the tap on, watching them disappear down the drain. It seemed I was. I don't know what that said about me. Maybe that I was even madder than she was.

The bed was cold when I got in, and I couldn't help but extend an arm across to the other side of it where Frankie had once lain. I could picture him there, could almost see the bright blue eyes, the way his lips had curved when he'd smiled, and how he'd sounded when he laughed. And even more painfully I could recall the way he'd looked when we'd made love, the sounds he'd made, and the way it had been so right between us.

I watched the hours tick by, the clock passing four in the morning before I finally fell asleep.

* * * *

The river was louder than usual, evidence, along with the dampness of the surrounding trees and the grass beneath my feet, that it had rained recently. I jogged through the undergrowth, eager to reach our meeting spot. It had been days since I'd last seen him, the opportunity to slip away without anyone asking questions not presenting itself. I hoped he'd be there. I needed to see him so desperately that it hurt. Feeling his bare skin against mine as his body arched up in the throes of passion was the only thing that made life worth living.

Looking back, I didn't know how I'd managed to spend so long denying my feelings for him. I'd watched him from afar but hadn't made any attempts to converse with him, looking away the moment his gaze strayed in my direction. I should probably thank my sister for forcing me into the position of finally making my desires known. It was only her expressing her own interests that had spurred me into action.

Wait! A sister? I didn't have a sister, did I? I was an only child. So why could I see a girl with long, red hair as clear as day in my head? And I knew that her name was Madeleine. She scared me. She did things, she and my mother, that weren't… normal. And it wasn't just the things they did. It was the fact that they enjoyed them. I wasn't like them. I didn't take enjoyment in other people's suffering. I would never be like them.

My enjoyment came from the man I was on my way to see, the man whose face I struggled to picture. Why was that? How could I see a sister I didn't have, but not the face of the man I loved? And I did love him. We'd whispered those words to each other on several occasions, the knowledge filling me full of a joy I'd never expected to experience.

The clearing was empty as I arrived. He wasn't here yet. It wasn't a problem. I could wait. There was no amount of time I wouldn't wait for him. Wait for who? I came to a halt at the side of the river, something stopping me from looking down into the rushing water.

Embrace the dreams!

I wasn't sure where the voice came from, only that it shouldn't exist in this place, in this time. It made me want to drop my gaze to the river in the hope of seeing my reflection. My heart started to pound, and I didn't know why the thought scared me so much. I knew what I looked like. I took a deep breath, gathering myself for what was about to come, and then I looked down.

The raging river settled immediately, the rushing waters going still, and the sun appearing from behind a cloud. The change in conditions provided a surface so clear that a mirror couldn't have given a better reflection. The face staring back at me was all wrong. I leaned forward to get a better look, lifting a hand to check that the red hair I could see was indeed mine. Red hair. An upturned nose. Green eyes clouded with confusion. It was me, but it wasn't me. Who was I? And who was I here to meet?

The river faded away to nothing, and I found myself back on the edge of the forest. It was another day. I didn't know how I knew that. I just did. Like I knew that whoever I was in this dream was a me that had lived long before. Pieces were starting to slot into place just like Gloria had said they would. Gloria! Who was Gloria? I didn't know a Gloria. Did I? My steps took me through the forest again, the path the same as the one I'd just taken. This time, I knew he was there waiting for me. Craving answers, I quickened my pace. If I dallied for too long, I might find myself back where I'd started, stuck in a never-ending loop that revealed nothing.

When I reached the river, there was a figure standing with his back to me. I stopped at the edge of the trees, something in my head telling me to leave while I still could, that nothing good would come of getting answers. The figure started to turn, and I took a step back. Run or stay? If I ran, I would never know.

And then it was too late. The man had seen me, a broad smile lighting up his face and those familiar blue eyes sparkling with joy. The man was Frankie. It had always been him. I think deep down, I'd always known that. But I'd hidden the truth from myself. I'd shied away from it. He ran toward me with his arms outstretched. "Estienne, I feared you would not be able to get away. I have waited a long time. But now that does not matter because you are here."

Despite the fact that he was speaking French, I could understand him. And then he was in my arms, and we were kissing hungrily as if we had not seen each other for weeks rather than days. He was the first to pull away and I could only stare at him, my gaze roving over every inch of his beautiful face. His brow furrowed and he reached up to palm my cheek. "Estienne, my love, what is wrong? Why do you look at me like that?"

Estienne. My name was Estienne. I lived on the outskirts of a French village with my mother and sister. And François was the light in my life that I'd never known I needed until I'd finally plucked up the courage to invite him to the river with me. It was there that I'd kissed him for the first time and been lucky enough that he'd returned my passion. He was everything to me, my friend, my lover, my husband, even if such a thing wasn't permitted.

How could he look exactly the same, when I knew that these events had happened hundreds of years ago? I lifted a trembling hand to his cheek, almost expecting him to be transparent and my hand to go straight through him. It didn't. Instead, his skin was warm and soft beneath my palm.

"I missed you, that's all." I was speaking French too, despite the fact that I'd only ever studied the language for a couple of years at school. But then, that was Daniel, not Estienne. Except, I knew I was both of them.

The dreams had never been dreams. They'd always been memories. Memories shaken loose by Frankie's reappearance in my life. Gloria had been right. I had been resistant to the truth, but it was right here in front of me, and it explained the instantaneous connection between myself and Frankie. We hadn't needed to fall in love because we'd already been in love. It was just that I'd been in a different body.

I lowered my lips to his and kissed him again. He tasted of sunlight and sugar, of days spent entwined together where nothing else mattered except for the two of us. I laughed and it was full of joy, full of optimism for the future. He was mine and I was his and no one could stand in our way.

Dark clouds started to gather above our heads, and Frankie looked up.

I shook my head in denial. "No!"

He lowered his gaze to mine, a question in his eyes.

"No, I won't let you take him from me."

Fingers curled around my shoulders. "Estienne, calm down. It's just a rainstorm. It can't hurt us."

But it could. I knew it could. And it would. It would rip us apart. It would change everything, and life would never be the same again. I blinked, and Frankie was gone. I wanted to cry. I wanted to rage at the world and ask it why.

I blinked again, and I was in the cottage where I knew I lived, but I was bound, my wrists and ankles tied tightly with thick rope. I was propped up against the bed, the same bed where François and I had just made love. I'd been stupid and reckless, making an assumption that my mother and sister would not be back 'til late. Only they'd returned early, and they'd caught us.

And then they'd taken him. They'd taken François.

I struggled against the bindings, desperation lending me greater strength. I needed to find him before they did him any harm. If I could get free, I could talk to my mother. I could reason with her and if that didn't work, I would beg. François and I would leave the village. We would travel far from here and my mother would never have to see me again. It didn't matter that we had no money. Nothing mattered except for the two of us being together.

We both knew farming. We could find work. They wouldn't even have to pay us. Food and shelter would be enough. We would need to pretend that we were brothers rather than lovers, but we would do whatever was necessary. We would be careful, just as we'd always been. Until today, when I'd thrown it all away for the sake of a few hours in the arms of the man I loved.

But first, before any of that could happen, I needed to find a way of getting free.

I cast an eye around the cottage. There was a knife in the cupboard, one that my mother used to skin rabbits. Was it in there? Or had she taken it with her? I prayed she hadn't, not just because I needed it, but because I didn't want to think about what she might be doing with it if it was on her person. I shuffled forward, managing to reach the cupboard in a series of awkward, halting movements that left me *panting with exertion. I hardly dared to look as I opened it with my bound hands.*

The knife was there in the back of the cupboard. It took lying on my side and maneuvering my body half into the cupboard to be able to reach it, but I finally had it in my hand. Progress was slow as I set to work on the rope binding my ankles. It didn't take long for blisters to appear on the hand holding the knife, but I didn't stop. I couldn't, not when François's life depended on it. No one else was going to save him. No one was going to venture this way in such bitter weather.

Therefore, I was the only one who could rescue him from my mother and sister's clutches. I kept telling myself that they wouldn't hurt him, that they would only be interested in scaring him enough to make him stay away from me, but I didn't really believe that. I'd seen what they were both capable of. I'd turned a blind eye to it because they were family, and they were the only one I had.

I made plans as I continued to saw through the rope. We'd go along with whatever they demanded. We wouldn't see each other, but when the time was right and we'd gathered enough provisions to last for at least a few weeks, we'd run away together.

It would be hard on François. He'd be leaving his brother alone to tend the land, but he would see that it was the only course of action. He wouldn't forsake me. He would realize that there was no alternative when my mother would be watching us like a hawk from this day forward.

The rope around my ankles gave way and I started on the one tethering my wrists, using my feet to steady the knife. Where had they taken him? The only shelter outside of the cottage was the barn, but there was nothing in there except for a few animals and… My pulse began to race. My mother kept things in there – dark things that she used for her magic that I'd been only too happy not to look too closely at. They wouldn't use them on François, would they? And if so, to what end?

Time kept ticking away, each separate strand of the rope seeming to take forever to get through, but eventually I was free. I didn't stop for a coat, stumbling shirtless and barefoot out into the snow, the cold air licking at my chest. I made straight for the barn, but I knew even before I got there that something was very wrong. The air wasn't right, the wind picking up and dragging the snow with it until it eddied around me like a whirlpool. Determined to get to François, I carried on regardless. I'd gotten no more than halfway when a flash of blue light came. It only lasted for a few seconds, but it was bright enough to illuminate the entire sky and make me cover my eyes with my hands.

Once the light had faded away, I broke into a run. What had they done? As I neared the barn, my mother and sister stepped out of it. I hid behind a tree, watching as they headed back to the cottage, their steps light and their backs ramrod straight. Once inside, they would realize that I had freed myself and they would come after me, which meant that there was no time to waste. They'd probably tied François up the same way they had me.

I winced at the creak of the barn door as I pushed it open and stepped inside. "François?"

My voice was barely a whisper. Had he been standing right next to me I doubt he would have heard me. Therefore, the lack of answer came as no surprise. I repeated it again, but this time louder as I peered into the gloom. "François, where are you? I've come to get you out of here."

Silence.

I crept forward, listening carefully for any sort of sound. Had they gagged him? Is that why he couldn't answer? I rounded a corner and stopped dead. They'd left a torch burning, which meant I had no problem seeing the thing that hadn't been there earlier. I swallowed nervously as I stepped closer to the stone gargoyle. I don't know how I knew, but there was no doubt in my mind that this was all that was left of François. I laid a hand on the cold stone, its façade blurring as tears streamed down my cheeks.

The surface was unyielding against my forehead as I rested my head against the hooked nose of the gargoyle, and I imagined that I could feel François in there, trapped and alone, because I'd been stupid and selfish and put him in harm's way for a few snatched hours together. A solid weight lodged in my chest and I recognized it as pure hopelessness. I wanted to crumple to the ground and wail. I wanted to hit something, but again, that would have been selfish. I'd done this to him, so the least I could do was stay strong. "I'm so sorry, my love. I'll talk to my mother. I'll make her see sense. I'll make her see that she has to reverse the spell and free you."

"I don't have to do anything."

I turned slowly to find my mother standing behind me. Of Madeleine, there was no sign. My mother had always made for a particularly intimidating figure, and being her son did not make me immune to it. She might love me, but she'd always resented the fact that I wasn't like her or my sister, that I would never be like them. That same streak of cruelty just didn't run through me like it did through them. I'd never known my father. I suspected my mother had killed him when she'd no longer had any use for him, but I assumed I'd taken after him rather than her, and I couldn't help being glad about it. "What have you done to him?"

My mother's smile was full of triumph. "I have been practicing some new spells." Her smile grew wider as her gaze strayed past me to the gargoyle. "I would say that they are sufficient, wouldn't you?"

I dashed away the remainder of the tears still on my cheeks. "Please..." I stood taller. My mother respected strength far more than she did a sniveling idiot. "Let him go. I promise never to see him again. You have my word. I just want him to live his life. He doesn't deserve this. He's a kind and gentle man."

My mother stepped forward and curled her fingers around the tip of the gargoyle's wing. "Oh, he'll get to live. Don't worry."

A beacon of hope ignited in my heart. "So, it is reversible? You'll let him go? He won't give you any trouble. You will have scared him enough that I doubt he will even look in my direction."

If my mother heard me, she gave no indication of it. "He'll get to live. He'll live for hundreds of years, the majority trapped in stone. The rest of his time he'll spend searching for something he can never have. It's exactly what a sinner like him deserves."

Anger bubbled within me, spilling over like the water in the river did after torrential rain. "What about me? Am I not a sinner too? I approached him. *I kissed* him. *There isn't a part of his body I haven't touched with my hands, with my mouth, with my tongue." It pleased me when my mother cringed away from me as if I'd burnt her. Good. Let her be disgusted. I didn't care anymore. If she wasn't going to release François, then my life was over. I would wither away to nothing like a dry leaf in the sun. It would prove a mercy if she killed me.*

Her face turned red, and for a few seconds we glowered at each other. Mother versus son locked in a battle of wills I had no chance of winning. Finally, her eyes narrowed. "I can fix you. I will find a spell that removes the perversion from your soul. It won't be a pleasant process, but when it's done, you will thank me for it."

"No!" I shook my head. "I will never thank you. I will always hate you for this, for what you've done. You and Madeleine."

Her mouth settled into a straight line, and then she darted forward. I was too slow, unable to avoid her as her fingers wrapped around my biceps in a grip so tight that I was sure the blood supply must have been cut off. "You will come back to the cottage, and we will start the process. We will purge you first. And then we will take it from there."

I attempted to dig my heels in, but she must have been exerting something stronger than pure physical strength on me, and I found myself dragged from the barn, and out into the snow. And more importantly, away from François. Or at least what was left of him. Was he conscious in there? Had he been able to hear me? Perhaps it was selfish that I hoped he'd at least heard my regret, that he would know that I'd never been complicit in any of this happening. My fate didn't look any brighter than his. I was glad. I didn't deserve to be happy when his existence had become so miserable.

I jerked upright, my gasping breaths sounding loud in the room. For the next few minutes, I was locked in a struggle to take in enough oxygen, my chest heaving with the effort. The sheets were drenched. I was drenched. And I couldn't slow the rapid pounding of my heart, my fingers trembling so much as I brought my hand to my face that it was an effort to guide them in the right direction to wipe the sweat off my brow. I concentrated on the simple action of taking in oxygen and then releasing it. At least it used to be simple. At the moment, it was anything but. It was a battle I wasn't sure I was going to win. Could you have a heart attack brought on by a nightmare? Except… I closed my eyes, images from the dream flickering behind my eyelids like the world's cruelest slideshow. As the light gradually grew brighter in the room, I was forced to face the truth.

Crazy as it seemed — and it was crazy — I'd been reliving memories of a past life. A life I'd lived hundreds of years ago that had involved Frankie. The two of us had loved intensely, even if only for a short time before being forcibly separated. I might inhabit a different body, but Frankie was still Frankie, trapped in the gargoyle by the actions of Estienne's mother, by *my* mother, and he'd barely aged. No wonder there'd been so many questions he couldn't answer. Poor Frankie.

I hung my head, grief welling up in me so intensely that it was all I could do not to scream. He'd suffered so much, was still suffering. Because I knew where he was now. He was back in the gargoyle, back in the statue I'd always felt strangely drawn to and had never been able to understand why. Well, it all made perfect sense now — my subconscious able to discern something my conscious mind couldn't.

The muscles of my calves trembled as I lowered my legs over the side of my bed. From shock? From adrenaline? I wasn't sure. Fate had brought Frankie back into my life and there had to be a reason. There had to be something I could do. But what? I was a history lecturer. I didn't have the skills to deal with… I swallowed. Witchcraft. There was no other word for it. Estienne had been brought up in a family practicing the dark arts, and even he had had no protection against it.

But as Daniel Smith, I was even less prepared. But I had to try. At the very least, I needed to go to Frankie. I needed to let him know that I knew the truth, and that I understood that he'd never left me.

Thoughts tumbled chaotically over and over in my brain as I stumbled to the bathroom and into the shower, still struggling with my new reality, with the fact that I was Estienne. Had Frankie known who I was? I didn't think he had. What did that mean? That he'd fallen for me in spite of that? Did he think I was a pale facsimile of the lover he'd been forced to leave hundreds of years ago? None of the answers mattered in the grand scheme of things, but that didn't stop them from plaguing me. All that mattered was freeing François, if such a thing was even possible.

I dressed in a daze, and didn't bother with breakfast, or even coffee, the desire to get to campus superseding everything. Despite the hopelessness of the situation, it seemed like the only option. Picking my car keys up from the table by the door, I wrenched the door open, only to find a figure standing on my doorstep.

Chapter Twenty-two

Daniel

"Richard, Jesus, you scared me. What are you doing lurking on my doorstep at…?" I checked my watch. "Not even seven."

His gaze trailed slowly over me. "I could ask you the same question."

I laughed. "It's my doorstep. I'm allowed to be on it whenever I want to be."

His nod was long and slow. "True. Are you going to work?"

I dropped my gaze to the clothes I wore, registering the items I'd chosen for the first time—suit trousers and a sweatshirt. Not the best combination. But then looking good hadn't exactly been at the forefront of my mind. Clothes had been nothing more than a means to an end. Something better than stepping out in my pajamas. "No. Imagine Marjorie's face if I turned up looking like this. She'd have a heart attack."

"She would." Richard turned his head to scan the street. At this time of the morning, it was almost empty, save for the occasional car passing. "So where are you going in such a rush?"

"Who said I'm rushing?"

He arched an eyebrow, dropping his gaze pointedly to the laces on my trainers, the ones I hadn't even bothered to tie. Crouching down, I tied first one, and then the other, Richard's gaze burning into the top of my bowed head the whole time. "I left you loads of messages, Dan. You never called me back."

Laces tied, I straightened again. "Sorry, I've been…"

"Been what?"

I shrugged. Richard still hadn't said what he was doing here. He lived on the other side of Sheffield, and even if he'd had a sudden attack of work-based conscientiousness — which was unlikely — my house wasn't on his route to the university. Was he that concerned about me? I clapped him on the arm, flashing a smile that I hoped went some way to being reassuring. "It's sweet of you to come and check up on me, but I'm absolutely fine."

I went to walk past him, but he moved to block me. "Are you?"

"Yeah, why wouldn't I be?"

"You look like hell, Dan."

I ran a hand through my hair, hair that I hadn't bothered to brush. I hadn't shaved either. "I'm fine." Besides, he was a fine one to talk. Richard didn't look too good himself. He was abnormally pale with dark shadows under his eyes and lines of strain etched around his mouth. I hadn't managed to convince him to see a doctor, but there was obviously something wrong with him.

I tried another sidestep, but Richard planted himself in my way again. What was he doing? I got that he was worried, but I didn't have time for this conversation. I had more important things to worry about, like my lover of hundreds of years being trapped in stone.

Richard's hand landed on my shoulder, the pressure firm but insistent. "Let's go inside and talk."

"Talk about what?"

He gave a shrug. "Anything you need to talk about. Sometimes we get confused about stuff. And it's better to talk it through rather than run off half-cocked and end up looking like an idiot."

The pressure on my shoulder increased, fingers trying to steer me back toward my front door as I stood my ground. There was a stillness to Richard's body language that I wasn't used to seeing, and a steadfastness in his gaze. It was like looking at a completely different person, and I didn't like it, tendrils of unease starting to snake their way down my spine. "I need to go somewhere."

"Where, Dan?"

Why was he so interested in where I was going? What was it to him? "My mum called, my dad's not been feeling too good, so I promised I'd go round and see them both. Give my considered medical opinion about whether he needs to see a doctor or not." The attempt at a joke fell flat, the steel in Richard's gaze not softening in the slightest. "So... if you'll excuse me." I levered Richard's fingers from my shoulder, almost pushing him out of the way in my haste to get past.

I'd made it halfway down the path when Richard spoke. "You don't want to go there, Dan. Nothing good can come of it."

I turned back to face him. "Go where? To my parents' house?"

He sauntered toward me, his steps measured. "To campus. That's where you're going, right?"

The trickle of unease grew into a flood. There was no way he could know that. He'd said it himself — that I wasn't dressed for work, so why else would he think I'd go there? "I'm not going to the campus. I told you where I'm going."

Richard's exhale was long and slow. He averted his gaze and stared into the distance for a few seconds, as if he was making his mind up about something. When his gaze settled back on me, there was something distinctly eerie about it. "Let's go inside, Daniel."

I took a step back, shaking my head as I did so. "I don't want to go inside with you."

"I see." Richard drew himself up to his full height. "I guess it's time we stopped playing games then. I won't let you go to him."

"Him?" My voice sounded impossibly reedy. It was the voice of someone already on the ropes, who wasn't sure why the punches kept coming. I already had enough to deal with without this, whatever this was.

Richard's mouth twisted into an ugly shape. "I won't use his name. He doesn't deserve it."

"You've never even met him."

Richard's laugh was decidedly condescending. "Oh, you still don't get it, do you, Daniel?"

"Get what?" I took another step back, the gate pressing into my back. All I had to do was open it and get in the car, but some sixth sense told me it wouldn't be that simple. Richard was too calm, too self-assured. His body language said that he had everything under control, that he had me under control. "Why don't you explain it to me?"

He prowled a step closer. "Did you sleep well last night?"

He knew about the dreams. It wasn't possible, but then my life had become a whole mass of things that weren't possible. What was one more? "Who are you?"

He came to a stop directly in front of me. "Who am I? I'm sure if you think about it for long enough you can work it out."

A trickle of blood appeared from one nostril and he swiped at it angrily. "This body is so damn resistant."

This body? I stared at him, unwilling to face the truth, even though I knew it was the only possible explanation. There was only one person who would do everything in their power to stop me from freeing Frankie, and that was the very same person who had put him there in the first place. "Cecile?"

Richard laughed, but it wasn't his laugh. It belonged to someone else. "Are you pleased to see me again? It's been a long time since you were able to look into my eyes and recognize me." I was numb with shock, incapable of doing anything to stop him as he lifted his hand and ran gentle fingers through my hair. I shuddered at the touch, Richard frowning, my reaction obviously displeasing him.

And then something changed in his face, the mask sliding away to reveal terror in its place, and I knew I was looking at Richard again. He grabbed hold of my sweatshirt, pulling me closer to him. "I can't stop her, Dan. She's too strong. I keep fighting her, but I'm getting weaker. I don't know how much longer I can hold her off. I'm sorry. She's said things, done things, that I wouldn't have done, but I couldn't stop her. I tried. I really did. I'm so sorry. I just want it to stop. Make it stop."

I covered his hands with mine. "You have to keep fighting. You can't let her win."

Richard's eyes were imploring. "I can't. She's in my head. At first, she was happy just to take over for short periods, but now she wants all of me. She's trying to push me so deep inside my own head that I won't be able to crawl out of there. I'll stop existing. Help me, Dan, please. Don't let her do it."

That's what the nosebleeds had been about. Now, I thought about it, they'd always preceded a change in his behavior in some way. Of course they had. That's when Cecile had taken over, the nosebleed a result—as were the headaches, no doubt—of Richard doing his best to fight it. "I'll—" But it was already too late, the mask sliding back into place. She shook her head. "See what I mean. So damn resistant." She let go of my sweatshirt, her fingers moving to my neck.

"You have to let him go."

She gave a little laugh. "I will, when I've finished with him, but I still need him at the moment. I can't be here without a body."

I tried to pull away from her, but she held me in place. "Don't worry, you can help your friend. I can make you forget. That sounds good, doesn't it? Things can go back to normal. No more stress. No more bad dreams. No more longing for things you can't have."

It became a struggle to keep my eyes open. I didn't know whether it was something Cecile was doing, or whether it was just a combination of a lack of sleep and the strange melodic quality her voice had taken on. All I knew was that staying awake had become an impossibility. I would just close my eyes for a minute. What harm could it do?

"That's it, give in to it, Daniel. And then you'll feel better. I'll make you forget."

Would that be good? It would certainly take the pain of losing Frankie away. But it would leave him trapped in the gargoyle forever, no one knowing, no one caring. For that reason, I fought whatever it was she was doing to me. Only, my eyelids were getting heavier and heavier. In fact, my whole body was. As if someone was pressing me down into the ground. I needed to close my eyes. I couldn't fight it any longer.

It was the screech of tires that brought me back to myself, Cecile's grip slackening as a police car pulled up at the curb. Not in front of my house, but in front of Gloria's, Gloria meeting them at the gate as two officers climbed out of the car — one male, one female.

She lifted an arm to point in our direction and I took the opportunity to put some distance between myself and Cecile, and whatever it was she'd been doing to me.

Gloria sniffed, the sound so loud that it carried across the space between the two gardens. "It was that man, the one with the blue coat. He was the one looking through my windows, officer. I called you straightaway so that you could come and deal with him. I've been an active member of neighborhood watch for years. It's part of my job to keep the neighborhood safe and I take that role extremely seriously. It might only be looking through windows today, but what will he be up to tomorrow? That's how sexual predators start. I watched a documentary about it once. You need to arrest him before his behavior escalates to something truly dangerous. People like him think they can get away with their questionable habits. He probably thought that I was too old to make a stand. Well, he's wrong. You need to arrest him for the good of the community."

Richard let out a snort as both officers turned their focus his way. The female police officer, who gave the impression of being the most senior, shared a look with her partner before both of them made their way toward my house, Gloria following in their wake. Why had Cecile been looking through her windows? Or had it been Richard, then? But then what reason would he have had to be looking through her windows? Gloria obviously knew something. She had after all been the one to tell me to let the dreams show me the truth. Did Cecile know that? Was that why she was interested in Gloria?

The two officers paused on the other side of the gate, the male officer unfastening the latch and pulling it open. He made a sweeping gesture with his arm. "If you could step outside, sir, so that we can talk about this, I would appreciate it."

When Richard made no move to do so, the female officer's eyebrows rose. "Sir, we can do this here, or down at the station. Your choice."

Richard's gaze moved to Gloria, reluctance etched in every atom of his being as he grudgingly followed their directive. "You do know how ridiculous this accusation is, don't you? I'm not in the habit of looking through anyone's windows, but if I was going to, I'd hardly choose some dried-up hag whose days when she *might* have been worth looking at are decades behind her."

I followed Richard out of the gate, mainly because that's the goal I'd been trying to achieve anyway, so it seemed stupid not to do it while I had the opportunity. The female officer didn't seem to take kindly to Richard's words, her straight back and set jaw clearly demonstrating the fact. "There's no need to be rude, sir. If there's been some sort of mistake, then we can work it out without resorting to petty insults. That's why we're here." She turned her attention to Gloria. "Now, if you could tell us exactly what happened, we can get to the bottom of this."

Gloria nodded eagerly. "I was in my living room." She pointed back to her house, indicating the closest window. "I was still in my nightgown at the time and when I looked up, he was there, just staring at me, his eyes roving all over me."

Richard's laugh was cut short as he received a searing glance from the female officer. Whether it was a case of a female solidarity or something else, she seemed far more inclined to accept Gloria's version of events, while the male officer seemed to be going through the motions as he scribbled a few notes on a notepad.

He glanced up from it. "Did you feel threatened?"

Gloria's nod was so pronounced that her chin wobbled. "I felt extremely threatened. For all I knew he could have had a knife, or even a gun. He might have been about to force his way in. I wasn't even sure I'd locked the door. I was so scared that I called you straightaway."

Richard's sigh was long and pronounced. "You don't actually believe this stuff that she's coming up with, do you? She's obviously living in a fantasy world. She's probably saying the stuff she wants to happen. I got straight out of my car and came here. Isn't that right, Dan? He'll tell you."

His gaze when it met mine held a level of challenge. I looked past him to Gloria. She glanced at the police to make sure they weren't looking her way and then mouthed the word "go."

I got it in a sudden rush of understanding. She was creating a diversion so that I could get to Frankie. I took back all the times—of which there were many—where I'd referred to her as an interfering busybody. "I wouldn't know. I was in the house. He was already here when I reached the front door."

The female officer cocked her head to one side. "So... he could have gone next door first?"

I deliberately didn't look Richard's way, fearing what I might see on his face. "It's possible. I can't account for what he was doing when I couldn't see him."

"And do you know this man?"

Not at the moment, not with the interloper he's harboring. "Vaguely. We work together."

The male officer made another note in his book.

I cast a quick look at my car. It was a tantalizing few meters away. "Listen, speaking of work, I really need to get there. Do you... need me for this conversation?"

The male officer's gaze slid to Gloria, and she shook her head vehemently. "I know Daniel. I've known him for years. He's a good man. He's not involved in this." She lifted her hand to point a finger at Richard. "It's all him."

Richard wasn't looking at Gloria, though. He was looking at me. "Don't do this, Dan. You'll regret it."

I slid a hand in my pocket to wrap my fingers around the reassuring outline of my car key.

"Dan!"

There was a whole world of warning wrapped up in that single word.

The female officer moved to block Richard's view of me. "Sir, I don't think you realize how serious this allegation is."

"Oh, I realize how serious it is. I just know that she's lying through her teeth."

Gloria pressed a hand to her chest and made a sound of shock. I had to admire her acting ability. "I would never... I know what I saw as clear as day. I'm not in the habit of dragging somebody's character through the mud for absolutely no reason. But I should be able to walk around my own house in my night clothes without fear of being watched."

"She's a barefaced liar!"

I didn't wait to hear anymore. It was likely the conversation would go on for some time, which was exactly what I needed. I just hoped Gloria was going to be okay, that Cecile wouldn't do anything to hurt her. I still hadn't recovered from that strange feeling that had stolen over me, simply from the touch of her fingers and the timbre of her voice. How had she done that? Except I knew the answer, didn't I? She was a witch. There'd been no words though, no incantation. She hadn't even had anything with her, or not that I'd been able to see. I supposed there could have been something in Richard's pocket. I didn't want to believe that she could be so powerful that she could perform magic with nothing but thought.

The idea made a shiver run down my spine as I slammed the car door shut, fastened my seatbelt, and started the engine. I could feel Richard's eyes burning into me, but I refused to look up and acknowledge it. Gloria had given me the gift of time, and I didn't intend to waste a single moment of it. Would the police arrest Richard? Given his demeanor when they'd questioned him, and the lack of respect he'd shown to Gloria, it was possible. If he'd had any sense, he wouldn't have denied it, and instead come up with a plausible excuse for peering through Gloria's windows, but I wasn't going to complain when his belligerence had worked in my favor.

I parked on the street outside the university instead of in my usual parking spot. The last thing I needed was to be spotted by Marjorie, who had a habit of getting there at the crack of dawn. Either that, or she didn't actually go home. I grimaced as I got out of the car and remembered my mismatched clothes. Being seen by anybody probably wasn't a good idea, but it was a little too late to worry about that. If any of my students did see me, they'd probably assume I was having some sort of breakdown, and they'd be half right.

As it was, the campus was empty apart from a couple of workers emptying the bins next to the dining hall. Figuring they were too busy doing their jobs to be interested in what I was up to, I made a beeline for the familiar stone figure on the far side of the campus, my pulse beating a rapid tattoo as I grew closer.

Once I came to a stop in front of it, I found I didn't know what to say. I was assuming Frankie had some level of consciousness within it, that Cecile hadn't been charitable enough to give him blessed oblivion. She'd want him to suffer. She'd want him to be aware of all the things he was missing out on and couldn't experience. Therefore, I needed to stop standing there like an idiot and say something.

Chapter Twenty-three

Frankie

After a long week of worrying why Daniel hadn't been at work, he was here. Right in front of me. He looked terrible. It was obvious he hadn't shaved in days, and the dark shadows under his eyes said that there hadn't been a lot of sleep going on either. Why? It couldn't just be about me, could it? Had something happened to his family?

It made me ache to reach out and console him. Except, without arms, or a voice, it wasn't possible. I was an inanimate lump of cold stone. Things would go the same way they had before. He would get what he needed to off his chest, and then he would walk away. And as for me, my heart would break that little bit more.

There was a slight tremor to his fingers as he laid them on the stone. I imagined lifting my hand and lining my fingers up with his so that our palms were pressed together. I closed my eyes — figuratively speaking anyway — and I recalled the feel of his skin, how soft it had been, how right it had felt. The memory was bittersweet.

"Frankie!"

The word was full of so much longing that my eyes snapped open. He was staring straight at me and if I'd had any breath to hold, I would have held it. He couldn't know that I was in here. Unless Gloria had gone back on her word and had told him, but even then, he wouldn't sound so sure. There'd been a certainty in the way he'd said it rather than it being a question.

When Daniel finally started talking, his words came out in a rush, his hand still resting against the stone. "I don't know what to say to you. There's so much and none of it seems enough." He shook his head and seemed to take a moment to gather himself, his voice firmer and his words slower. "I can feel you in there. I've always been able to feel you in there, even though I didn't know it. That's why I was drawn to you. That's why I came here and kept talking to you." He paused to give a humorless laugh. "You must have listened to me for hours. All those things I told you about Calvin, and I dread to think what else I droned on about. Maybe you liked to listen, though. Maybe it gave you a break from the nothingness you've had to endure. I hope so."

He glanced back over his shoulder, almost as if he was expecting to find someone standing there. There wasn't, the lawn behind him empty of anything except for a couple of birds pecking at the grass. When he turned back to face me, there were deep furrows on his brow. "I don't know how much time we've got before Richard gets here. Richard is… Wait, I need to tell you some other things before I get to that. You remember my dreams? Well, it turns out they were never dreams. They were memories. Only they were fuzzy and indistinct, and I guess I was doing my best to ignore what they were trying to tell me. Deep down I knew it would be painful and confusing."

I didn't have a clue what he was trying to say. What did his dreams have to do with anything? Or Richard come to that? He'd looked fearful when he'd said the name, but Richard was a friend of his. Why would he be scared of his friend? I had a million questions I wanted to ask and no voice to do it with. All I could do was listen.

"I don't know if you know who I am."

Of course I knew who he was. He was Daniel, the man I'd fallen in love with.

"Maybe on some deeper subconscious level, you do. I think we both did. Either that or its true what they say about soulmates." He gave a wry smile. "Would you listen to me... one day I don't believe in soulmates and reincarnation, and the next..."

Reincarnation?

Daniel took a deep breath in and then let it out slowly. "The dreams were about me and you, but not as we are now. Back when I was..." He swallowed, the action so drawn out that it seemed almost painful. "When I was Estienne."

A ringing started up in my ears. What was he talking about? He couldn't be Estienne. The notion was ridiculous. Except... the more I thought about it, the more it made sense. Daniel had fallen too fast and too hard, even for a man who admitted to having gotten married too quickly. And it explained that instantaneous connection we'd had. If he was Estienne, then... The wave of sadness was intense and all-consuming. If he was the reincarnation of Estienne, it didn't change a single thing. Because even that love — a love that had apparently lasted for centuries hadn't been enough to break the curse.

My time inside the gargoyle would be eternal.

Refusing to give in to a wave of self-pity, I forced myself to focus on what Daniel was saying. "I dreamt it all last night. I remembered everything, and I relived it all. I'm so damn sorry, Frankie, for everything. All of this is my fault. I was selfish. Even from the start, I was selfish. I'd wanted you for so long, but I knew it wasn't a good idea, that it would make life difficult for both of us."

"*It was worth it.*" I knew he couldn't hear me, but even so I needed to say it.

"And then that day... I don't know what I was thinking. It was a huge risk to invite you back to my family's cottage. I knew it, and I did it anyway because I was so desperate to spend time with you. I may not have known that she would do this" — he lifted his hand and slammed it against the stone—"But I knew what she was like, what she was capable of. I turned a blind eye to it, but I knew nonetheless. My mother and my sister both had a darkness inside them, and I worried for years that I carried it as well, that I would wake up one morning and surrender to it."

"You're not like that."

Daniel shook his head. "I did everything I could to get her to reverse the spell, but it was no good. I didn't give up on you, even when you were gone, and she wouldn't tell me where she'd sent you." He rested his head against the stone, and it was like I could feel his frustration and sadness leaching into me. Or maybe that was because I felt the same. I didn't know what to make of Daniel knowing the truth. It made it worse in some ways. Now, we would both be miserable. Daniel would continue to come here, and we would be stuck in an endless loop where he couldn't do anything to help me and he couldn't move on, and I was forced to watch him age.

"I don't know how to get you out." His voice was full of anguish.

"You can't."

Daniel flicked another glance over his shoulder. "She'll be here soon."

"Who?"

"She already tried to stop me once. She said she was going to make me forget, but Gloria intervened. She called the police on Richard, but I don't know how long that'll delay her. She'll talk her way out of it. And she knew everything. She even knew I was coming here."

Daniel wasn't making sense. There was only one person who would be that determined to keep us apart, and she'd been dead for centuries. Was that what Gloria had meant when she'd said that there were still dark forces at play?

Daniel took in a shuddering breath. "Cecile… I don't know how, but she's… in Richard. She's controlling him and he's not strong enough to get rid of her."

"Merde!" Could Cecile do that? But then why would I believe she couldn't? She'd had the power to curse me, so why would it be surprising that she could take over someone's body? Daniel had spoken of his friend numerous times. He'd always been there in the background, offering opinions on our relationship, and expressing a constant desire to meet me and get to know me. Daniel had confided in him, and in doing so had played right into Cecile's hands.

What were the chances of the three of us all finding ourselves in the same place? What did that mean? Gloria had said there would be an end. Was this it? It struck me that she had never said the end would be a happy one. I'd made that assumption because I'd needed something to latch on to, something to keep me going.

"He's here."

There was a man coming across the lawn toward us. It was no surprise to find that it was the same one who had waylaid me at Daniel's house. Even then Cecile had been whispering words of poison into my ear in a bid to separate us. And not just words of poison. There'd been that feeling that I had to do his bidding. It was obvious now that there'd been magic involved. It made me feel better in some way, to know that my decision to leave that day had been based on more than just being susceptible to suggestion. It was lucky that I'd had enough presence of mind to return of my own accord.

I studied him as he drew closer. He didn't look good. There was a sheen of sweat on his forehead, and his skin was pale to the point of making him look sickly. It wasn't until he drew close that I realized he was carrying a sledgehammer. It didn't take a genius to work out what he intended. It wasn't an end I'd ever foreseen. What would happen to me if he smashed the gargoyle to smithereens? Would my consciousness just blink out of existence as if it had never been? The life I'd been living may not have been a life, but it was all I had, and I suddenly wanted to cling on to it with every fiber of my being.

Richard came to a stop in front of us, lifting a shaky hand to wipe the sweat off his brow as his eyes locked on Daniel. "She didn't like that stroke you pulled, Dan."

So, this was Richard then. Not Cecile. That had to be good, right? It meant he was back in control.

Daniel squared his shoulders, and I was proud of him for standing up for himself despite knowing what lurked beneath the surface of his friend. How long could Richard stay in control? Minutes? Hours? If Cecile took over, it would be like a fly taking on a spider. There could only ever be one outcome.

"I didn't pull any stroke. I just didn't dispute it. I assume the police let you go?"

"Once I showed them my credentials, of course they did. They were hardly going to take the word of an old woman over that of an academic."

Daniel nodded as he dropped his gaze. "What's with the sledgehammer?"

"I need her gone, Dan." His gaze skipped past Daniel to land on me. "This is what she wants. She wants this thing gone. I don't know why the hell it's so important to her, but it is. Once I've destroyed it, she'll get out of my head. She'll leave me alone. And I need that, Dan. Surely, you can understand that." He lifted a trembling hand to gesture at himself. "Look at me. My body is breaking down. If I don't do what she wants, she's going to kill me."

He lifted the sledgehammer off the ground and leaned it against his shoulder.

Daniel held his hand up, his expression placating. "You can't do this. There's a person inside this statue. I know it sounds crazy, but Frankie is in there. *She* put him in there, hundreds of years ago. If you destroy it, you destroy him."

Richard gave a short, sharp laugh. When Daniel's countenance didn't change, he sobered quickly. He swallowed, more sweat dripping from his brow. "I'm sorry. I have to do this. It's the only way it ends."

Chapter Twenty-four

Daniel

I lost the ability to breathe as I realized that Richard couldn't be swayed from his intention to destroy the gargoyle. I'd thought that the danger came from the person inside him, that if I could somehow reach *him*, he would be able to keep her at bay, but it seemed that he was as much of a danger as she was.

My gaze darted around the campus in search of salvation, seizing on the sight of a student out for a run. "Do you really think that no one is going to try and stop you? Someone will call the police, and you'll find it much more difficult to wriggle out of their grasp when you're facing charges of criminal damage."

Richard tilted his head to one side as if he was listening, and then nodded. "She says that no one can see us."

Cecile could talk to him. I didn't know why I was still capable of being surprised. His words had been spoken with such a quiet assurance that they sent a chill down my spine. "You're lying."

There was a long pause while I assumed Richard held a conversation in his head. "Try it! Shout for help. See if you can get anyone's attention." He pointed across the campus to where a couple of female students, looking decidedly worse for wear, were wending a none-too-straight route down the path after what appeared to be an all-night bender. "Why don't you try and get their attention?"

"Hey!" They didn't even glance my way. I tried again, louder this time. It had the exact same result, the women continuing on their way.

"I tried to tell you, Dan."

"Shut up." I didn't want to listen to him anymore. He might not be Cecile, but given that he was in league with her, it made him the enemy too. He wasn't a friend. Not any longer. A friend would listen to me. A friend would fight her. But perhaps I was being unfair. The gargoyle was just a gargoyle to him. To me, it was the past and the future all rolled into one, and I would fight for it for as long as I still had breath left in my body.

Richard came forward a step, and I moved to block him, keeping my body between him and the gargoyle, my gaze fixed on the sledgehammer. I wasn't a fighter. I never had been. Estienne hadn't been one either, but it didn't matter. Richard was flesh and blood, and without Cecile in control I had a chance against him. Cecile had already taken Frankie away from me once. Neither her nor one of her minions was going to do it again.

Richard's expression was pained. "Do you really think you can stop me? Have you ever thrown a punch, Dan? Do you remember that time when a fight kicked off in the city center? You almost crapped yourself, and I had to rescue you. Do you remember? What makes you think this time will be any different?"

I looked him dead in the eye. "Because there's a lot more at stake. And I can't let her win."

He stepped to the left, and I shadowed him. He shook his head. "I don't want to hurt you. You're my friend. All you have to do is step aside and let me do this."

"I can't do that."

"Step aside, Dan. I won't ask you again."

There was a wealth of pleading in his voice, but I wasn't about to let it get to me. "No. If you want to get to him, you'll have to come through me. You don't get to kill him without killing me first." Adrenaline coursed through my veins—a dizzying mixture of fear and anticipation taking root.

I saw the sledgehammer swing my way, but there wasn't time to do anything else but twist my body slightly to one side, the head glancing off my arm. It hurt but it hadn't done any real damage.

The next blow slammed into my chest just below my ribs, knocking the wind out of me and sending me staggering backwards. A bit harder and he would have broken something.

Richard backed off a step. "Don't make me do this."

I rubbed a hand over the sore spot on my abdomen. "I'm not making you do anything. If anyone is, it's her."

Richard circled me. "You don't know what it's like, having someone else in your head, someone who can take over at any time and force you not to have control over your own body."

I kept my distance from him, moving as he did. "No, I don't, but you have to know that she's evil, that what she wants you to do is evil. And you're just going to do it."

Richard screwed his face up, almost spitting the words at me. "I have no choice."

"There's always a choice."

He came at me with a far more vicious intent. I ducked out of the way, narrowly avoiding the sledgehammer hitting my left knee.

"She says that he's not worth this."

I avoided another blow. "He is worth it."

"How? What's so special about him?"

"He's sweet, and he's kind, and we belong together."

"She says that in that case you can die together."

The next blow was aimed at my knee again. Only this time it made contact, my knee giving way beneath me as a sharp blast of pain filled my body. I crumpled to the ground, the pain so sharp that it was accompanied by a wave of nausea. Richard went to walk around me, but I launched myself at him, both of us toppling to the ground, the sledgehammer trapped uselessly between our bodies as I pinned him.

I raised my fist and planted it in his face. His expression of shock might have been comical under other circumstances. Pressing my advantage, I did it again, Richard seeming to have no defense for the physical assault. I didn't need to kill him. I just needed to render him unconscious. If he was unconscious then Cecile was too. Or at least that's how I hoped it would work.

I hit him again. I would have kept hitting him, but an invisible force propelled me backwards and I knew what had happened even before I managed to struggle upright and saw Richard's face, or should I say Cecile's face. She'd taken over.

I struggled to my feet, my injured knee unable to bear my full weight. Cecile's gaze was fixed on me as she picked herself up off the ground too. "I should have known that that idiot was incapable of getting the job done." She threw a scathing glance at the discarded sledgehammer. "I won't be needing anything as crude as that."

Maybe I could get to it? Any weapon was better than none. Especially now that I was facing a far worse enemy than simply a determined Richard. Her gaze skirted past me to the gargoyle. "How are you doing, François? How do you like the gift I gave you? It really does keep on giving, doesn't it? It may sound like boasting but you are one of my greatest success stories. I have to say that I'm surprised you have survived this long with your mind intact. You should have gone mad years ago. But then, you always were stubborn. You and your whole family. I remember a summer when you were only a small boy when your crops should have perished. Yet somehow your father managed to tease enough out of the ground to keep your family alive with nothing but sheer bloody-minded persistence. And yes, I did know of you before you decided to defile my son."

Could she see him? At least it told me one thing. He did have a consciousness inside the gargoyle or she wouldn't be wasting her time talking to him. Could he talk back?

She shook her head. "So silent. Always so silent, François. Surely you have things you want to say to me."

I guessed that even if he could, he wouldn't give her the satisfaction.

She laughed and I could hear Cecile in it, even though it was delivered through Richard's voice box. "No matter. It's time to end this once and for all anyway. Although it's been amusing over the years to watch you whore yourself out in an effort to make someone love you, that amusement has grown thin."

I would beg for Frankie's life if I had to. After all, no one was pure evil, not even Cecile. Perhaps there was a shred of goodness in her, if I could only find the right words. "Please… don't do this. I love him. I've always loved him. Even when I couldn't remember him, I loved him." I clasped a hand to my chest to accentuate the point, laying my palm over the place where my heart lay. "You can kill everything else, but you'll never kill that."

A muscle twitched in Cecile's cheek. "So dramatic. So doomed."

I tried a different tack. "Surely, you must realize by now how wrong you were. I can understand thinking that homosexuality was a sin back in the 16th century, but if you've lived since then, you must know that…" It was useless. There was no reasoning with her. She didn't need a reason to hate. She just did. And even the fact that I'd once been her son Estienne didn't matter to her. She'd done horrible things to him once, and she would again given the opportunity.

She lifted her hands, an incantation spilling from her lips, and a bright ball of blue energy started to form between her hands. I planted myself squarely in front of the gargoyle. Frankie was sweet and pure, and I would rather die than see his light go out forever. The ball of energy grew bigger, gathering mass and power.

Something caught my eye on the opposite side of campus, and I tore my gaze away from Cecile to consider the strange sight. Marjorie Rutherford was walking toward us, her long, red hair, which I was used to seeing tied back in some strict authoritarian style, flowing behind her. She was crossing the lawn diagonally, her path bringing her straight to us. Only that would mean that she could see us. How was that possible if no one else could?

Her lips were moving, but she was too far away for me to be able to tell what she was saying. I tore my gaze away from her to find that the ball of blue light had reached epic proportions. Cecile would aim it my way and it would consume me. Would it hurt? Would it be hot? Or cold? Would death be instantaneous, or would it be a long, slow process?

The incantations stopped, the silence almost deafening, and all the time Marjorie grew closer.

Cecile smiled. It was a cold, malicious smile. "Step aside."

The same words that Richard had spoken. Perhaps they were no longer separate entities, but one and the same. Perhaps he no longer existed, bent beneath her will—just another victim of her eternal hatred. My heart was pounding so hard that I could feel it in my throat and my legs were shaking, but I would not move. If she was going to kill Frankie, then I didn't want to remain here anyway. I would embrace my fate.

She sighed. "As you wish."

She pushed the ball of energy my way and I braced myself as it came spinning toward me, its center a mass of raging blue fire.

And then it stopped.

It hung there in the air, as if it couldn't quite decide what it was supposed to do. It was close enough that I could have reached out and touched it. Although, something told me that would have been a very bad idea. There were words being spoken, words like the ones Cecile had said, but they weren't coming from her lips. The words got louder, the ball of light seeming to pulsate in response. It flickered once. Twice. And then it seemed to cave in on itself, going from a raging mass to barely a pin prick in less than the time it would have taken me to blink.

A strange sound came from behind me, and I spun around. I blinked, convinced that the crack that had opened up in the stone façade of the gargoyle must be nothing more than wishful thinking. As I watched, several smaller cracks radiated out from the larger one.

"No!"

Richard's voice. Cecile wasn't happy.

And Marjorie was there. She was happy, a smile on her face. She'd stopped the ball of fire. How? Why?

And then came a flash of light so bright I had to turn my head away or risk being blinded. When it faded, there was no gargoyle, and standing in its place instead was Frankie. I limped over to him, his blue eyes containing a mixture of confusion and wonder. We fell into each other's arms with an instinct as natural as breathing. I held him so tight that it must have bordered on painful, but I couldn't force myself to slacken my grip in case he disappeared. He held on to me just as tightly, the dampness on my neck giving away the fact that there were tears. I buried my nose in his hair breathed him in.

"Well, isn't this a sweet reunion."

Frankie lifted his head to face Cecile, his eyes fierce. "Why do you hate me so much?"

She let out a laugh. "You're a worm, François Damont. You've always been a worm. Your whole family were worms. You should have stayed crawling around in your pitifully small plot of land that you toiled over for so little reward. And you should have stayed away from my family."

I pulled Frankie tight against me. "Leave him alone."

Cecile narrowed her eyes. "Or what?"

Marjorie stepped forward. "Enough! This ends today. I'm sick of us all being tied together century after century. I'm sick of watching the same thing happen over and over again. I want peace. I want to stay dead. Surely, that shouldn't be too much to ask for."

I stared at her, everything clicking into place. Marjorie had changed, just like Richard had changed. Only her personality had changed for the better. And there was only one person missing from this little reunion.

"Madeleine?"

She turned her head my way, her red hair blowing in the breeze. "Hello, Estienne."

Frankie was staring at her like he'd seen a ghost. I could only imagine how overwhelming this was for him. There were four people in this reunion. Except really, there were seven. He was the only one who had stayed the same, the only one who hadn't changed over the centuries—not physically anyway. I took his hand, interlocking our fingers together in a way that I hoped broadcasted that I was there, that whatever happened I wasn't going anywhere.

Gaze fixed on Madeleine, Cecile lifted her hands again. "You can't win."

Madeleine lifted hers too. "We'll see."

They both started to chant, the archaic language spilling from their lips. Sweat appeared on both of their brows, whatever they were trying to do seeming to take a great deal of effort. And all Frankie and I could do was watch, and hope that the right side prevailed in the end. I had to assume that was Madeleine. She'd managed to stop Cecile before, but there was a big difference between catching her unawares and taking her on face to face. The air started to crackle with electricity, both the antagonists speaking faster, the foreign-sounding words harsh and guttural.

My heart leapt as Cecile staggered backwards, but she regained her composure within seconds. The words were coming thick and fast now, aimed like bullets. Cecile seemed to be weakening, her back—Richard's back—bending under the onslaught, and her speech becoming less strident the longer it went on. Did that mean Madeleine was winning?

And then Richard crumpled to the ground and lay still. The air settled again, like it would after an electric storm, and I was surprised to see the world continuing as normal outside our little bubble—students walking past laughing, a man walking his dog.

I inclined my head toward Richard. "Is he…?"

Madeleine shook her head. "No. He'll be okay." She crouched over him and pressed two fingers to his forehead. She uttered a few words, the bruises on his face disappearing. "He won't remember what happened. He'll wake soon."

Frankie cleared his throat. "And Cecile?"

"Gone. For good."

God, I hoped that was true.

Madeleine straightened, brushing her hands over her skirt. "I don't have much longer. I haven't had as much trouble with Marjorie as Cecile did with Richard, but she's starting to get restless. Actually, you should be grateful that Richard was so resistant. It took a lot of Cecile's power away. I doubt you would have gotten to this point had she had an easier ride. If you have any questions to ask me, I'd ask them now."

Questions. It was hard to know where to start. I shook my head, Frankie not seeming to be faring much better.

Madeleine smiled. "Okay. I'll tell you what I can, what I think you'll wish you knew when everything stops being so much of a shock. I don't know if she did it deliberately, but the curse tied us all together irrevocably." She frowned. "I assume she did, that she wanted to make sure that it could never be broken, and the only way she could do that was to ensure a way of returning. But then the same was true for all of us."

"Why?"

Madeleine laughed. "Why did she do anything? Because she could. Because it made her happy to watch others suffer. It might have been triggered by your sexual preferences, but it was never about that. Not really. She lived to hate. She fed upon people's pain." She lifted a hand to point at me. "You were always there whenever Frankie was freed."

I frowned. "I don't think…"

"You were. You just don't remember it."

She turned her attention to Frankie. "Raphael. Jeremy. The rest. They were all Estienne. It was just that sometimes that connection was easier to make than at other times."

Frankie looked like someone had slapped him in the face with a wet fish. I got it. It was a lot to take in, but Madeleine hadn't finished yet. "And as soon as your souls were together, as soon as you'd spoken your first words, it triggered the reappearance of both Cecile and me. But we could only exist in someone else's body, someone who was already on the periphery of your life." She looked down. "I liked this one. I got to have red hair again." She picked up a strand of it and ran it between her fingers. It reminded me of how much she'd liked her hair when we were growing up. "I have to admit that at first,

I meddled as much as Cecile did, that I took delight in keeping you both apart." She grimaced, her expression showing regret. "And I'm truly sorry for that."

I squeezed Frankie's hand tighter, and he squeezed back. "What changed?"

She sighed. "I don't know. I guess I never had the same hatred that Cecille had to fuel me." Her gaze skipped over to Frankie. "In many ways, I was stuck in the same cycle as you were, the only difference is that there was nothing but oblivion in between. That, and I always had to borrow someone else's body. I grew tired of it a long time ago. I stepped back from it in the twentieth century. I left you all to it and used the time for something else instead. I visited museums and went to art galleries. I went for walks and rode horses."

She shook her head, her gaze encompassing them both. "But that was selfish of me. And I realized that the only person who could bring an end to this was me."

"Did the dreams have anything to do with you?"

Madeleine shook her head. "No, that was all you. The only thing I did was prepare for this moment."

"Did Cecile know that Marjorie was you?"

She nodded. "She knew, but she was so used to me floating around in the background that she didn't think anything of it. She never saw me as a threat, which was to my advantage."

"How was the curse broken?" That was Frankie, his voice decidedly croaky.

She smiled. "Estienne..." She corrected herself. "Daniel protected you. He was prepared to die rather than let you be destroyed. That was always the parameters of the curse. Cecille just didn't think it would ever be met. And it hasn't been for hundreds of years. That was why I waited until the moment I did. Any sooner and I could have gotten rid of Cecile, but I wouldn't have been able to break the curse."

She staggered back a step and pressed a hand to her forehead. "The bond is breaking. It's time for me to go. You should leave before Marjorie comes back. I'm not sure what she will make of finding you here."

I nodded. I was in full agreement with that. "Thank you, Madeleine."

Her smile was tinged with sadness. "You're welcome, big brother. And all I did was make amends for past mistakes."

For a moment, we just stared at each other. It felt like there was a lot that I wanted to say but no time in which to say it.

Madeleine let out a sigh. "I wish we had more time."

"Me too."

She inclined her head toward where I'd left my car. "Go."

I went, holding tight to Frankie's hand and not caring who might see us as we made our way across campus.

We were halfway across the lawn when the voices came from behind us.

"Mr. Yates. Would you care to explain to me why you are sprawled on the lawn in the middle of campus as if you do not have a care in the world?"

"I don't remember." Not surprisingly, Richard sounded confused.

"Do you think it is a good example to set to students?"

"Probably not."

"Then I suggest you get up and go back to wherever it is that you should be. And I would also suggest that it does not happen again."

We reached my car and I opened the passenger door for Frankie. "Let's go home."

He lowered himself into the seat. "This is real, Daniel, right?"

I bent down to kiss him on the cheek. "Yeah, it's real. Enjoy it."

Epilogue

Three months later

Frankie

I loved watching Daniel sleep, but then I loved everything about him. Daniel. Estienne. They'd both blurred into each other, and I was amazed that I'd never been able to see it before. They might not look similar, but in spirit, in what made a person who they were, the two men were virtually indistinguishable.

His eyes flickered open, and I smiled as his gaze found mine. "I could hear you thinking. It was really loud."

I snuggled closer, abandoning my pillow for his until our noses were touching in our customary way of lying together. I lifted my fingers to trail them gently over his cheek, all the way to the crease that appeared as his lips curved at my touch. "Did you dream?"

Daniel shook his head. He might not have admitted it, but I knew he'd been just as scared as I was that his subconscious might be determined to fill in the blanks, that it might replay whatever had happened at Cecile's hands after she'd turned me into a gargoyle. The more time that passed, the more relaxed we both became that it wasn't going to happen.

Neither of us needed to know what twisted methods she might have had for purging the gay away. Daniel shifted slightly to drop a kiss on my forehead. "Nothing bad anyway. What about you?"

My dreams were to be expected—dreams of being back in the gargoyle, where this part of the day, the part where I got to lie next to Daniel and touch him, were actually the dream. They left me feeling like I wasn't sure what was real and what wasn't.

"They're getting less frequent."

"Good."

I smiled as the bedroom door creaked open and seconds later a black, furry projectile launched itself off the floor and did its best to get in the middle of us. I dug my fingers into Napoleon's fur, tickling him under the chin the way he liked. "Are we late giving you breakfast?" I got an indignant meow for that comment. "You need to start catching mice. There's loads of them out there."

There were. Daniel had handed in his resignation, using owed holiday time to ensure that he didn't have to set foot back on campus, and then we'd relocated to a village on the outskirts of Manchester, moving into an idyllic cottage with a stream at the bottom of the garden. It was peaceful, the closest house more than a mile away. Daniel worried that it would be too quiet for me when I'd spent enough time away from people, but I didn't need people. All I needed was freedom—and him. Maybe I'd change my mind later, and I'd had to promise him that should that happen he'd be the first to know, but for now, we were both content.

It had taken Napoleon a little longer to adapt. He'd seemed confused by the distinct lack of concrete, and hadn't been too sure about the stream either, but at least we'd stopped worrying that he might try and find his way back to Sheffield.

"I need to call my mum today."

I grimaced. "Give me some warning first so I can make sure I just happen not to be here."

Daniel chuckled. "Where are you going to go?"

"I'll walk down to the village."

"We don't need anything. We went shopping yesterday."

"I'll find something." I lifted my head to look at Napoleon, who having decided that breakfast wasn't going to be forthcoming, had curled up between us. "You want some tuna, right, Napoleon?"

He gave a long, drawn-out meow, followed by two shorter ones, and we both laughed. "See. It's an emergency."

"My mother is not that bad."

"She hates me."

"Not true."

I gave him a look. "She blames me for you moving out of Sheffield, which technically she's right to. It is my fault."

Daniel's brow furrowed. "How did you work that one out?"

"You'd still be there if I hadn't come into your life."

Daniel's eyes softened. "And I'd still be unhappy. I'd still be beating myself up for not being successful in a marriage that was never going to work. And I'd still be being berated daily by a certain dean determined to make my life miserable."

"She had her uses."

Daniel chuckled. "Yeah, I guess she did. She's probably still recovering from being seen on campus without her hair being tied back."

We both lapsed into silence, until Daniel broke it. "And my mother's not that bad."

"She's better than your other one. I'll give you that."

A wry smile played on Daniel's lips for a few seconds. "She'll be happier once I've gone back to work. I'm convinced she thinks I'm making the new job at Manchester University up." He propped himself up on one elbow. "Hey! Stop looking sad. We've still got two weeks until then."

In truth, I probably did look sad. Daniel's lack of a job had meant that I'd had him all to myself for months, but I'd always known it wouldn't last forever. After all, we were both living off his savings. It wasn't like I had anything to bring to the relationship.

As usual, Daniel read my mind. "Stop!"

"Stop what?"

"Feeling like you're not enough. You are more than enough. We said we were just going to live, remember. I agreed not to blame myself for the past, and you agreed not to feel bad about the circumstances you were left with, which were beyond your control."

Daniel was referring to the fact that after the initial buzz of freedom had worn off, we'd realized that there were a lot of practical obstacles to our life together. Not least the fact that I had no identification. No identification meant no driver's license or passport, and that even something as simple as getting a job was going to be nigh on impossible. "I don't want you to feel trapped with me. Not when I'm going to stop you from doing so many things like going on holiday, and…" I stopped when I saw Daniel's expression. "Why are you smiling? I'm being serious."

He leaned closer until his lips were barely a hair's breadth away from mine. "I don't give a rat's ass about any of those things. We'll work it out. All that matters is that I love you."

I never tired of those words, and no matter how many times I heard them, they still caused the same burst of euphoria in my chest. "I love you too. Always and forever."

Daniel pulled back a little so that I could see his face. "And no truer words have ever been spoken."

Our lips met in a passionate kiss, unfortunately ruined by the furry monstrosity deciding he needed breakfast more than sleep after all. Kissing wasn't the same when it was accompanied by a mouthful of fur.

****

Daniel spread the sheets of paper across the kitchen table. "Are you sure about this?"

When I'd first broached the subject of him looking into the past and trying to find out what had happened to my family, it was with the expectation of him drawing a blank because it was so long ago. That hadn't been the case. We'd decided that he wouldn't share anything until his research reached the inevitable dead end.

I picked up one of the pieces of paper and stared at it, but despite the fact that Daniel had been teaching me to read and write, I still hadn't progressed much beyond the *'Run Spot, run'* level. Besides, Daniel's handwriting was a messy scrawl. Even if I'd been literate, it was debatable whether I would have been able to make head nor tail of it. I placed the paper back on the table and nodded. "I need to know. Even if it's stuff I don't want to hear, I'd rather know about it. It's the not knowing that has driven me crazy all these years."

Daniel gave me an assessing look. "Just bear in mind that I had to sift through an awful lot of information in order to build up any sort of picture. It's like…" He frowned. "I don't know, I guess… it's like a plate that's been dropped, and I've glued it back together. There's going to be pieces that I couldn't find, ones that are missing."

I stared resolutely at him until he took the hint. "Okay. Here goes. Here's what I found." He cleared his throat. "The piece of land you told me about stayed in the Damont family for another couple of centuries, so that would mean that your brother, Antoine, must have married and had a family of his own, and it was passed down through his relatives—your relatives. I couldn't find any specific information about him. There was a mention of an Antoine, who died as an old man, but the year is hazy, so I can't guarantee it was your brother."

It made me feel somewhat better to know that Antoine had lived on, that my disappearance hadn't changed his life too much. I hoped he'd been happy. "What about my parents?"

Daniel dropped the piece of paper and picked up another, glancing over the top of it. "You said your father's name was Olivier?"

He was stalling. I could see it in his face. "Just tell me."

"All the information points to him having died in 1572. There's a gravestone which matches the name Olivier Damont. I got a contact to send me photos, but it's very faded. It's hard to make out anything except for the name and year."

I sat back and took a moment to digest that piece of information. "That's only one year after I disappeared. He'd been ill... before. We'd thought he was getting better, but maybe..."

Daniel nodded. "I think your mother married again. There were records of a Isabeau Damont and then after a certain date, the only records I could find mentioned an Isabeau Courtier. I can't see any reason for her to have changed her name unless she remarried."

Neither could I. It was a strange thought to consider my maman getting over my father's death to the point where she'd married again, but maybe she'd needed to. Maybe that's how they'd survived and managed to keep the land. I wasn't there so I could hardly judge her for it. "Do you know when she died?"

Daniel shook his head. "Like I said, there's pieces missing. That may have been a different Isabeau. Do you recognize the name Courtier?"

I wracked my brain, but I couldn't recall anyone in Domme who'd had that surname. If my mother had remarried, it was most likely to a stranger. "No."

"You probably expected me to find out more."

"I didn't think you'd find anything."

"There is one more thing." I raised an eyebrow in question, Daniel continuing. "There are still Damonts living in Domme. I would assume they're your relatives. If you wanted, we could contact them."

I stared at him. "And say what? Hi, you don't know me, but it's likely that I'm your great, great, great uncle, even though I'm younger than you." I shook my head. "No. I just wanted some sort of closure. To know that my whole family didn't perish. I've got that." I propped my head on my hand. "What about you?"

Daniel shifted uncomfortably on the chair. "What about me?"

I reached across the table and took his hand. "I know you. There's no way you weren't curious enough to look into Cecile and Madeleine." And although, I didn't say his name, I knew it would have been impossible to research the two women without bringing Estienne into the equation. "Is it bad? Is that why you don't want to say anything?"

"It's…"

I gave his hand a reassuring squeeze when he fell silent. "You don't have to tell me." I gestured at the pieces of paper. "We could just burn all these and forget they ever existed."

Daniel ran a hand through his hair. "Are you suggesting I keep secrets from you?"

"No. Yes. I don't know. Some secrets are good, though, right?"

He narrowed his eyes at me. "Like what?"

"Well… like if I'd invited someone to come and stay with us, who I knew you wouldn't be exactly overjoyed about, and I figured I'd leave it until nearer the time before telling you, so that you wouldn't get too annoyed about it."

"Who?"

"Gloria."

Daniel's face said it all.

"We owe her a lot."

"I know, but can't we owe her our gratitude from afar?"

He'd come around. I knew he would. "It could be worse. It could be Richard."

Daniel grimaced. "That's true."

There'd been no fixing that relationship. It would be difficult for Daniel to ever get past the knowledge that Richard had been prepared to do whatever it took to get rid of Cecile, and of course with Richard being oblivious to everything that had gone on, there was no explaining it to him. As far as Richard was concerned, Daniel was too consumed by his new relationship to have any time for old friends, and Daniel was happy to let him believe that. Maybe one day he would see his way to forgiving him once the memories weren't quite so raw, but we hadn't reached that point yet. I waved a hand at the piece of paper. "Come on. Get it over and done with. We can talk about Gloria later."

Daniel sighed. "Estienne, he… I…" He was never sure what pronoun to use when referring to Estienne. "He disappeared, not long after the date you did. Either he managed to get away, or she killed him."

We both fell silent, probably contemplating that the latter was far more likely.

"And Cecile?"

Daniel's lips turned up at the corners. "Her physical body died from plague by all accounts. It would seem that even magic can't keep the Black Death from your door."

"Good. It's just a shame she didn't stay dead."

Daniel nodded in agreement. "I couldn't find anything about Madeleine. Maybe she left when Cecile died."

"Maybe."

I got up from the table and squeezed myself onto Daniel's lap, looping my arms around his neck and staring into his eyes. "The past is done."

"Is it?"

I thought about all the things I'd endured, about the years of torment, and all those failed attempts at love in the vague hope that the man of the moment might be the one to break the curse, not knowing that they'd all been the same man. The time and circumstances had just never been right, mainly thanks to Cecile's constant meddling. But here with Daniel, safe in his arms, it all seemed like a distant memory, like something that had happened to someone else.

"Yeah, it is." I lowered my lips to his. "There's only the future, and that's going to be beautiful."

Daniel's nod was long and considered, his smile the best tonic that anyone could ask for. "You're right. It will be. Because it's us."

Thanks

Thanks for reading this book. If you can take the time to leave a review, I would really appreciate it.

You can receive a number of FREE short stories and bonus chapters by signing up to my mailing list. You'll also be informed about new releases and get other exclusive stuff.

Want to see what I am working on before anyone else? Subscribe to my Patreon for WIP chapters and a version of A Temporary Situation written from Tristan's point of view. I'll also be writing bonus stories about established characters exclusive to my patrons.

Other places you can find me

Twitter. Bookbub Instagram Facebook. Website Days Den

More MM romance books by H.L Day

Romantic comedies

A Temporary Situation

A Christmas Situation

Temporary Insanity

Taking Love's Lead

Suspense

A Dance too Far

A Step too Far

Contemporary

Eager For You

Eager For More

Edge of Living

Kept in the Dark

Time for a Change

Christmas Riches

Post-apocalyptic Sci-fi

Refuge

Rebellion

Exposed

Paranormal

The Longest Night

Read the blurb for these books through H.L Day's website or on H.L Day's Amazon page.

Available In audio

Kept in the Dark

Edge of Living

A Dance too Far

A Step too Far

Exposed

If you liked this book, you may also like

A Temporary Situation: An employee/boss gay romantic comedy
(Temporary; Tristan and Dom #1)

Personal assistant Dominic is a consummate professional. Funny then, that he harbors such unprofessional feelings toward Tristan Maxwell, the CEO of the company. No, not in that way. The man may be the walking epitome of gorgeousness dressed up in a designer suit. But, Dominic's immune. Unlike most of the workforce, he can see through the pretty facade to the arrogant, self-entitled asshole below. It's lucky then, that the man's easy enough to avoid.

Disaster strikes when Dominic finds himself having to work in close proximity as Tristan's P.A. The man is infuriatingly unflappable, infuriatingly good-humored, and infuriatingly unorthodox. In short, just infuriating. A late-night rescue leading to a drunken pass only complicates matters further, especially with the discovery that Tristan is both straight and engaged.

Hatred turns to tolerance, tolerance to friendship, and friendship to mutual passion. One thing's for sure, if Tristan sets his sights on Dominic, there's no way Dominic has the necessary armor or willpower to keep a force of nature like Tristan at bay for long, no matter how unprofessional a relationship with the boss might be. He may just have to revise everything he previously thought and believed in for a chance at love.

Temporary Insanity: An enemies to lover gay romantic comedy.
(Temporary; Paul and Indy #1)

Sleeping with the enemy never felt so good.

When Paul Davenport comes face to face with the man he caught in bed with his boyfriend years before, it's hate at first sight. Well, second sight. Indy should be apologizing, not flirting. Except the gorgeous barman is completely oblivious to their paths ever having crossed before.

Despite his feelings, Paul's powerless to resist the full-on charm offensive that follows. It's fine though. It's just sex. No emotions. No getting to know each other. Just a bout of temporary insanity that's sure to run its course once the simmering passion starts to wear off.

Only what if it's not? Indy's nothing like the man Paul expected him to be from his past actions. What if they're perfect for each other and Paul's just too stubborn to see it? Forging a relationship with him would require an emotional U-turn Paul might not be capable of making.

There's a thin line between love and hate, and Paul's about to discover just how thin it really is. He can't possibly be falling for the man that ruined his life. Can he?

Warning: This book contains hate sex – sort of, lots of banter, and a pink elephant. No, really it does. Actually, two elephants.

Please note: Although this book is in the Temporary series, it occurs during the same timeline as A Temporary Situation. Therefore, both books can be read as standalones and in any order.

Time for a Change: A Grumpy vs Sunshine gay romance

What if the last thing you want, might be the very thing you need?

Stuffy and uptight accountant Michael's life is exactly the way he likes it: ordered, routine and risk-free. He doesn't need chaos and he doesn't need anything shaking it up and causing him anxiety. The only blot on the horizon is the small matter of getting his ex-boyfriend Christian back. That's exactly the type of man Michael goes for: cultured, suave and sophisticated.

Coffee shop employee Sam is none of those things. He's a ball of energy and happiness who thinks nothing of flaunting his half-naked muscular body and devastating smile in front of Michael when he's trying to work. He knows what he wants—and that's Michael. And no matter how much Michael tries to resist him, he's not going to take no for an answer.

Sam eventually chips through Michael's barriers and straight into his bed. But Michael's already made some questionable decisions that might just come back to haunt him. He's got some difficult choices to make if he's ever going to find love. And he might just find that he's too set in his ways to make the right ones quickly enough. If Michael's not careful, the best thing that's ever happened to him might just slip right through his fingers. Because even a patient man like Sam has his limits.

Kept in the Dark: An escort gay romance

Struggling actor Dean only escorts occasionally to pay the bills. So, his first instinct on being offered a job with a strange set of conditions is to turn it down. No date. Don't switch the lights on. Don't touch him. I mean, what's that all about? What's the man trying to hide? Dean certainly doesn't expect sex with a faceless stranger to spark so much passion inside him. It's just business though, right? He can put a stop to it whenever he wants.

When Dean meets Justin—a scarred, ex-army soldier unlucky in love. Dean's given a chance at a proper relationship. He can see past the scars to the man underneath. He's everything Dean could possibly wish for in a boyfriend: kind, caring and sweet. All Dean needs to do is be honest. Easy, right? But, Justin's holding back and Dean can't work out why. But whatever it is, it's enough to give him second thoughts.

They both have secrets which could shatter their fledgling relationship. After all, secrets have a nasty habit of coming out eventually. The question is when they do, will they be able to piece their relationship back together? Or will they be left with nothing but memories of bad decisions and the promise of the love they could have had, if only they'd both been honest and fought harder.

Edge of Living: A hurt/comfort gay romance

Sometimes, death can feel like the only escape.

It's been a year since Alex stopped living. He exists. He breathes. He pretends to be like everyone else. But, he doesn't live. Burdened by memories, he dreams of the day when he can finally be free. Until that time comes, he keeps everybody at bay. It's been easy so far. But he never factored in meeting a man like Austin.

Hard-working mechanic Austin has always gone for men as muscular as himself. So, it's a mystery why he's so bewitched by the slim, quiet man with the soulful brown eyes who works in the library. The magnetic attraction is one thing, but the protective instincts are harder to fathom. Austin's sure, though, that if he can only earn Alex's trust, then the two of them could be perfect together.

A tentative relationship begins. But Alex's secrets run deep. Far deeper than Austin could ever envisage. Time is ticking. Events are coming to a head, and love is never a magic cure. Oblivious to the extent of Alex's pain, can Austin discover the truth? Or is he destined to be left alone, only able to piece together the fragments of his boyfriend's history, once it's already too late?

Trigger warning: Please be aware that this story deals with suicidal ideation and other dark themes. If this is a subject you find uncomfortable, then this book is not recommended.
Despite this, there is a guaranteed HEA.

Printed in Great Britain
by Amazon